Baron's War

Book 3

in the

Border Knight Series

By

Griff Hosker

Published by Sword Books Ltd 2018

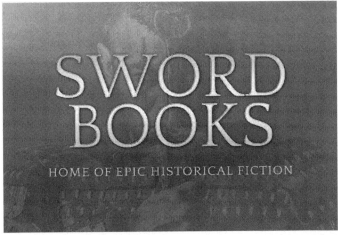

Dedicated to Isabelle May Hosker, my first granddaughter!

Prologue

When my family had lost the title of Earl of Cleveland I thought that my world had ended. Through hard work and raw courage, I had clawed back some of that power and I hoped that someday I would have the title returned too. Prince Arthur had lost his title but he had not been patient. I had thought that Prince Arthur would have realised that he had allies other than the French King. He was young and he still believed that King Phillip was looking after his interests. He was not. He had one aim and that was to recover Normandy, Anjou and Maine. Instead of trusting in me and in knights such as William des Rocher, Arthur had gathered an army and was marching on Mirebeau to take his mother and sister away from King John's mother, Eleanor. It was a catastrophic mistake. Constance had taken her daughter there for safe keeping and now King John was heading to Mirebeau. All my good work and the men I had lost had been in vain! To make matters worse King Phillip now had an army and he was threatening the Norman borders. I was in great danger of being caught in the middle as King John fought King Phillip and Arthur. Whoever won I would be the loser!

I could do nothing about either Prince Arthur or King Phillip. I commanded a few knights and less than a hundred men at arms. All we could was to weather the storm. We made preparations for war. We had good defences and we had strong warriors. We had, however, lost warriors when we had returned from doing a favour for William des Roches. There was no use bleating about my position. I had made my own bed. I had chosen to oppose King John. I had defied him in his court. I had killed his Bishop of Durham and now, thanks to my manor in Anjou, I was a thorn in his side. I wondered why he did not come to squash me. My castle was a strong one but King John commanded many

3

hundreds of knights. If he came it would fall. It would be a bloody battle but we would lose.

Sir Richard of East Harlsey, who had fled King John too and was now one of my household knights, had a theory about that, "He cannot risk losing to you. You bested him when you defied him in England and did not bend the knee. He has sent killers after you and they have failed. He will hope that you are defeated by King Phillip. The French have tried to take this castle and failed. He is not the best general that I have ever seen. If it was not for William des Roches then King John might have lost already and might still be in England, hiding in the White Tower. Now that Longchamp has added defences that will be where he will hide."

I was not certain. Normandy and Anjou were too valuable for him to let them go. He would fight. What would happen when Phillip got his hands on Arthur's mother and sister did not bear thinking about. "Perhaps you are right but we will prepare for war. I will send to England. We need news of how the land lies. I cannot believe that there are not more Barons such as you who wish to shake off the shackles of this monster."

Sir Richard shook his head, "They need a figurehead for them to follow and to replace King John. I fear that the English need a King and, sad though it is, King John is the one we have."

"Then when Prince Arthur has rid himself of this foolishness we must bring him here and use him to rally the loyal barons here and in England."

Disaster at Mirebeau

Chapter 1

My home at La Flèche was still secure; for the time being. *'Swan of Stockton'* had just returned from England when a rider galloped in with the news. It was one of Sir Guy's men. The livery was recognised. We knew Sir Guy de Changé and I trusted him. There were few men I did trust.

"Sir Thomas, King John has captured Prince Arthur and the Maid of Brittany. He is taking them to Falaise. Sir Hubert de Burgh is to be his gaoler."

"And his sister?"

"Sir Guy believes that she is to be taken to England." The messenger lowered his voice. "My lord begs you to do nothing impetuous. Prince Arthur is escorted by the whole of King John's army. The King hopes that you will try to take him. William des Roches believes that this is an attempt to draw you from your castle."

I nodded, "And King Phillip?"

"There is good news. Now that he has been thwarted he has retired to the border."

Handing a silver coin to the messenger I said, "I know that this message comes from the seneschal at Angers. I pray he continues to keep me informed."

"I believe he will."

When he had gone I summoned my knights. I included Edward for he would soon be knighted. Sir William had been my squire. Sir Henry had come to me as a penniless knight and Sir Richard and his nephew, Ralph, had been driven from their homes by King John. It was not the largest conroi in Anjou but, for me, it was the best.

"Once again, my friends, disaster has struck. Prince Arthur is now a prisoner of King John. My hope lies in the fact that he will be a prisoner at Falaise. That is not too far from here. His gaoler is also a kind man. My aim is to find some way to extricate him from King John's clutches."

"Will he not try to trap you, lord?"

"I would expect nothing less but I will first send a couple of trusted men to scout it out for me. I tell you this for I fear that when King Phillip recovers from the loss of Prince Arthur and Lady Eleanor then he will turn his eye to us. We must be ready. Sir Henry, you have Bazouges. How are the defences?"

"We are still building them, lord. We have the outer wall built and we have the keep begun but we need another six months to finish."

"I hope we are granted six months. Just do your best." I turned to my former squire. "And La Lude?"

"We began the work some time ago. The workmen are almost finished." He smiled, "We both know, lord, that one can never finish building defences but if the French come then we can give you warning and, I believe, hold out until you arrive."

"I know you both lack numbers and I promise that as soon as more men come from England then they shall join you."

Sir Richard asked, "What about Bretons, lord? Would they not fight for their Duke?"

"From what I learned at Le Goulet they have abandoned him. They now play games to gain thrones. They vie with each other for the favour of John or Phillip. It is Englishmen and Welshmen that we can rely on."

Edward asked, "Lord, what news did the *'Swan'* bring?"

"I know not. When the rider arrived, I spoke with him and I had forgotten our ship. Edward go and speak with the captain and see what he has brought."

Geoffrey, my steward arrived, "Wine, my lord?"

"I think so, Geoffrey. I have used King John's name too many times and I need the taste removing from my tongue."

Sir Henry said, "They must fear you, lord."

"They may but that brings me no comfort."

Sir Henry was a thoughtful knight. He had come to me with little hope of becoming a knight despite the training. It had made him cautious. "Lord, the estate you have in Whorlton, you may be able to use that to your advantage."

"How so?"

"The Dowager Queen said that so long as you did not rebel then it was yours. She was quite clear on the matter."

"And?"

"You could send Sir William or Sir Edward to take charge of the manor. It would give you better access to the lady in England and you would know what was going on. Sir William and Edward have never rebelled." I had not thought of that and the idea deserved merit. It is much to put on the shoulders of one so young." Sir Henry pressed his point home. "Lord, you have given them their spurs. When a man becomes a knight then they have to change."

I looked at Sir William, "How would you feel about going to England?" He hesitated and, in that hesitation, I knew his heart. I waved my hand as though to make the question vanish. "You have answered me. I will think on this. Say nothing to Edward. He has much to think of with the ceremony."

Sir William said, "I am sorry, lord, I feel that I have let you down but my wife is happy and settled in La Lude."

"William, you know me. I want honesty above all things."

Edward returned with ten men and a piece of parchment. "Lord here are four archers and six men at arms. They have come to join us."

I nodded, "Sir Henry, Sir William, they are your men. Speak with them while I read this missive. Edward, I need to speak with you too."

"Aye lord."

I slit the seal on the parchment.

You know who you are and you know that we think about you each day.

England is a troubled land. There are spies everywhere. Men cannot speak with their neighbours for fear of the Sheriffs. The barons have no power and there is a feeling that they need to change the way the country is ruled. Rebellion and the talk of rebellion fills the halls of the lords of this land. Our only hope is Arthur or his sister.

I know that you are an island of hope in a sea of treachery but I pray that you can summon some of the power of the Warlord. The land needs a hero. We need someone behind whom we can unite. My grandfather did so when King Henry II was just a boy. I know that you have it in you. Our family's name still commands respect. We may have

7

lost our lands but we have not lost the support of the people of the valley.

I do not ask you to come back to England yet; you have a family and there is too much treachery but you need to come soon.

She who prays for you each night and yearns for the day when the knight returns whence he came.

I read it over and over. My knights looked at me as I folded the letter. I smiled, "This was not a happy missive. Our homeland is troubled and while we are safe here, or relatively safe, our people at home suffer. We must rescue the Prince!"

I saw, from their faces, that the prospect daunted my knights. It was a hundred miles to Falaise. It would take, whichever men I sent, at least ten days to get there and assess the situation and return.

I stood, "I know this is hard but we are true knights and a true knight does not baulk at that which seems impossible. We think our way through the problem. Until then we are on a war footing. I cannot see King Phillip resting too long. We are a thorn in his side and close enough to his borders for us to be seen as something he can remove." They stood. "Sir William, Sir Henry, return to your castles and make them as strong as they can be."

I sought out Griff Jameson and Tom Robertson. Both were fine archers and, more importantly, had been born in this land. I had others who were as good as archers and scouts but I needed two men who could blend in. I would not order them to go. The journey was both dangerous and difficult. "I would ask you to travel to Falaise and discover where they are holding Arthur, Duke of Brittany. I will not order you to go for you would be putting yourselves in harm's way and if you decline I will not think any less of you."

Griff looked at Tom, "Lord we know how important the Duke is to this land. We will go. As for the danger? The only safe places in this land lie within ten miles of this castle. We will go." He looked at Tom, "Perhaps we will go to see William of La Flèche. We could take samples of wine and pretend to be wine merchants."

I cocked an eye at them, "With bows?"

He shook his head, "Lord, if we travel with bows we sign our own death warrant for all know that the only men who travel with bows are your archers.

Besides we know wine. It would seem natural. Falaise is known for cider and not wine. It would not seem unusual."

Tom nodded, "We could say that we came from Chinon. The red wine from there tastes similar to that in this valley. It would work, lord."

I nodded. They were both clever men. I was lucky to have them serve me. I might be sending them to their deaths yet they were happy to serve me. "I leave it to you." I took a purse of coins. "If you are merchants then you had best dress as such. Buy clothes and take money for lodgings. Wine merchants do not sleep beneath the trees."

After they had gone I sought James Broadsword. He was one of my older warriors. He would no longer ride to war. He was a greybeard but he knew how to defend and he commanded my garrison. "James, war may be coming." I told him of the disaster of Mirebeau. He nodded as though such events were expected. He had come to me after another such calamity. The lords would normally survive but the ordinary men would not. He had been lucky to find me and was as loyal a man as I had ever met.

"King Phillip will send men here." It was obvious to me that the French would attack my strategically placed town. If it was taken it would open up the whole of the Loire valley.

"If he sends men to La Flèche then they will bleed on our defences. It would take the whole of the French army to reduce these walls, lord. If I were the French then I would take La Lude or Bazouges. Both are smaller and less well made. To get to Bazouges an army would have to pass here. I would say that they would try to take La Lude first. With that in their hands they have a crossing of Le Loir."

"You are right. Then we need to be able to move quickly when they do attack."

"You have the watch towers, lord and the signal fires. If they bring war machines to reduce the walls then we will know in plenty of time. A ram moves slowly. On the other hand, if they arrive swiftly and build machines at the castle then we have time enough but Sir Richard will need to be ready."

He was right. My former squire now had a family. They would be in danger too. The next day, taking Fótr and Edward with me, I rode the few miles to La Lude. As we rode I spoke with Edward. "Edward are you ready for the ceremony of the knight?"

"I believe so, lord but, in truth, I am fearful."

9

I laughed, "A warrior who has faced overwhelming odds fears to be dubbed and given spurs?"

"No lord. It is the responsibility. I will have a squire to train and I have not found one yet. I will have men to find and to pay. I know how to fight and yet I know not how to be a lord. Does that make sense?"

"It does. I suppose I was lucky. I became a knight almost by accident. I had just one squire to worry about. The Holy Land taught me how to be a lord." I had not thought of how he would pay for men. I was more concerned that I would have another knight in my conroi. I looked north. "There is a small manor at Saint-Jean. Four or five farmers till the land there. I would give you the manor and help you to build a small keep there. It is close enough for you to return to La Flèche if danger threatens and yet will give you an income. At the moment I take the tax but I have enough from my town,"

"What of Sir Richard? Would he not want the manor?"

Shaking my head, I said, "Sir Richard still harbours a dream of his home in East Harlsey. Since I have been given Whorlton the two are not far from each other."

When we reached La Lude, I saw that William had begun work on improving his defences. His new men toiled alongside the older warriors. I dismounted and Fótr took Skuld away to be watered and fed. William was wearing a kyrtle and worked alongside his men deepening the ditch and making the bailey higher. "I did not expect you so soon, lord."

"I spoke with James Broadsword. He has a wise old head upon his shoulders. He pointed out that it is you who will be in the greatest danger. I know you have a family and I am concerned."

"Marguerite is a warrior's daughter and a warrior's wife. She is not afraid of danger. My ditches will be deeper and my walls higher when the enemy come. My farmers all train each Sunday with the bow and their sons with the sling. My walls will be defended."

I nodded, "Then keep men patrolling the border. As James Broadsword pointed out they can either bring war machines or build them close by. Cut down as many trees as you can. It will make your walls stronger and deny the enemy the means to make machines. As soon as you spy them then let me know! I promise that I will come with my horsemen."

"Of course, lord."

That evening I dined with Sir Richard, our squires and my wife. I could tell that something was on my wife's mind. She was distracted. Alfred was now old enough to sit at our table and it amused me to see him trying to copy the squires for they were the closest in age to him. I knew my wife was distracted when he reached for the jug of wine Fótr had just replaced in the middle, "Alfred!"

"But Fótr…"

My voice was stern. It sounded harsher than my wife's. I could not help it. That was the way I had been brought up. "Fótr is almost a man grown. Until I say then it is milk for you."

I saw Margaret look up at my sharp words, "I am sorry, my lord, I should have been watching him. Come Alfred, it is time for your bed."

"But…"

"Do as your mother says."

He would learn his lesson. He would not reach for the wine again. Being taken from the table was the worst of punishments for he loved to listen in to our conversations. When they had gone I said, "Sir Richard I have decided to give Edward the manor of Saint-Jean when he is knighted."

I saw Edward look at Sir Richard. There was apprehension on his face. Sir Richard beamed, "An excellent decision, lord. You are lucky, Edward. It is a small manor but it will help you to become a lord."

I smiled at the relief on Edward's face. "Then I would have you and your men go with Edward on the morrow and begin to build the mound. He will not need a large hall. At the moment he does not even have a squire but when the castle is built then we will have another line of defence."

We spoke at length on the design and position of the castle. Saint-Jean was close enough for us to be familiar with the land. There was a small stream which could easily be diverted and dammed to give a good moat and a nearby wood would provide the timber. When they left for their quarters we were all happy.

When I retired I found that Lady Margaret was not asleep. She had a candle and was sewing. That was unusual. She was frugal and candles were expensive. She looked up as I entered. I smiled, "Tell me what troubles you, my love. I can see it writ clear across your face."

She laid down the sewing and then smiled. She reached up, held my beard and kissed me, "You are to be a father."

"Why did you not tell me sooner?"

"It was only this afternoon that I visited the women who deliver babies. Clothilde confirmed it. I am with child."

I nodded, "And that is why you sew. I am pleased. I wondered if Alfred was to be our only child."

"No, lord, I will bear you as many as I am able."

The news had a two-fold effect on me. It made me more worried about our position and so I worked even harder on the defences and it set me thinking about the future. I liked my home here but it could not compare with England. I would return and the Dowager Queen's gift had made it more likely that I would be able to return to my home and my beloved valley. I just had to work out how to do so.

We took not only Sir Richard's men but also most of the garrison to help build the new castle. We were close enough to La Flèche to return if danger threatened. We built the biggest mound I had ever seen. Sir Richard told me that it matched the one the first Bishop of Durham had built at his first home, Bishopton. I remembered the castle well. It was a good sign for although the castle had only been occupied for a year or two, a hundred and forty years later, it still stood. We built a dam and diverted the stream. My men cut down the trees so that there was no cover within four hundred paces of the castle. When Edward gained more archers, they had a killing zone.

The locals were so impressed with the castle that they began to talk of their home as Saint-Jean-de-la-Motte. The name stuck.

We were still working on the walls when Tom and Griff returned. I had been watching the road from the north while we had been toiling. They dismounted. "Well?"

"He is in the keep, lord. King John is also there." Griff shook his head. "You cannot spirit him from the castle, lord for it has a high wall and the keep is perched upon a rock. The walls of the keep are also high. Lord, I have yet to see a mightier castle save, perhaps, Chateau Galliard."

My archer would not exaggerate. I nodded. "I thank you for your efforts."

Griff held out the purse I had given him. "We did not need all of the coin lord. Here is what we did not spend."

"No, keep that for your trouble. I must now find another way to rescue the Duke of Brittany."

The bad news spurred me on and we had the wooden walls and the keep finished by the end of the month. "Come Edward, we return to my castle. It is time that you were knighted. This night you stand vigil and I will summon my other knights to witness your dubbing on the morrow."

When I returned to my castle Griff and Tom were waiting for me. "Lord, what we did not tell you was that we discovered that there are many barons who are unhappy with John as Duke of Normandy. Playing wine merchants, we heard much dissension in the taverns. We fear that the French King may try to take advantage of this. There is rebellion in the air and the barons may make war."

"Thank you for that. You are right. While I would support a baron's war against John I would not do so if the French were the beneficiaries."

"There is something else, lord. When we spoke with William of La Flèche before we left, he was most helpful and he asked a boon. His son, Gilles, wishes to be a warrior. He is too old to be trained as an archer but, perhaps he could be a man at arms?"

I smiled. Sometimes fate came to the rescue. "I can do better than that. Edward, my captain of men, will be knighted tomorrow. He needs a squire. Have you met the youth?"

"Yes lord. He has seen sixteen summers. He worked in his father's winery and is not afraid of hard work. I fear that he may not have a warrior's skills yet."

"They can be taught. Have the young man and his father come to see me."

I summoned Edward and told him of my idea. Edward had been the son of a hawker. He had been surprised when I had said that I would knight him. The fact that I had secured him a squire further humbled him. When they returned I saw what his father had meant about the young man and his physique. Gilles was broad in the chest and almost as tall as me. "Gilles, your father wishes you to be a warrior. What do you say?"

His face told me all, "Lord it is my dream."

"Can you ride?" His face fell. "You will learn, Gilles that I value honesty above all things. Do not give me the answer you think I want to hear." I saw Edward smile. Edward knew how to train men. He could teach Gilles how to ride.

"I can sit on the back of a horse without falling off, lord."

"Can you use a sword?"

"I know the hilt from the handle but I would be lying if I said I could use one." He shook his head. "I am sorry, lord. I am not yet ready to be a warrior."

"That is for me to decide. Edward here is to be knighted tomorrow. He needs a squire. That means that you would be his servant but, in return he would train you. He would teach you to ride and to use a sword. Does that suit?"

13

He dropped to a knee, "Aye lord and I swear I will be the best squire that I can be."

"What say you Edward?"

"I am happy, lord. Gilles will have no bad habits for him to unlearn. It is good."

His father beamed, "I know the expense involved. I will buy his horse, mail helmet and sword. I am grateful, lord that you have given my son this chance. We are lucky to live under your benevolent rule."

And so, Edward spent the night in the church. He prayed and he contemplated. His world would change the moment I touched his shoulders with my sword and gave him his spurs. After he was knighted we celebrated and I told my knights of my wife's news. The feast was a joyful one.

The Knife in the Night

Chapter 2

The men who occupied the tower at the south side of the river signalled across the river that riders were approaching. Riders from the south were normally a sign of danger and so I had the garrison stand to. We saw many men approaching. There were six banners which meant six knights but I relaxed when I saw the Duchess Constance and the Dowager Queen Eleanor. My wife, when I told her, took charge, "We will need quarters for them. Husband you will sleep with the other knights and I with my ladies."

"If they come at such short notice then they must expect basic accommodation."

She shook her head, "Men!" and she left.

It always took time to cross the river for we had a ferry rather than a bridge. A ferry meant that ships could sail up unhindered and we had better protection should the southern bastion fall. Eleanor and the Duchess were the first to land from the ferry. The Queen Mother looked at my town. "When the Empress gave this to your father it was a tiny, insignificant manor. It is good to see that it has grown into the citadel it has become." She smiled, "I am sorry that we did not warn you of our arrival. Put it down to old age."

"It is not a problem, Your Majesty."

She laughed, "And I would wager that your wife would not agree. She will be racing around your hall now making sure that all is well for the visit of the cantankerous old woman and her court!" She took my arm. "Come and I will tell you why I visit."

We walked through my town. The townsfolk, recognising the grand matriarch, all bowed and curtsied as we passed. She waved a hand at them. "As you know, Sir Thomas, Duke Arthur has been captured and is in Falaise. As for Eleanor, it is rumoured, and that is all it is, a rumour, that she is in the White Tower in London. We travel to Falaise so that I can ask my son for the truth. The Duchess would be with her daughter."

I looked at the Duchess, "Not your son?"

She shook her head, "When he allied with the French I knew he was lost to me. I hope that King John will keep him from harm but his people did not take kindly to the act and I have done with him. My daughter, on the other hand, is an innocent in all of this."

"Then welcome to my home." My wife and Alfred stood in the doorway to my hall. She had managed to change and to make Alfred presentable.

My wife curtsied, "Welcome, Your Majesty. I am afraid that our home is humble. If there is aught you wish then I pray you let us know. This is our son, Alfred."

The Queen Mother smiled and ruffled Alfred's hair, "It is good that you named him after the Warlord. He was the greatest knight in Christendom. Will you grow up to be such as he?"

Alfred nodded eagerly, "I will and I will help my father drive King John from England!"

I shook my head and my wife said, "Alfred!"

Eleanor laughed, "Oh the innocence of honest children! You know, young man that I am King John's mother?"

"I did not and I am sorry for he is a bad man!"

"Many think so but I hope that he will learn greatness." She turned to me. "When we have cleaned up after our journey I would speak with you. I have something to ask of you."

"Of course."

I was intrigued. While my wife saw to the ladies I went with Fótr to make arrangements for the knights and men at arms who accompanied them. It took some time. It was fortunate that Sir Edward had taken some of the garrison to help finish work on his castle or we would have struggled to accommodate them all.

Eleanor of Aquitaine and the Duchess Constance were with my wife in my hall when I returned. Of Alfred there was no sign. I think my wife had sent him off with a servant to keep him from mischief! They had goblets of wine. "This is good wine, Thomas. It reminds me of the red wine of Chinon."

"Thank you, majesty."

16

"My visit here is deliberate. I would have you accompany me to Falaise."

"I am not certain that your son will be happy about that."

"Leave my son to me. This will be my last act as Dowager Queen for after we have discovered the whereabouts of Eleanor, Fair Maid of Brittany, I will retire to Fontevraud Abbey. I will become a nun. I tire of this world of politics. I have outlived all but two of my children and I wish to prepare myself to meet my maker."

"But I still do not know why you wish me to come with you."

"I have seen in you hope for you are true to that in which you believe and that is rare. You are not swayed by money or by land. You fight for that which is right. Like Constance I believe that Arthur has now burned all of his bridges but I would not have harm come to him. I intend to make my son guarantee your right to La Flèche and Whorlton. I want him to know your feelings about Arthur. It may, perhaps, dissuade him from some rash deed. It will be my last act as Dowager Queen and I would see things right. I owe your family much. If it were not for the Warlord then John might not have been born nor Richard nor any of my other children. If I can I will protect his last heir."

And so, when they left the next day, I accompanied them. I took Fótr, ten men at arms and ten archers. We rode north. I was going to meet the King who had sworn to have my head. As we passed my new castle the Queen Mother said, wryly, "I see you do not let the grass grow beneath your feet."

"My priority is the safety of my people. We are surrounded by enemies. Strong walls will deter them."

"You may be right. King Phillip is merely regrouping. He sees Brittany as something he can take and Normandy is not as strong as it was. I thank God for William des Roches. He is well named for he is a rock."

The journey north opened my eyes for we were travelling with the most famous and powerful woman in the land. We were feted. Even I was accorded respect. I wondered how I would have been greeted if I had travelled just with my men. We did learn much, as we travelled. My men spoke with the garrisons of the halls. We discovered, as Griff and Tom had that there was great unrest in the land. It was the barons of Normandy and Maine who were unhappy. Some feared France and others wished France to take over Maine and Normandy. Civil war loomed large.

When we neared the mighty castle, I saw that Griff and Tom had been correct. Falaise would be impossible to take. I could have held it with a handful of knights, men at arms and archers. Sir Hubert himself greeted us, "I am sorry, majesty, but the King is absent. He rode to Rouen two days since. I expect him to return with the next day or so."

"In fact, when you saw our approach you sent a rider to fetch him hence." She smiled to take the sting from her words, "Good then I can have the royal quarters and I think that the Duchess of Brittany would like to see her son. Make it so."

He nodded and looked at me, "And Sir Thomas?"

"Sir Thomas and his squire are my guests. They will stay in the castle too." She turned to me and smiled.

While the castellan was unhappy he could do little about it. No one argued with Eleanor of Aquitaine.

The chamber we were given was a small one. I did not mind. Fótr would have to sleep on the floor. I changed from my mail into something more suitable and, leaving Fótr to see to the horses, I descended to the Great Hall. There was no sign of Eleanor but Arthur was there with his mother. I was about to turn and leave when Arthur waved me over. "My lord I would speak with you."

I wandered over and the would-be Duke stood, "I have to thank you for saving my mother and sister. I must also apologise. You were right about Phillip of France and I should have trusted you."

"You are young and you will learn from your mistakes."

"If I am given the opportunity. I confess, Sir Thomas that I fear for my life. My uncle has murderous intentions."

The Duchess said, "That is why the Dowager Queen is here. She will ensure your safety."

"I pray that you are right. And my sister?"

"That is what we need to ask King John."

The King did not arrive until after dark. It was an interesting moment and showed that while John was King his mother knew how to show where the power lay. She insisted upon eating when it suited her. The result was that King John arrived half way through the feast. I was seated next to Duchess Constance. Her son was seated between Eleanor and the Duchess. I saw King John's face darken. He then saw me and he coloured. He was angry. Sir Hubert left his seat next to the Dowager Queen and hurried to speak with the King. The two of them left the hall.

Eleanor nibbled the fowl before her and said, mildly, "It seems someone has upset my son." She put down the bone, wiped her mouth on her napkin and looked down the table towards me. "I am guessing it is you, Sir Thomas." She had a cheeky smile upon her face. She still knew how to play games.

I smiled back, "And I made certain that I had my beard and moustache combed!"

She nodded as she laughed at my attempt at humour, "You will do, Sir Thomas, you will do." She leaned closer and said quietly, "Just hold your tongue and your temper. All will be well. There will be a storm. We shall weather it."

When King John came in it was without Sir Hubert. King John sat next to his mother. He took out the knife he used for eating and pointed it at me, "What is that traitor doing here?"

I was mindful of his mother's words and I bit back my retort.

Eleanor put her hand on her chest, "What a fine welcome for a guest! I thought I had brought you up better than this! Sir Thomas is my guest. As he prevented King Phillip from getting his hands on the Duchess and her daughter I assumed that, like me, you would wish to thank him."

She was a clever woman. King John hacked a large piece of meat from the wild boar before him. He began to chew. It gave him thinking time. How could he gain from this situation? He did not know, yet, of Whorlton nor did he know of his mother's decision to go to a nunnery. He ate the meat and then washed it down with wine.

"I suppose I should be grateful. At least I now have the Fair Maid of Brittany safe from Phillip's tentacles!"

The Duchess said, quietly, "And where would that be, my lord?"

He frowned, "She is safe in England."

The Duchess looked hard at King John, "Where in England?" King John did not reply. "I should like to go to her. I am her mother and I can assure you I pose no threat!"

He still said nothing. Eleanor nodded, "Very wise, my son. You know not whom you can trust among your barons I hear. Better to let the Duchess know when we three are alone, eh?"

He had been outwitted again, "Yes mother. That would be best."

She smiled, "And now I will retire. Sir Thomas, would you be so good as to accompany me to my room?"

"Of course, Your Majesty. Fótr!"

The two of us each took an arm and we walked her to her chamber. As we reached her door and her ladies came she said, quietly. "The storm has yet to break Sir Thomas. I hope you did not drink too much. You will need your wits about you this night."

The door closed and we headed to the upper floor and our room. I turned to Fótr. "That was as clear a warning as I have ever had. Go back to the Great Hall and fetch an empty wine jug. Pretend, when you bring it, that it is full."

"Aye lord."

The Dowager Queen had given me a clear warning. I would heed it. I reached our room and I pushed the door open. There was a burning brand in the sconce next to the door and I took it. There was no one in the room. I pulled back the bed sheets. There was no venomous creature lurking there to sink its fangs into me. I now knew why Eleanor had left the hall so quickly. She wanted to avoid any chance that my room could have been tampered with. I lit the brand in the room and replaced the one in the hall. I had gone to the meal with just my eating knife. Now I drew my sword and laid it on the bed.

Fótr arrived. I asked him, "Did anyone say anything?"

"No lord but I saw some men watching me. I pretended that the jug was full."

"Good. Close the door and arm yourself." I took the jug from him. It had contained white wine. It mattered not. I wrapped my arming hood around the jug and, using the hilt of my dagger smashed the jug. I emptied the broken pieces along the inside of the doorway. The door opened out into the corridor. We would hear when anyone stepped upon them. Fótr had his sword and dagger in his hand. "Now we wait." I sat on the chair in the corner. I laid my sword and my dagger on my lap. Fótr sat on the floor in the other corner. We could both see the door. The brand in the sconce would soon burn out. If someone wished us harm then they would wait until no light shone beneath the door.

The light sputtered and then the room became dark. By my estimate it had burned for an hour. Now we waited in the darkness. Time passed. We heard noises in the distance but they did not appear sinister. I had begun to think that the Dowager Queen's fears were unfounded when I heard something in the corridor. I stood with my dagger and sword in hand. Fótr also rose. The noise had been outside and could have been innocent. It sounded like something catching on the stones. Another guest might have had too much to drink and be staggering back to their room. However, the Dowager Queen's warning had been good enough for me. I saw that the light in the hallway had been extinguished. That in itself was sinister for servants kept those burning all night. They would replace the ones which burned out.

Whoever came in was quiet. I barely heard the handle turn but there was the slightest of sounds and I did hear it. The door opened so slowly that the movement was almost imperceptible. I moved closer to the broken pieces of wine jug. The room was, ostensibly, totally black but my eyes had become accustomed to the dark and I saw the hand on the edge of the door. I saw the sword as it entered the room. The first foot in scraped across the shards of pot. It made a noise. It triggered the trap. Three men leapt into the room. The broken jug took the first man unawares. His shoes must have had thin soles and he lurched to one side. Fótr's sword darted out and struck him in the throat. I brought my sword down on the hand which held the second sword. Freshly sharpened it hacked through flesh and bone. He was a small man but incredibly tough for he uttered not a sound. He had a dagger in his left hand and he lunged at me. My own dagger slashed across his throat. The last man stepped into the room. He was a bigger man than the first two. He swung his sword blindly. It was a lucky blow for it would have hit my head had I not had fast reactions and my dagger came up to block the blow. Sparks flew as the sword and dagger clashed. I felt myself falling backwards. The man raised his sword and then had a surprised expression on his face as Fótr's sword slid from his back and out of the front of his chest. All was silent. Save for the clash of swords not a sound had been uttered. All three had died silently.

"Fótr, fetch a light. I would see what we can learn from these killers before someone else comes."

When the light was brought I saw that the first two men who had come to kill us were small and dark. I opened the eye of one of them and saw that they were wide. I recognised the signs. I had seen them in the Holy Land. "These two are assassins. They take hashish so that they will feel no pain." I turned to the other man. He was a Templar knight. He wore no mail but he had tanned skin and, about his neck, bore the Templar sign. I had seen enough of them when they had tried to abduct the Fair Maid of Brittany. "Search them."

We discovered coins but they were French and not Norman. Had the killers been sent by King Phillip or was this a complicated plot and they had been sent by King John?

"Fótr, fetch Sir Hubert. This is his castle."

I pocketed the coins. They might tell us more later on. I examined the weapons. They all came from the Holy Land.

21

Sir Hubert and his guards appeared with Fótr. He looked at the bodies. I could see the surprise upon his face, he knew nothing about this. "Do you recognise them, Sir Hubert?"

"The knight is vaguely familiar. He came here last year with a party of Templars on their way to England. I did not know he was back in the castle and as for the other two? I have never seen their like."

I stood, "I do not like to point fingers Sir Hubert but how did three killers, two of them strangers, get into your castle and come close to killing me and my squire? The Duke of Brittany is a more valuable prize. Is he safe?"

Sir Hubert nodded, "I passed his room on the way here. The guards are still outside. And as for how they came to be inside? I cannot give an answer. The castle is full. This man is a knight albeit one with a dark skin. I am sorry, lord."

I took him to one side, "I pray you keep a good watch on the Duke. If anything happened to him then you would answer to me."

"I swear he is safe in my keeping."

I believed him. As events transpired he kept his word.

He had his men dispose of the bodies and had our chamber cleansed. It was almost dawn by the time it was done and I knew that I would not be able to sleep. We washed and we dressed. Sir Hubert took us to the Great Hall. Food was being prepared. Sir Hubert poured us some small beer and asked, "Did *you* know them, lord?"

"One was a Templar and the other two were assassins. They come from a mountainous area of the Holy Land and they are deadly killers. We were lucky."

He smiled, "I think, lord, that you are a man who makes his own luck and for that I am grateful. The Queen would be less than happy if anything untoward had occurred."

It was the Dowager Queen who rose next and she joined me. We said nothing. "You had a restful night's sleep, Sir Thomas?"

I looked at Sir Hubert. The guards who had taken away the bodies would have spread the word. There was nothing to be gained from discretion. "No, Your Majesty. Three killers came to my room. They are dead."

For once she was taken aback. "I expected something, Sir Thomas, but not this. Did you know them?"

"A Templar and two assassins. They had French coins in their purses."

"Phillip's hired killers."

"Or perhaps someone closer to home who wishes to throw us off the scent. They are dead now and we could not question them."

"Sorry, lord." Fótr looked contrite.

"You saved my life Fótr, do not be sorry."

The Dowager Queen put her skeletal hand on mine, "And I too am sorry. I appear to have brought you into danger when I thought to make your life easier."

"When I was in the Baltic on the crusade some of the older warriors, you might call them Vikings, believed in three sisters who spin webs. It is not a Christian idea but it might explain much. Perhaps there are things which happen and they are beyond our control. It may have been that the killers might have gone to my home to kill me. I would rather they tried to kill me here and leave my family safe."

She nodded, "You are a wise man. As soon as my son rises I will broach the issue with him. The sooner you leave for your family the better."

John was a late riser. I suspect the fact that he had been ousted from his own bed by his mother had not pleased him. Everyone else was up and had partaken of food by the time he arrived. I had been questioned by everyone about the killers in the night. As I had expected the guards had not held their tongues. This was not my castle and they were not my men.

King John avoided me. Eleanor of Aquitaine had been seated with me. She saw the slight and she sighed and rose. She walked over to him. There was an animated conversation which went on for longer than I had expected and then he nodded. The Dowager Queen waved over one of her ladies and then returned to me. "Come, my son has a chamber we can use. Give me your arm. I will not use a stick! It makes me look old. If I lean on you it is just a lady with an eye for a handsome young knight." She took my arm and I realised how frail she was. "He knew nothing of the killers. I know my son and I know when he is lying. He might wish you harm; in fact, I know he does. That is why I gave you warning but I think he is too clever to risk hurting you here. I would keep my eyes open on the road." She laughed, "What am I doing telling one of Alfred's blood what to do? It is in your nature! You are a survivor."

The room we entered was a large one. There was a table and around it six finely made chairs. The castle had been built by the first King Henry. I wondered if the Warlord had sat at this table. The Duchess and her son arrived next. Arthur said, "Lord, I have heard that assassins came for you in the night. They were sent by Phillip?"

"They are dead, Duke Arthur. And as for their master? It could have been King Phillip. He wishes me gone from my land. It would make the taking of Anjou and Brittany so much easier."

He sat and I saw that my words had given him much to ponder. His mother stroked my hand. "I am pleased that you live. Whilst you do there is hope for Brittany."

King John came in with Sir Hubert and a cleric. He stared at me, "I am sorry that your life and that of your squire was put in danger. This is my castle and my guests should be safe. I have punished the guards. It was not of my doing."

I nodded, "Thank you, Your Majesty. I have met these killers when on Crusade. God watched over us."

King John made the sign of the cross. "Good fortune and God; you are indeed a lucky knight. Now, mother, what is this meeting about? I have much to do. King Phillip still threatens my land."

She nodded, "And Sir Thomas is a bastion for you against him but we will come to Sir Thomas later. Firstly, I wish to know where is Eleanor, Fair Maid of Brittany? Her mother and I wish to know."

He looked first at his mother and then at Arthur. "I have sent her to Brough Castle in England. There she will be safe until I return home."

The Duchess looked confused, "Brough Castle? Where is that?"

I said, "It is in the north of England. It is just south of the Roman wall." I looked at King John. "It is a bleak and desolate part of England."

King John smiled, "And therefore easy to watch. She will be safe from King Phillip's clutches."

"I would go to my daughter."

"I cannot allow that... yet. When I have returned to England and secured her in another castle, further south, I will send for you. Until then, Duchess, I suggest you return to Brittany and rally your knights to defend the land against the voracious French." He held his hand up for his mother was about to speak. "I will have no argument in this matter mother."

Eleanor nodded. She had not finished with her requests. "That will have to do Constance. Now, my son, with regard to Arthur. He is the rightful lord of Brittany." She paused and King John nodded. "And as such I would have him safe. I am pleased you have brought a cleric for I would have you swear that you will keep him safe and you will ensure that he lives."

I thought that he would stand and leave for his fists knuckled on the table and his face reddened.

The Dowager Queen smiled, "I am old. Soon I will be with God. I have made a will. It would pain me to leave my lands in Poitou and Aquitaine to another. Perhaps your sister would make a better ruler." It was a direct threat. Joan was married to King Alphonso of Castile. If he was to gain control of Aquitaine and Poitou it would be an end to the Angevin empire. John had no choice. I was not sure if the Dowager Queen would carry out her threat but neither did John.

He nodded and turned to the cleric. "I swear that I will keep my nephew alive." He looked at his mother. "There! Satisfied?"

She shook her head, "Father would you fetch a Bible. I would have the oath taken on one." The priest hurried out. "And now we come to the matter of Sir Thomas. I have given him the manor of Whorlton. It is mine to give. I wrote to you some months ago to tell you of this but you have not replied."

"He killed the Bishop of Durham! How can he rule a manor?"

She waved an irritated hand, "And he did penance in the Baltic Crusade much as your father did penance for the death of Thomas Becket. You knew that my son! I would have you recognise him as lord of the manor of Whorlton and La Flèche." The priest returned. "The Bible is there and I would have you swear. And swear that he has done penance. There is no crime for which he is accountable! He can travel where he will in England; even to Stockton and Durham!"

"Mother you are asking much for a traitor."

I was about to speak and she put her hand on mine, "My son sometimes you are a fool! Sir Thomas has defended your land against the French when other lords turned traitor. The only time he fought against you was when you sent men to take his castle! When I was at Mirebeau I was not closeted in isolation. I heard what happened around me. I would have you swear. If not then I will ride home, change my will and you will lose one half of your empire."

The King had nowhere to go. In that moment I became his greatest enemy. He would have to swear; that much was obvious. He could not take away my lands. The Dowager Queen had made me secure but he could still have me killed. He could hire killers. I would have a price upon my head.

He nodded and put his hands on the Bible. "I swear that Arthur will be safe in my care and Sir Thomas is the rightful lord of Whorlton and La Flèche." His mother looked at him until he continued. "And I also swear that, as he has

25

done penance for his crime he is free to travel my realm unhindered." As he took his hands from the Bible he added, "But if Sir Thomas rebels against me then I will wipe him and his brood from the face of the earth!"

It was a threat he could not carry out and I just smiled. His mother, in contrast, became angry, "Have you no spark of nobility in you? I am pleased that I have chosen a life in a nunnery for I can pray for your soul! You have much need of prayer!"

Insulted, he stormed out. The priest was about to leave but Eleanor said, "I would have you write down what transpired. Give one copy to Sir Thomas and one to the Duchess."

"Yes, Your Majesty."

He left. "Sir Hubert you are the castellan. Do you swear to keep Arthur safe?"

"I do and you have no need for me to swear on a book. I am a true knight and my word is my bond. I will die before I let anything happen to the Duke."

Eleanor nodded. "Then I am satisfied." She looked at me. "I owed much to the Warlord. I pray that I have done enough for his heir to keep him safe. If you are safe then the north of my husband's realm will be safe." She patted my hand and then turned to the Duchess of Brittany, "I am sorry, Constance. I could not get you close to your daughter but there is hope that you can see her and I have ensured that Arthur will live. He might be a prisoner but he has life and while he does then there is hope."

Ambush

Chapter 3

I bade farewell to the Queen. I never saw her again. She had been the most powerful woman in the world. She had brought her husband half of his empire and she had ruled it with him. She was a throwback to the time of my sire, the Warlord, and, I confess that I knew I would never see her like again. The world would be a sadder place without Eleanor of Aquitaine.

It was noon by the time we left. My men had heard of the attempt on my life and cast murderous looks at all whom they passed. Their hands were never far from their weapons. The did not like other men's warriors guarding me. The attempt had confirmed their opinion. We would have left earlier had we not had to wait for the parchment from the priest.

Ridley the Giant said, "We will not get far this day lord, and we do not have the protection of the Queen."

I nodded. "We will avoid Alençon and Le Mans. I know not if we would be safe. We will take the other road, further west. It is quieter."

Griff said, "Aye lord but it passes through forest for most of the way."

I smiled at Griff and spread my arm around, "And I have, with me, the best archers in the land. I trust to you and your archers to keep us safe."

As we headed towards Le Grais, eighteen miles away Fótr asked, "The Fair Maid, she is lost to us?"

I saw him fingering the half locket she had given him. I would not give him false hope nor would I dash them. "She is in England and that means she is safe. She is in the north of England and the people there have good hearts." I patted my saddlebag which contained the parchment. "And now we can visit England. We can go to Whorlton. It is not far to Brough. If we can"

He brightened. "Thank you, lord."

Griff and Tom were at the fore. Fótr and I rode mailed and with arming caps. I was under no illusions. King John hated me and he would send men to hurt me. They would not be his knights. They would be hired swords. I knew that there were many of them to be had. When we had been at Le Goulet we had met them. Landless lords, they would do anything for coin. Then there were brigands and bandits who had lost lords. The good ones, like James Broadsword, came to lords like me. The ones with murderous intent found likeminded masters. We would keep our eyes and ears open until we were safe in my manor.

Le Grais had a castle. It was on a higher piece of ground and was made of stone. We were spied as we approached and a pair of riders came towards us. I had intended staying in the town and wondered if this approach was to keep us moving. We reined in and my men closed up on me.

"You are Sir Thomas of La Flèche?"

"I am."

"Our lord, Baron Odo de Le Grais invites you and your men to his castle. He would entertain you."

I could not refuse. I was duty bound to enter the castle but I did not know this knight. He had heard of me but I had not heard of him. It would pay to be cautious. I smiled, "Excellent. We will be delighted to accept the baron's offer." The two men led the way. I said, quietly to Ridley, "Have the men drink little and keep their ears open."

"Aye lord." The look he gave me suggested that my words were unnecessary.

I saw that the castle had been made of wood but the keep was now built in stone. It looked substantial although the curtain walls were still made of wood as was the gatehouse. I saw that there were men wearing the baron's livery. He had coin. There was a stable too and, when we dismounted, I saw that he had twenty horses at least. There were two war horses. This was not an impoverished knight.

Odo de Le Grais was a little older than I. His wife was a small shrew of a woman who greeted me and then disappeared. I never saw her again. The Baron clasped my arm. "I recognised your standard. I had to meet you. It is an honour to meet the hero of Arsuf! I look forward to hearing all about it!"

After we had washed up Fótr and I were taken to the Great Hall. It was not particularly large and the table looked barely big enough for ten people. As it was there were just four. The Baron's squire, Gilles, joined us. The tale of Arsuf and the Baltic Crusade were payment for the accommodation and the food. I did not mind. I liked to tell the story of Arsuf if only to give the true version and not the legend which had grown up around the young squire defending the standard and his father's body.

When I had finished the Baron topped up my goblet. "I can see why men follow you. That is quite a tale and I now understand you a little more. You have quite a reputation here in Normandy and Maine. You are the only man to defy the Duke of Normandy and live. That is quite remarkable."

I said nothing but inclined my head and sipped the wine. It was not the best wine. Whatever he had paid for it had been too much. I did not know this man. For all I knew he was a spy for King John and he was attempting to make me say something injudicious. That would render the parchment I bore useless.

"Think you that the French will try to take our land once more?"

I nodded, "I can guarantee that. The Vexin remains in Norman hands and Phillip does not like that. His men are camped on the borders even as we speak."

Odo nodded and, after sipping his wine, looked at his squire, "John Lackland is not the man to defeat Phillip."

I had just spoken with King John. Odo's words invited agreement. Perhaps I was right and this was a spy sent to entrap me. I would not put it past the King. "His victory at Mirebeau halted the French did it not?"

"Pah! They were Bretons he defeated! They were led by a boy!"

"Then you do not put your faith in Prince Arthur?"

"He knows not which way to jump. First it is with Phillip, then John, then Phillip. No, lord, I have no faith in him."

"Then you must put your faith in King John of England. He is the rightful Duke of Normandy."

The silence which followed was eloquent. He was not a spy. He was one of the barons who wished to make war on King John. I was about to retire when he said, "What if there was another who could be Duke of Normandy?"

"There is none. The only other who might have a claim is Queen Isabella of Castile."

He smiled, "I did not say they had a blood claim but perhaps there are knights who could be Duke and a strong Duke. This land was founded on such men. Rollo, William Broadsword, William the Bastard, Henry; all were strong men. Perhaps we need another such one."

I stood, "I should warn you, Odo, that you speak treason. I put it down to bad wine and I will forget what I have heard."

He looked as though I had slapped his face, "But I thought that you of all people would support a revolt by barons!"

"You thought I would support a greedy baron who wished power? I may have no love for the Duke of Normandy but I would not give the title to one who was not of royal blood. Can I give you counsel?" He nodded, "Worry more about the French and less about the Duke!"

When we left, just after dawn Ridley reported that he, too, had heard treasonous talk in the warrior hall. He even had more information. "It seems, lord, that the land around Mayenne is where the treason emanates. Guy of Laval has made no secret of the fact that he wishes to be Duke of Normandy."

I nodded, "Even though his lands are in Maine. Then we will avoid Laval on our way south. In fact, I think it better if we sleep beneath the trees from now on. It will be safer." I closed my eyes to see the map I had in my hall. "We will head to Saint-Jean-sur-Evre. It is forty miles but there is no castle there. Griff, scout out the road ahead. We ride hard!"

The forest through which we rode was sparsely populated. We spied the fires of charcoal burners and the occasional forester but other than that we saw nothing. Our twenty-five horses made such a noise on the road that the men who lived close by the road fled and hid. Such a large number of horsemen did not bode well for those who lived in the forests. We had travelled ten miles when the heavens opened and it rained. We had good cloaks but I knew that Fótr would have his work cut out to clean my mail when we stopped. The storm lasted but two miles and then stopped. The sun came out and steam rose from our cloaks as they dried.

I decided that we would stop, while the sun shone. Riding in such wet clothes was not comfortable. Griff and Tom found a clearing where we stopped to water our horses at the small stream which passed nearby. We ate some of our rations. We were down to salted meat for we had not had the opportunity to buy food. I hoped that the ones who live in Saint-Jean-sur-Evre might have food for us to buy.

Dick One Arrow went into the forest to empty his bowels. When he returned he had a worried look on his face. Tom bantered, "I told you that woman in Falaise was not the cleanest of women!" My men laughed.

"Lord, I had seen tracks in the forest. They were in the mud. Someone passed this way after the rain. From the depth of the hoof prints there were men with mail."

"And numbers?"

30

"Sorry lord, they rode in single file."

That changed everything. My archers strung their bows. The blue skies suggested it would not rain; at least not for a while. Rain made bow strings less effective. The rest of us hung our shields from our cantles where we could reach them easily. We took our spears from our horses. We donned helmets. Our archers had the eyes and ears to listen for the ambush. I was in no doubt that we would be ambushed. All that I did not know was who would be the ambushers. Perhaps Baron Odo feared I would betray him and had sent men to silence us or King John might send killers so that he would not need to break his oath. It mattered not. We still had seventy miles to go and the journey would be fraught with danger.

My archers left us. They would leave the road and use the woods. That was where they were comfortable. I trusted both them and their judgement. The twelve of us and our three horses rode closely together. We had to make the ones waiting for us believe that we knew nothing of the ambush. We were the live bait. I was lucky in that all of the men I led were experienced. Some had been with me in the Baltic. They knew about ambush. It did not matter how many men we faced, I would back my men against any, including knights. All of my men had hauberks. Their helmets were full face ones and well made. They had mail mittens and their legs were protected by simple greaves. We would give a good account of ourselves.

I disliked wearing the helmet. It meant I had a restricted view and it was hot. That day my helmet saved my life. The cross-bow bolt struck my helmet and lodged in one of the holes of my visor. My arming cap stopped further penetration.

"Ambush!" Even as I shouted I pulled my shield up to protect my left side. The bolt had come from that side. I levelled my spear and I peered through my slits. I saw a figure some hundred or so paces from me. I spurred Skuld and my horse leapt off. Even as I charged at the figure I saw Godwin of Battle tumble from his horse. I could not afford to lose men. I hoped that my archers were close by. Another two bolts smacked into my shield. One had been released so close that the tip came through the leather cover and laminated wood. The man who stepped out of the wood with an axe swinging mistimed his swing. I jerked Skuld around and, as the axe struck fresh air I rammed the spear into his chest. His dying hands tore it from my grip and I drew my sword.

I saw the crossbowman as he frantically wound back the cord. He wore no mail. I brought my sword back and hacked up through his chest and into his skin.

31

Even as I did so I saw two horsemen ride at me. Neither were knights or, if they were then they were impoverished for they had leather jerkins studded with metal. They had swords. I rode at the two of them. Fótr would be close behind me and I trusted my squire. He knew how to fight in a mêlée. Skuld was flying. To fight from the back of a fast horse requires fast reactions. I had them. I pulled Skuld to the right. That meant only one horseman could get at me. Standing in my stirrups I brought my sword down. He tried to block it with his shield but the blow was so hard that it split his shield. I wheeled Skuld around to the left. I left the one with the broken shield and galloped after his companion who was trying to turn. I saw Fótr with his spear levelled as he charged the man with the broken shield.

The man I faced had an open helmet. The flecks of grey in his beard told me that he had experience. I gambled upon slower reactions. He was trying to turn when, instead of sweeping, I punched with my sword and lunged at his middle. His shield was slow to block the blow and my sword came away bloody. As he passed I punched with my shield and I saw him reel. Skuld almost anticipated my command and she pulled around so that I was facing his back. I rose and brought my sword down to split his back open to the spine. Fótr's spear took the other man in the throat.

I turned and saw that there were just my men left. Eight were mounted. Godwin of Battle had fallen earlier on and Godfrey of Lancaster was being helped to his feet by Ridley. Godfrey's horse lay dead. Griff and Tom ran up, "Sorry lord, we were slow. The rest of the ambushers are dead."

"Search their bodies. I would know who sent them. See if any survive."

Fótr said, "Lord, there is a bolt in your helmet."

I took off my helmet and pulled it out. It was cooler without the helmet. "How are you Godfrey?"

"I had the wind knocked from me but the bastard killed Anna!" My men were all attached to their mounts.

"How is Godwin?" I could not see him. I spurred Skuld to the place I had seen him fall. His horse was nearby grazing and he lay still. I saw a bolt in his shoulder. "Ridley, Fótr! We have a wounded man!"

They galloped up. I took off Godwin's helmet and put my ear close to his mouth. He was breathing. I saw blood by his arming cap. He had been knocked unconscious. Head wounds were always unpredictable. Ridley was good when it came to tending wounds. He took charge immediately. "Master Fótr, fetch the vinegar and honey from my saddle bags." As my squire hurried off Ridley said,

32

"It is good that he is unconscious. It will make this easier." He handed me a piece of cloth. "Lord, when I take out the bolt press this to the wound."

"Should we not take the mail from him?"

"Not with a bolt lord. We stanch the bleeding and then take off his hauberk. I fear we will not make Saint-Jean-sur-Evre this night. I dare not hurry this or we may lose him."

"We can camp here."

"Ready lord!" Ridley was a strong man and he easily pulled out the bolt. I jammed the cloth there and managed to stem the bleeding. Ridley nodded his approval. "Good." Fótr arrived with the vinegar and honey. He laid them on the ground as Godfrey of Lancaster appeared. "Godfrey and Fótr, you two take his arms from the hauberk. Loosen the ties around the neck and see if you can get it over his head before he wakes. Lord, you must maintain the pressure."

I had the easier task. Taking mail from an unconscious man is never easy. Trying to do so while his wound is being tended is almost impossible. The two of them managed to do as Ridley had asked. The hauberk was now pressing against my hand.

"Lord, we will take off the hauberk. Move the cloth and as soon as we have taken the hauberk apply the pressure." I nodded and watched as the three of them held the hauberk. Ridley said, "Now lord!"

I took off the cloth. Blood seeped rather than spurted and I took that as a good sign. They managed to get the hauberk off and then Ridley tore the gambeson apart to reveal flesh. He nodded to me and I applied pressure. "We are lucky. The bolt did not strike a vein and is only as wide as the bolt. I will not need to stitch. Honey and vinegar will do it."

It did not take long to clean the wound with vinegar and then to use honey to seal it. With a bandage applied he would heal.

"Now we see what damage there is to the head." We carefully took off the helmet and the arming cap. There was a tendril of blood. "We wait to see when he wakes. If you wish to push on, lord, I can wait here with him."

"No Ridley we all stay or we all leave."

I stood and my men gathered around. We had captured three horses. Only Godfrey had lost his horse. Griff said, "There were twenty of them lord." He shook his head, "They must have been desperate to take on twenty-two of us. Did they not know your reputation? One looked to have been a knight once. He had spurs and a faded tunic but he had fallen on hard times. His mail hauberk was rusted. He fell to Tom's arrow." He held a purse. It was full. "We collected

33

the coins from the dead. They are fresh minted Norman coins. They bear the face of King John."

I nodded, "Then we know who sent them. King John, it seems, regrets writing that decree. We will make camp here and wait until Godwin awakes before we ride. Lay traps around the camp."

Will son of Robin said, "They had food and wine in their saddlebags, lord. I am guessing that they anticipated a long chase."

As we ate I pondered the events. I nodded to Griff, "You were right Griff, they would not have ambushed us with so few men. Some escaped. This is not over. They will ride back to Falaise and report to whoever sent them."

"King John."

"I doubt it Fótr. He would have given the orders but one of his men would have been charged with the deed. We leave tomorrow before dawn. If Godwin is not yet awake then we tie him to the back of a horse."

"That may kill him."

"I know, Ridley, but if we wait until he awakes we may have more enemies and then he would surely die."

Godwin was tough and he woke in the middle of the night. The men watching him came to fetch me. Godwin looked unhappy, "I am sorry to have inconvenienced you lord. I am ready to travel now."

"No, eat and drink. You lost blood. We leave before dawn and you will ride with Godfrey. You were both wounded. Let others fight if we have to."

I was glad when we managed to leave the forest. We did so in the third hour of the day. We were now in open country. They could stop us but they could not ambush us. My archers rode ahead but were within sight of us. We spied Saint-Jean-sur-Evre in the late afternoon. There was no hall and no castle. The villagers wisely kept in their homes. I walked up to the largest and banged upon it.

A frightened looking man peered out, "Yes lord?"

"We would buy bread and food from you. We have coins."

He looked relieved, "We only have rye bread, lord and bean stew."

"That will do."

He hurried inside and then came back out to go to the other houses. The freshly minted coins ensured that we were able to buy plenty of food. The villagers were happy with the trade. If they went hungry they had money to spend. It was better for them. They even had rough cider for us to drink.

"Did you see any other men coming down the road?"

The head man, Hugh, looked around as though someone might overhear. "Yes lord. Last night horsemen galloped through the town. We had our doors barred but we heard them."

"They headed south?"

"Aye lord but I have no idea of numbers."

I gave him another coin. "Thank you." I waved over Griff and Ridley. "There were more men. I am guessing that they had two ambushes. When the first one failed then the survivors went to fetch the others. They will attack us tomorrow."

"But where? There are no more forests."

"No but there are woods. This is not a Roman Road. It is not straight. There are places they can attack."

Griff nodded his head grimly, "This time, lord, we will not let you down. We will not be caught unawares!" With David of Wales guarding my home Griff commanded my archers. He understood the responsibility.

We had less than thirty miles to go. I could, if I had more men, have sent one for help. We would have to deal with the ambush with the men that I had with me. Hindsight is always perfect. As we rode, in a tight formation, I speculated where the attack might come. South of Louailles there was a wood. It was forty paces from the road but if they had crossbows then we could be hurt. Griff and my archers had taken great delight in destroying the ten crossbows amongst the dead men. The lack of quality of our attackers was shown in the poor nature of their weapons. Cheap crossbows are a poor investment.

I turned to Fótr, "Ride to Tom and ask him to send men to Louailles. I would have them scout out the woods. Tell Griff to slow down our approach to allow them to discover the danger."

"What makes you think the attack will come there, lord?"

"If I was setting an ambush that is where I would choose. It is just five miles ahead. Tell them, if it is an ambush not to spring it. I would have us surprise them by being ready for it."

He galloped off and Ridley rode next to me. "We should have brought more men, lord."

It was not a criticism, just a comment. He was correct but I had just been asked to bring a handful of men to escort the Dowager Queen. Had I known what she intended then I might have done things differently. "You are right but it is too late now. The carrots are out of the ground. We deal with the problem ahead. How are you Godwin?" I shouted the comment over my shoulder.

"I have a headache and the next man with a crossbow that I see will be gutted. My left arm aches!"

"There may be an ambush. If there is then you and Godfrey stay with the horses."

Godfrey shouted, "We can fight, lord!"

"And you can obey orders too! Stay with the horses and the baggage."

I saw Fótr speak with Tom. He and Mordaf galloped off across country. We were far enough away from Louailles that they would not be seen and it would allow them to approach through the woods from the west. I had my helmet hung from my saddle. At the first sign of danger I would don it but I wanted a clear line of sight. If I donned it then the ambushers would know that we expected trouble. We passed through Louailles. There was a horse trough and we stopped to water the horses. As we did so it allowed us to look ahead. Tom and Mordaf had not returned. That could mean that they had not discovered the ambush and were still looking but my archers were so skilful that it might mean they had seen it and thought to ambush the ambushers. If the enemy were using crossbows then the two bows could send far more arrows towards them than they could send bolts.

"Fótr, fetch me a spear." Some of my men at arms had already sought a spear from Godwin. I would try one. If these were armed the same as the ones in the earlier ambush then they would have leather mail. A spear could kill!

With the spear in my hand I spurred Skuld to catch up with my archers. I saw that they had their bows strung and each carried three arrows. If there was danger then they would dismount and send three arrows towards the brigands in a heartbeat.

Ridley said, "Remember, lads, it is we who protect Sir Thomas now. We are not pox ridden half-wits like those at Falaise!"

In the end we saw them first. There were twelve riders across the road. They had spears. I saw, on the side of the road, stakes embedded in the ground. Behind them were men. I suspected there would be men at arms and crossbows. The woods to the side looked like the kind of place men would be hiding. I saw Griff and my eight archers halt just three hundred paces from the enemy. They knew the range of crossbows and there were aware of the speed of charging horsemen. My archers trusted that the ten of us would protect them.

I slipped my helmet on to my head. "Form line." By forming line, we threatened the horsemen. I watched as my archers spread out and headed towards the woods. I knew not where Tom and Mordaf were but whoever was in the woods were dead men. This was the time to trust my archers. The ten of us would charge the horsemen. Their crossbows, I could not see exactly how many there were, would be aimed at us but my archers would target the crossbows. Once they were eliminated then the men at arms would be the target. I saw that my line had spread out. We would not charge boot to boot. We had to give a target which was hard to hit.

I watched as Griff drew back and sent his first arrow to plunge into the shoulder of one of the crossbowmen. It made then loose their crossbows too early. Most hit the trees behind which my archers sheltered. Griff had realised that he had the wind with him. He had taken cover behind a stunted tree. Arrows could be released over such an obstacle. A crossbow had a flat trajectory. I spurred Skuld as my archers moved forward and sent eight arrows towards the enemy. I saw the crossbowmen frantically reloading. I spurred Skuld. We had to reach the horsemen before the crossbows could be reloaded. Their horsemen realised their dilemma and belatedly spurred their own horses. We had momentum. I lowered my spear and aimed Skuld at the one horseman with a mail hauberk. He had been a knight. My archers had the range. The crossbows were eliminated and I saw the men behind the stakes close ranks to make a shield wall. Ignoring the men on foot I concentrated upon the horsemen.

The man who had once been a knight had a lance. That showed his heritage. I guessed he had not used it much lately for it wavered up and down. The lance was longer than my spear. It hit me on the top part of my shield. I angled my shield so that the sliding lance hit the air above my left shoulder. I rammed my spear towards his middle. His mail was old and his shield slow to block the strike. My spear tore into his middle and the speed of our collision meant that the shaft was shattered. I let go and drew my sword. I saw the remaining men on foot looking at me. They turned and fled. I saw their horses waiting just twenty paces down the road. They were sumpters. One man stood to face me. Perhaps he was a former squire of the knight. I used Skuld's skill to fool the warrior. He slashed at air as I stood in the stirrups and hacked across his neck.

My men at arms and squires were urging their horses on. We had to get to the men before they reached their horses. I could not afford a chase through Maine. Leaning to the side I swung my sword across the back of a luckless man at arms who had been slower than his comrades. My sword grated along his spine. Fótr caught another with his spear. Ridley the Giant and Padraig the Wanderer managed to reach two more before they could mount their horses.

Their deaths saved four others who made their horses and galloped off. My archers had followed through the trees. They slew another five. I reined in. It would be a fruitless chase and I would learn nothing.

I looked around and counted my men at arms. Not all had survived. I had one dead man. Even as Griff and my archers searched the bodies I saw Tom and Mordaf emerge from the woods. They rode their horses and raised their bows. They had killed those waiting to ambush us. King John had failed. Would he try again?

William des Roches

Chapter 4

The attack had been repulsed and we had won but we had lost men. Jean de la Mont lay dead and we had two more wounded men. We did not have far to go to reach my manor and so we took Jean's body back with the five horses we had captured. We burned the bodies of the attackers. As we headed south the black smoke rose behind us. Tom and Mordaf had told us that they had come across ten men with crossbows in the woods. Their skills as both archers and foresters had helped them to slay them all without suffering a wound. The crossbows which had been intended to kill us made good kindling for the funeral pyre.

Ridley had examined the bodies before they had been burned. "There was one amongst them who had been a knight, lord. He had spurs. None had good swords and the mail we found was not worth saving. They were swords for hire. The men were desperate."

"As was John. He could not afford to use men who might be traced back to him. He will have used someone like de Ferrers to hire the killers. It is known that there is a blood feud between us. I have no doubt that there will be another manor in England for de Ferrers."

Sir Edward was in his new castle and working with his men on the tower above the gate. He saw the body draped over the horse. "You had trouble, lord?"

"We were ambushed twice. Keep your eyes open for a half dozen or so men who may have escaped us. I am not sure they would risk my wrath by attacking this close to my home but these are desperate times." I told him the news and my parchment.

He smiled, "Eleanor of Aquitaine is a wise old bird, lord. It is sad that she will retire to a nunnery. I will miss her." He looked up at Fótr who was talking to Gilles, Edward's squire, and added quietly, "And how did Fótr take the news that the Maid was in England?"

"Better than I might have hoped. There is now a chance that he might get to see her. We can now go to England without fear of arrest."

"But will you, lord?"

"Not yet for we need to deal with whatever Phillip throws at us first but we shall go and soon."

Alfred ran to me as soon as we rode through the town gate. He had watched our approach from the keep. He was a clever boy with sharp eyes. He, like Edward, had seen the body on the horse and also the bandaged Godwin. "You fought?"

I dismounted and picked him up. "That is my welcome? Where is the, '*I am glad you are home father for I have missed you*'?"

He hugged me, "You know that I have missed you but how many men did you kill?"

"There was no honour in their deaths for they were desperate men, hired to kill me." I saw his eyes widen. "We are safe here. Fear not."

Margaret was a kind woman. She had known Jean and her eyes were sad when I told her of his death. She looked at me for signs of a wound. My scarred face was a reminder of the dangers of combat. "But you are safe?"

I nodded, "And I have a document which guarantees our safety. I will rest for a day or so and then ride to Angers to speak with William des Roches. Would you wish to come with me?"

She nodded, "Soon I may not be able to travel and they have merchants there with goods we cannot buy here. Geoffrey has told me that we have coin aplenty. I would use some to make our home more pleasant before you hire more men!"

"Those men keep us safe." I took out one of the bags of coins we had taken from the killers. The other I had split amongst my men. "And I have more coins here. Spend what you will. We will not need more men for a while."

Many of my men were now married. They hurried to their families. Fótr saw to the horses. I took the document to my hall. I waved over Geoffrey. "I am pleased to see you well lord."

I showed him the parchment. "I would have a copy made of this. Can you make a fair copy?"

He shook his head, "I can write lord. Father James has a young priest just come to him, Father Abelard. He has a fair hand. He has been making a second Bible. Father James wishes one in each church."

"He sent for the priest?"

Geoffrey nodded, "Father Abelard comes from the monastery at Chinon where Father James trained. He keeps in contact with the abbot there. Father Abelard no longer wished the life of a monk. He is young."

"Then have him brought here. I would not let this out of my sight."

"Of course, lord."

After he had gone I sat in my chair in the west tower and drank some heady wine. The parchment was all important. Father Abelard's copy would not have the same weight as the original but if anything happened to the original then the priest could attest to the existence of the document. I did not trust John. The two ambushes had shown that he paid lip service to his mother. When she died he would renege on his oath; of that I was certain. He had done so when annulling his first marriage. He had made up some nonsense about not seeking the Pope's permission to marry. Isabella of Angoulême was a pretty twelve-year-old when he married her. John had been attracted to her by her looks but also because she had been engaged to Hugh le Bruin. He was devious. The plan had not worked as well as King John might have hoped for it alienated the Lusignan faction. That meant more enemies in the south. I needed to visit with William des Roches. Although John's seneschal, he had shown me both respect and had prevented others from attacking me. He had to see the parchment. Like Father Abelard he could attest to its existence.

When Father Abelard arrived, I was amazed at how young he was. He was, however, delighted to copy the document. He was honoured to have been given the task. "My copy, lord, will not be legal. It will not have the signatures nor the seals."

I nodded, "I know but you have now seen the original. If anything happens to the first document then we can produce this and you can testify to the existence of the other."

He smiled, "I heard that you were a clever man, lord. I look forward to serving you."

Over the next few days I busied myself with my men and my defences. James Broadsword knew better than any what we needed. "James, I would have you accompany me to Angers when we go to speak with Sir William. We will leave Ridley the Giant in command."

"You take Sir Richard with you, lord?"

"Aye." I had decided to take fewer men with me. I did not wish to appear to be intimidating the seneschal with large numbers. Now that I had Whorlton I needed to speak with Sir Richard. This would also be the first time that Alfred had left La Flèche. He was excited. We had a small pony for him and he would ride with me. I charged Fótr with watching him.

We left seven days after my return. I had a chest of coins for my wife and James to spend. Geoffrey, my steward came with us. I had plans for him. My wife travelled in a closed carriage. She was with child and I did not wish to risk damaging my unborn child. We also took a wagon for the goods we would buy.

"The document lord, it is good news?" Sir Richard rode with me.

"Aye Sir Richard. It means we can return home to England one day. Not yet for I would not leave this land while the French threaten."

Sir Richard looked back to where his squire and nephew, Ralph, was speaking with Fótr and Alfred. His young son, Dick rode with them. "Lord before we do return I would have my nephew knighted."

I nodded, "You are a knight. You need not my permission."

"Yet I would have you dub him lord. He admires you and it would mean much to me."

"Then I will be happy to do so. And would you and your son return to England with me when I go?"

He was silent for a moment and stared into the distance as though gathering his thoughts. "Lord, it pained me to leave England. I left many good men there. I cannot return to England. I am sorry. I would stay here. I like La Flèche. I would end my days here, if you and the good Lord permit it."

"But Ralph?"

"My nephew would return to England. He has told me, often, how he misses the land. The hills where he grew up are wild and he likes them. And his father is buried in England. I think he would like to visit his grave. There is another reason for his spurs, lord. You will need a household knight to accompany you."

"I think that Sir Edward will wish to return too but you are right. I will need knights with me. However, that is some time off." My mind was already working on the plans I knew I had to make. I could see the dangers which were growing in Normandy and Anjou. I had a wife and family. I could face trials and tribulations but I would not inflict that upon my family.

My livery was recognised as we approached the gate of Angers. We were allowed in immediately. I would not impose upon William des Roches for it might put him in a difficult position. I had plans to buy a home in Angers. I had coin enough and we could use it for Geoffrey to come and buy that which my wife needed. We went to the large inn by the river. The innkeeper was more than happy to accommodate us.

"James, I would have you buy the weapons and mail that we need."

"Aye lord."

"Geoffrey, you will accompany my wife but I would also have you search out a small house that we might buy. Close to the river would be good. Four sleeping chambers would be all that we need." We had spoken of my idea before and he nodded. "Alfred, would you accompany and guard your mother or would you come with me?"

My wife laughed, "My lord, that is no choice! He will go with you!" Alfred's face was eloquent.

I took just Sir Richard, his squire, Fótr and Alfred with me. The rest of my men guarded my wife and James. They had coin about them and there were cut purses in Angers.

We walked to the castle. We were bareheaded but we had swords. We were admitted but asked to leave our weapons with the chamberlain at the guard house. I did not mind. The weapon I held in my hand, the parchment, was more powerful than my sword.

We were taken to the Great Hall and wine was brought. William des Roches did not keep us waiting. Often the great and the mighty did so just to show their power. William was not like that.

He held out his hand, "Sir Thomas. It has been some time." I bowed. "And this must be your son."

"Aye lord, Alfred. The knight is Sir Richard of East Harlsey."

"You are all welcome, sit. What brings you here?"

I knew that he would know why I had come. Messengers travelled almost daily from Rouen to Angers. William des Roches was vital to John. He guarded the Loire.

I took out the parchment and handed it to the seneschal. He read it carefully. Smiling he said, "The Dowager Queen's hand is all over this. You have done well. This gives you security."

"From the Duke but not from the French. Another reason for my visit was to discover if there is danger from that quarter."

"There is always danger. However, King Phillip and his army are close by the Vexin. I think that the army which lies across the border from our lands is not yet a threat. I have my barons at the border keeping a good watch."

I had something delicate to broach, "Lord, when I travelled south from Falaise my men and I discovered that there is unrest amongst the barons of Maine and Normandy."

His steely eyes were piercing, "And you heard my name mentioned."

I nodded, "I did but as I did not know the men who suggested you as a future Duke I ignored it."

"Thank you for your honesty. Aye I have been approached but I am loyal to the Duke. He has treated me well." I was relieved. I did not want to fight William des Roches. His face darkened. "There is something else. Following the departure of you and the Dowager Queen Arthur of Brittany was moved to Rouen. William de Braose is lord there."

That was unwelcome news. "Was he not involved in the Abergavenny massacre? He is one of King John's lap dogs."

William smiled, "Lap dog is a little strong but he was involved in the massacre. He is a hard man."

"And is Prince Arthur safe?"

"I hope so." He leaned forward. "If I could speak in confidence?" Sir Richard nodded as did I. "I am disturbed that many of the prisoners King John took after Mirebeau lie in dungeons and I have heard they are being mistreated. I have written to King John to ask about them and their safety. I also asked for assurances about Arthur. I know the boy is foolish but he is the rightful Duke of Brittany. He has yet to reply to me."

These were worrying developments. Sir Hubert had been an honourable man. "Thank you, lord. That has given me much to ponder."

"Like you I believe in the young Prince and I would not wish harm to come to him but, at the same time, I had no desire to be Duke. You need to know that."

I believed him. He was many things but a liar was not one of them. When he heard that Ralph was to be knighted he insisted upon giving him a pair of spurs. I saw the look of envy on Fótr's face. He was desperate to be a knight. We spent half a day with William des Roches. I learned much about the politics of the south. King John had made a bad judgement of error when he had married Isabella. He now had the most power faction in Poitou against him. The barons

44

were rising in all of his lands save Aquitaine and they were loyal only because of his mother.

William took me on a tour of the castle. We met many of his household knights. They were devoted to Sir William for he was a charismatic man and the fact that he spoke to me as a friend meant that I was treated well by his knights. I was not the enemy and that was important. Alfred loved the tour. Angers was a bigger castle than mine. The sentries all had fine tunics and helmets. He would have stayed all day if I had allowed it.

Before we left William took me aside to speak to me alone. "Sir Thomas you and your family are in a parlous position. I can only protect you while King John is Duke and I can offer him my support. If I was not here… well let us say that the French wish to have your castle, Saumur, Tours and Angers. Those four are their avowed targets. If I were you I would make plans to go to England. The parchment you hold is a passport for you. It guarantees safety. England is an island. King Phillip may wish to rule it but it will be a harder nut to crack than Normandy or Maine."

"Thank you, lord. Your advice is sage."

When we left to return to the inn I thought about his words. They had been a warning. He was leaving the camp of John. Which side would he choose?

I was distracted for the whole afternoon. Alfred chattered on about the castle and the defences that he had seen. Ralph was excited about his spurs and spoke animatedly to Fótr about the ceremony of knighthood. I could not rouse interest in the items which were for sale. I had thought the parchment meant security. I was wrong.

"You are troubled lord?" Sir Richard recognised the signs.

I nodded, "I am Sir Richard. This revolt by the barons is more widespread than I had thought. King John's ill treatment of prisoners will sour relations further. If they rise against him what then?"

"Then we will be rid of him and can live in peace."

I shook my head. "Who would be Duke? Remember that King John is supposed to owe fealty as Duke to King Phillip. He has never acknowledged that. Would a new Duke bow the knee? Could I bow the knee? I think not. I have much to think about."

My wife was even more excited than Alfred when she returned. She had spent all of my coin on furnishings, cloth, dishes, pots; in fact, everything that held no interest for me whatsoever! I smiled and looked as though I was pleased. It was not her fault. William des Roches had sown the seeds of doubt in my mind. James Broadsword had also done well. He had not only bought all the weapons and mail I had asked of him, he had even found six English men at arms who were keen to serve me. What brought me the most delight was that Geoffrey had managed to find a house by the river. Although it only had three sleeping chambers it had a stable and secure gate. I asked him to find two housekeepers at La Flèche to maintain it.

The six months leading up to the birth of Rebekah, my first daughter, were the most peaceful I had ever known. The French did not come. King John battled with barons in Normandy and there was a civil war in both Maine and Normandy but it did not affect me. William des Roches, the seneschal, kept peace along the Loire. His strength protected us and we prospered. Ralph was knighted two months before the birth of Rebekah and his uncle and I sat with him. I had a proposal.

"Sir Ralph you are now a knight. I have no more manors here in the Loir valley to give you."

He shook his head, "I need no manor."

I waved my hand, "Yet I have a task for you."

"Yes lord?"

"Whorlton, in England, is unoccupied. The longer it remains so the more chance of damage and disrepair. I would have you, if you will, go to England and become my castellan and run the manor." He looked at his uncle. "If you say no then I will ask Sir Edward but, to speak truly, I would rather he stayed here."

"Of course, I will go, lord. It is just that I am not certain that I am up to the task."

"You are but you would not go alone. James Broadsword has told me that he would end his days in England. There are other men at arms and archers who wish to travel thence. You will have a good garrison. I will have Father Abelard make another copy of King John's command but I would have you just make the castle strong and the people prosperous. If this civil war escalates then I wish a place of safety that my family can use."

"Then I would be honoured to go lord."

It took half a month to organise. I sent with my captain, Henry, a letter to my aunt. Her own letters to me had spoken of banditry in the north. The Sheriffs were not doing their job and so I wanted her to know that she had my men upon whom she could call. When he returned Sir Ralph left with James and a boat load of men at arms and archers. It was a sad parting but the feast we held the night before they left was a merry one. For some of the men at arms they were leaving shield brothers. That was hard.

When my daughter was born I was relieved that all had gone well and that we had had so much peace. It seemed strange but Eleanor of Aquitaine died the same day as my daughter was born. Those of my men who had come from the Baltic saw it as a sign. They saw in my daughter the spirit of Eleanor. I was not so certain. I was sad for I liked the old lady. I wondered what her son might do now that he was free from her fetters. A week after Rebekah's birth William des Roches and his knights and men at arms appeared at my gate. I could see from his face that something had happened.

He would not enter my castle and we spoke in the guardhouse of the east gate. I sent the men thence so that we could be alone. "Sir Thomas, I have left the service of King John. He has gone beyond the pale." I waited. "Prince Arthur has been murdered in Rouen. It is rumoured that it was de Braose who did the deed but I believe it was King John himself. The body was found in the Seine. I believe that with his mother dead he feels he does not have to adhere to her edicts. With his mother's death it seems all restraint has gone. If I were you I would watch your back."

"What will you do?"

He looked sad and placed his hand on my shoulder, "I have offered my support to King Phillip. I take my men back to Le Mans. We will take Maine and then Normandy."

"Then we are enemies once more."

"I will not fight you. I am still your friend and ally. King Phillip is no fool. He knows he would lose too many men taking this castle. The greater danger comes from the new seneschal. Brice the Chamberlain is a mercenary paid for by John. If he is ordered to crush you then he will. Only Aquitaine will be free from war. Lock your gates and prepare to weather the storm." He clasped my arm, "Farewell. I am still your friend and will do all that I can to help you but as I said many months ago, England might be your best hope."

After he had gone I told my wife all. She was sad, "I liked Arthur. He made mistakes. It is a shame, for others who are not dukes and princes can make mistakes and they live. He made errors of judgement and has paid for them with his life. I will say prayers for him." She picked up our daughter and went to nurse her.

I sent for Fótr and summoned my household knights. We held a counsel of war. I told them William's news. Like me they were shattered by it. While

47

Arthur lived then we had hope that he might become Duke of Normandy. Now the choice was John or Phillip and neither appealed to me.

"So lord, what do you do?"

"My heart tells me to ride to Rouen and kill de Braose but that would not bring back Arthur and, as Sir William said, it is likely that it was King John who did the deed. I am loath to leave this land. We are all settled here but if life becomes impossible then I will return to England. I have Whorlton." I poured some wine. "I would have honesty from you. Do not give me the answer you think I seek."

William of La Lude said, "I am settled at La Lude. I now have three children and we are settled. I will stay lord." He shrugged. Whoever rules I may be able to come to some arrangement."

Sir Henry said, "I too like this land and I would stay here. For me England is no longer my home. Like Sir William I would seek an arrangement. I am sorry, lord, for you have done all for me."

"Do not worry about my feelings. None of you owe me anything. The six months of peace we have had is down to you four as much as anyone." I turned, "Sir Richard?"

"My nephew is in England but I like it here. My son likes it here. I could see Dick becoming a knight here but not in England." He shook his head. "I do not know, lord and that is the honest truth."

I was being deserted, "Sir Edward?"

He laughed, "Need you ask? As much as I like my castle my men and I would take ship to England in a heartbeat."

I knew where I stood. Like most of my knights I was reluctant to give up La Flèche but I had a family to think of and I would not come to an arrangement.

"Then we prepare to ride the storm. When it has abated we can then decide our course! Thank you for your honesty. A lord never led better nor more resolute warriors."

Baron's War

Chapter 5

When the war came it was not from the north nor the east. I had expected King Phillip to take advantage of the situation but he did not. Instead he joined William des Roches and they took control of the land around Le Mans. It was Brice the Chamberlain who led his forces north. I suspect it was on the orders of King John. If so it was foolish for I was the best defence against the French. I was summoned to the bastion on the southern side of the river. Sir Richard and his son Dick, now acting as his squire, were already there. The walls were manned and archers had arrows nocked. The new Seneschal wore no helmet and he was open palmed. Behind him was a column of household knights. I could see that he was there to talk. "Sir Thomas I am here to demand that you turn over your castles to me! William des Roches is no longer the seneschal, I am. King John is Duke of Normandy and you are his liege lord. Turn over your castles and you may leave this land and return to England."

I studied the man. He was a greybeard and had an enormous frame. He was a huge bull of a man. He had a cruel face. You could see his past in his face and hear it in his voice. I had heard of him. He was known as a cruel lord. William des Roches had told me, before he left, that it had been he who had starved to death twenty-seven knights of Brittany. It was said it was on the orders of King John but he looked like the kind of man who would enjoy it. He had the look of a bandit.

"This castle is mine. I hold a parchment signed by King John which guarantees my rights as lord of the manor."

"The document is no longer legal. King John's mother is dead! Heed my words or I will take your castle by force."

"Better men than you have tried and failed."

"Then be it on your own head. I will take this castle and you will die by my hand!" He whipped his horse around and dug in his spurs so hard that I saw flecks of blood.

I turned to Sir Richard, "Send riders to warn my other castles. Prepare for a siege."

After crossing my river, I told my burghers of the situation. I allowed them to discuss the situation amongst themselves. Like my knights they were worried. They knew that William des Roches had been a friend. We were now deserted and alone. Guillaume de La Flèche appeared to speak for all of the merchants and powerful men of my town for when he stood to speak they all looked to be in agreement. "Sir Thomas this town has grown and prospered under your rule but it seems to us that we are now in an impossible situation. If King Phillip comes he will conquer us. We have heard, through our customers that many barons have joined this revolt against John, Duke of Normandy."

"Have you any names?"

Alain the wine merchant said, "Aye lord. Robert of Sees and Ralph of Beaumont have sided with King Phillip in return for certain considerations. Maine is now French. William des Roches has helped to clear the land of those barons who were loyal to King John."

Guillaume continued, "So you see, lord, King John, the Duke, call him what you will, cannot win. If William des Roches had remained as seneschal of Angers then it might have been different. We have heard that Tours and Saumur are besieged."

I nodded. "And what would you have me do?"

"The men who come to attack us from Angers must be defeated. We will fight on the walls with your men and we will stand by you. However, if King Phillip comes then we would beg of you to bow the knee to King Phillip. We would come to an arrangement with the French. You have a noble name. You are well respected even by your enemies. Do not allow a stiff neck bring disaster to our town."

I might have become angered by the insult but I knew that he meant nothing by it. I stood and Guillaume de La Flèche sat. "I have listened to your words. We are in agreement. The immediate threat to this town comes from Brice the Chamberlain. We will fight him. However, I am a knight and took certain vows. You did not. When we have dealt with the attack from the south I will speak with you again."

I knew it was not the answer they wanted. They were merchants and business men. They did not want war. They wanted profits. My six months of peace had been brought to a catastrophic end by the murder of Duke Arthur. I wondered if I should have killed King John when I had had the chance. If I had done so then Arthur might be alive and he might be King of England. I dismissed the thought immediately. Arthur had proved that he could not be a leader. At least King John was fighting for his land. Arthur might have lost Normandy, Brittany, Maine and England. That I could not bear. When I had been first knighted I had learned to be pragmatic. That had continued in the Baltic. I needed to deal with the situation before me and then plan for the future. I was no longer alone. I had a wife and children. I had four knights, and more than one hundred and forty men at arms and archers. Perhaps I would have to take a knee. I did not want to but it might be inevitable.

That night, as I lay with my wife I could not sleep. The baby was asleep and Margaret cuddled in closer to whisper in my ear. She did not want the child awoken. "What troubles you, lord?"

I whispered in her ear and told her. She sat up. I sat up too. She spoke quietly, "This is simple, lord. We are happy here but this is not your home. We came here because we had nowhere else to go when we left Sweden. If you wish to live here then there is no choice. It is obvious to me that King John is finished here. If you stay here you have to acknowledge King Phillip as your master. Can you do that?"

I was silent. My sire, the Warlord, had fought all of his life to get Henry crowned King of England. John was Henry's son. Richard had been King and my father had given his life to save that of the Lionheart. My family had dedicated their lives to the Plantagenet dynasty. I might not like the way he ruled but I had to believe that blood would out. Perhaps when John had children they might be good kings. "No," I said, "I cannot."

She snuggled beneath the sheets, "Then you have your answer. You either fight Phillip, without the support of either your knights or your people, or you leave for England."

"You are a wise woman!"

My knights knew that danger was coming. My townsfolk were ready. We had supplies and our defences were good. It was late the next day when the sentries on the town's eastern gate shouted to me, "Lord, two men riding in. One looks hurt!"

I shouted for Father James and ran for the gate. I arrived to see Sir Guy de Changé fall from his horse. His tunic was bloody and he was unconscious. Father James took one look and said, "Get him to the church. Father Abelard, fetch my medical kit."

Sir Guy's squire dismounted. I shouted, "Wine!" I could see that the youth was shocked. This was not the squire he had had when he had helped get us across the Loire. Ridley the Giant handed me a wine skin and I gave it to the squire. "Drink and then tell me all."

He drank. He kept hold of the skin and nodded, "I needed that, lord. I am Stephen of Tours. I was one of Sir Guy's squires. Sulpice d'Ambroise attacked Tours. We could have held if many barons had not deserted us and joined the enemy. We lost the town but Sir Guy took charge of the citadel. We fought for two days. All the other squires died." He shook his head. "I am the youngest and I am the last. Why did God spare me?"

"I know not, son. God works in mysterious ways. How did you escape? I assume the citadel fell?"

He nodded. "The other barons accepted the offer to surrender. Sir Guy would not. We escaped on two horses. We would have made it had we not run into a band of knights wearing the livery of Angers. My lord took a lance to the side. I killed the knight and we escaped. We hid in woods. I tried to stem the bleeding. We were too far north to make La Lude and Sir Guy said to come here. He knew that you were a faithful and loyal knight."

"Fótr stable these horses. Come Stephen of Tours. We will see how your lord fares. He is a courageous man."

As soon as I entered I knew that it was hopeless. The two priests were covered in blood. They looked like the men who worked at the abattoir. Father James came to me, "I am sorry, lord but I cannot work miracles. The lance tore through his insides. I have cleaned the wound and stitched him to stem the bleeding. I have given him, perhaps, one more night on this earth." He nodded to Father Abelard, "He is confessing."

I turned to Stephen of Tours whose face showed that he was distraught to the point of tears, "You must be strong. You have done your duty and brought your master here. You can be proud of yourself."

Eventually Father Abelard rose and waved us over. Stephen of Tours dropped to his knees, "I am sorry that I was so slow lord!"

Sir Guy gave a wan smile, "No, Stephen you did all that you could. Go and fetch me some of Sir Thomas' renowned red wine."

He hurried off and Sir Guy gripped my hand, "I am dying, Thomas. I have done my duty and I can face God with a clear conscience. Would that others could say the same. Save yourself. We cannot win. King Phillip has suborned too many men. Barons now fight with each other for land and not for the rightful ruler. They seek estates."

I nodded, "I know."

"I beg a boon, lord. Stephen is a good squire. I would have him serve a good knight. I pray you find him one."

"I swear that I shall." I would keep that oath for one did not break an oath to a dying man.

Stephen of Tours and Fótr arrived. Fótr held out a goblet. Sir Guy drank deeply. He handed the goblet to Fótr. Holding out his hand he clasped Stephen's arm, "Stephen I am doomed to die. Do not grieve for me. I died as I lived, with honour. Sir Thomas has sworn to find you a knight to serve. I leave you my mail and my horses. I would that my sword be buried with me. I am the last of my line." It was too much for Stephen. He broke down and sobbed. Fótr put his hand on the squire's shoulder. Sir Guy smiled, "This is good wine, lord, I shall have, with your permission, a little more."

"Of course, and I shall join you." I picked up a goblet from the altar rail and poured us both a good portion., I saw the shock on Fótr's face that I was using the goblet for the sacrament. It seemed appropriate to me. "Here is a toast to good causes and knights to fight for them. Death to those with no honour!"

"Good causes and knights to fight for them. Death to those with no honour." Guy's voice was strong despite his wound. He was a true knight.

Sir Guy was drunk just before the end came. He had no pain. The four of us spoke long into the night and when he passed I knew that he had died as peacefully as was possible. We buried him the next day in my churchyard. Sir Richard attended. As Stephen of Tours prostrated himself on the grave I said. "Sir Richard you have no squire. What say you to taking on Stephen of Tours?"

He nodded, "Lord, it would be an honour." Stephen of Tours was happy too.

I sent riders to inform my knights of the loss of Tours. It meant that we could expect a French army as well as Brice the Chamberlain. The time of peace was over. It was now a time of war.

The men of Angers arrived two days later. They marched behind two banners: the familiar banner of Anjou and a red standard with a pair of yellow axes upon it. As I could see a warrior wearing the same design as a surcoat I identified Brice the Chamberlain. I thought it foolish. If Sulpice d'Ambroise had taken Tours then there would be another army coming for Angers. That would not help us and we had the bastion south of the river well manned. Every ship we had was ready at the river bank to ferry men back if the bastion fell or to take reinforcements across if they were needed. I stood on the wall with Sir Richard and my best men. Ralph of Appleby commanded my castle.

As we watched them approach Sir Richard said, "This makes no sense, lord. They will lose men attacking us. They should be defending their own castle."

I nodded, "And there is a reason. I think that King John has told this mercenary to make an example of me. Perhaps he has put a price on my head." I pointed. "They bring no rams and only pavise and ladders. They intend to take this bastion and close the river. When they attack they will come for me."

David of Wales commanded my archers, "He will have to endure a storm of our arrows if he is to do so. We have more than sixty archers and they are the finest I have ever commanded."

The approach of the men of Angers was ponderous. We would be outnumbered but there were no archers and remarkably few knights for us to fight. It looked to me like an army of mercenaries. Angers had a full treasury. They had emptied it to pay for hired swords. They must had spied out my land for they knew of the water filled ditch which was the southern defence. They used pavise and willow boards to cross it. When the ditch had been dug we had known that it would not hold an enemy for long. Its purpose was to slow up an attack for, as men approached it they came within range of my archers.

David gave the command and the arrows flew. They were mercenaries who were attacking us. Some had been more successful than others and that was reflected in their helmets and mail. I saw one man struck in the helmet by an arrow and the tip penetrated his skull. Others with superior mail and helmets fared better. Save for an arming cap I was bareheaded for I wanted to see clearly the attack unfold.

I heard David shout, "Ware crossbows!" My archers not only hated crossbows they recognised their danger. Standing behind my parapet we were a target for them. Brice the Chamberlain brought up his crossbows in an attempt to slow down the arrow storm. The tactic worked although it cost him his crossbows. My archers switched targets and slew the crossbow men. The warriors with the pavise and willow boards managed to make the bridges over the ditch and ones with the ladders poured across. The closer they came to the bastion the less effective our arrows would be.

The bastion itself was only twenty paces square and just two stories high. There was no gate on the southern side. There was one entrance and that was on the river side where it could be protected from attack by the town walls. The single entrance had been a risk but it gave the bastion a strength which belied its small size. It would soon be time for my men at arms. "Sir Richard take the west wall and I will take the east. Ridley the Giant, you and David stay on this wall but send some archers to the east and west walls. Come Fótr!"

The enemy, grateful that the arrows had slowed were eager to climb the walls of what they saw as little more than a glorified hall. I drew my sword and swung my shield around from my back. Fótr asked, "Will you not need your helmet, lord?"

"No Fótr for we shall be striking down on the enemy. You use your spear."

"Aye lord."

Ascending a ladder with a shield and a sword is never easy. Most of the those who climbed had their shields around their backs and carried their swords. I saw one of my men pitch from the walls as a spear struck him in the chest. These were mercenaries. They had skills with many weapons. I was just grateful that they did not know how to use the bow. The first man up the ladder was close to Fótr and I swashed his sword above his head. It clanged and clashed off my sword. Fótr chose his moment and, as the man's head came level with the top of the ladder he rammed his spear into the chest of the man. Even though he wore a hauberk, the spear was sharp and Fótr strong. My squire twisted the shaft of the spear as it entered the man and he fell, screaming from the ladder. His fall took two men from the ladder.

Dick, Sir Richard's son was fearless and he joined in with the men pushing the enemy from the walls. He was young but when he grew he would be a fine knight. Now that his father had a new squire Dick was keen to show that he was worthy to fight alongside his father. Stephen of Tours stood on the other side of Sir Richard and the three of them fought valiantly.

I saw that the archers on our walls had gone to the corners of the bastion so that they could send their arrows into the sides of the men climbing. They began to thin out the attackers so that the one or two who reached the top were easily dealt with. When the horn sounded and they began to fall back then I knew that they were regrouping. They pulled back beyond the ditch and out of bow range.

They had brought up more crossbows and they were giving the survivors some cover as they pulled back. I went to the south wall again and peered at the knot of knights who gathered around Brice the Chamberlain. I saw men pointing to the south west. Something had happened. His few knights and mounted men at arms suddenly turned their horses and galloped off in the direction of Angers. The others followed.

Sir Richard joined me. "I do not understand this, lord. He lost less than a hundred and odd men. He has many more than we do. Why did he break off the attack?"

"I know not. Let us not speculate. It will not give us the answer. Have the wounded despatched and clear the bodies. Take anything of value. If this war goes on we may need even base metal! I shall return to the castle."

Just then Stephen of Tours ran up to me. He looked not at me but Sir Richard, "Lord, Dick was killed in the last attack. A lucky bolt struck him. He knew nothing of it."

It was though Sir Richard had taken the blow himself. He ran to his son and cradled the body in his arms. We stood by him and said nothing. He had lost his wife, his lands and now he had lost his son. We buried him the next day. Sir Richard kept himself busy repairing the bastion while we wondered why Brice the Chamberlain had broken off the attack. The presence of Stephen of Tours helped Sir Richard. They had both lost someone dear to them and, in their grief, a bond was made.

Two days later we had our answer to the puzzle. One of our ships had tried to sail downstream but was prevented. There were warriors there. William des Roches had brought an army and was besieging Angers. Unlike Brice the Chamberlain he had war machines. I sent messages to my knights at Bazouges, Saint-Jean and La Lude. With Tours fallen and Angers under a siege we were surrounded.

We had news from the north of the war. It was not going well for King John. He was having to cling on to Normandy. Maine had gone. The presence of William des Roches and King Phillip had proved too powerful a combination. King John was now in Argentan trying to stem the loss of barons who were deserting him. William des Roches had come south and King Phillip had taken those barons who had defected to him, north to face John. There were now few barons who were loyal to King John. His cruelty had worked against him. His father had been a hard man but he had been strong and knew how to both persuade and force his barons to his will. The Warlord had taught him well. John had never been taught. They used a phrase about the Plantagenets style of rule, 'vis et voluntas'. It meant force and will. It needed someone who was strong to be able to rule in that manner. John had not been expected to be King. He had not been trained. He had been indulged. When Richard had gone on Crusade he had been able to enjoy all the trappings of power without any of the responsibilities. Richard's death had been a surprise.

When Angers fell, a few days later, William des Roches sent a message to me that my ships could use the river once more. That was all that the message said but I also took it to mean that he would not attack me. There was still another army to the east and Sulpice d'Ambroise owed me nothing. He would attack.

Saumur and Chinon also fell to the French. Their Breton allies, now fully behind the French King following the murder of the rightful lord, Arthur, were advancing towards Caen. John held Argentan but with the French coming from the recently captured Chateau Galliard it was only a matter of time before he would have to fall back to Rouen. Those were black days.

Refugees fled west to my town as Sulpice d'Ambroise headed towards us. That was our salvation. The refugees slowed up the advance and kept us apprised of his whereabouts. Most were trying to get to the sea. They were heading for Poitou and Aquitaine. Ships' captains soon heard of this and my town was filled with ships eager to make money from those barons and their people who had made the wrong choice. Many of those who spoke to me before boarding ships told me that they had estates in Aquitaine. I knew then that Aquitaine would remain loyal to King John.

I sent for Sir Henry and Sir Edward. "I want your mounted men. I do not intend to allow La Lude to be besieged. I will strike at this French army and defeat it before it reaches La Lude."

Edward was happy about that but Sir Henry had recently taken a wife, "What of my castle?"

"You are to the west. William des Roches will not attack you. Leave a strong garrison. I do not need your archers but I want your mounted men."

He nodded, but he looked less than happy, "Aye lord."

I sent David of Wales and all of my archers to La Lude. They would help to protect Sir William and his family. I led my mounted men to the woods north and east of La Lude. The river would dictate the approach of the French and I would use the land to defeat them. I would be behind their line of attack. I only had, including myself, four knights but I had twenty men at arms who were as good as knights and another forty who were almost as good. Most importantly every man who rode with me was mailed and all had a good horse. None was forced to ride a sumpter. Knowing the area as well as I did I planned on using a deep ford to attack the French in the flank as they approached La Lude. Men on foot could not use the ford but we could.

We waited in the woods while Robert de La Flèche scouted out the enemy. There was little point in crossing the river until the French were close. The woods afforded cover. We reached them at noon and we dismounted to rest our horses. I went to make water and when I returned I heard a heated debate between my three knights. "He is our lord and we should support him whatever he does!"

"Sir Edward you do not have a family to consider."

In response to Sir Henry's words Edward jabbed a finger at Sir Richard, "And neither does Sir Richard!"

I stepped between them, "Stop! Sir Edward you have gone too far! Sir Richard has recently lost his son. You will apologise."

Edward looked contrite. It had only happened recently and yet he had forgotten the death of brave Dick. "I am sorry, Sir Richard, my words were ill advised. I just do not like to see Sir Thomas treated in this way."

I shook my head, "My feelings are unimportant. This is unseemly in any man but more so in knights! I will not have this dissention! Why are you arguing? We are here to stop the French from attacking a brother knight. This will not decide who goes and who stays." I turned to Sir Henry and Sir Richard, "I am disappointed in you two. You, Sir Henry, have not had to fight yet. You Sir Richard have been victorious in all of our battles and yet you now seem to lack confidence in our cause." I pointed west. "If you cannot fight alongside me then return to your castles. I would fight with men who are loyal to me. I will have no doubters."

Sir Richard looked appalled, "Lord you misunderstand! Sir Henry and I merely said to Sir Edward that we hoped we could come to an arrangement with King Phillip."

I now saw why Edward had been angry, "Is King Phillip here? Is he even close? It seems to me that you go into this battle half-hearted. Decide now, both of you or leave me. We stop this French army. We stop every French army which comes our way until we face one which would result in the destruction of all that we hold dear. I do not fear Sulpice d'Ambroise. Do you?"

They shook their heads.

"Then no more talk of arrangements. Go and speak with your men. Put their minds at rest. I would have us all fight as one this day!"

An hour later Robert rode in, "Lord, their army is six miles from La Lude. They are making a camp." I nodded. "There is more. They have sent forty knights with men at arms. They are mounted and I think they are heading for this ford."

That changed everything. I should have known that they would have scouted out the river. They intended to try to take the bridge to La Lude. A mounted force could do so. I turned, "Mount and prepare lances. We wait in the woods and when they cross the ford we hit them hard."

The horses could swim the river both up and downstream from the ford but I doubted that they would do so. Knights and men at arms preferred their mail dry. Cleaning rust was a time-consuming activity. Fótr handed me my helmet and spear. We were far enough from the edge of the woods to be hidden. We would see their banners when they crested the rise and then they would drop down to the ford. The bank on our side was also steep. We would have momentum when we struck them. Some would escape and warn Sulpice but that could not be helped. Forty knights would be a loss to the French and might weaken their resolve. I had not misled my knights. Until King Phillip himself arrived then I was convinced that we could hold the French.

I did not don my helmet. I held it. I heard the French before I saw them. The jingle of mail, the hooves of the horses and the noisy chatter of men confident that they were safe told me that they were close. Then I spied their banners as they crested the rise. They rode in an untidy muddle of knights. They were relaxed. None wore helmets. Their shields were hanging from their cantles and their spears were with the baggage. I could understand their over-confidence. They had taken Tours and Saumur with ease. They had driven the last barons west and all that they faced were five barons in four small castles. Once our enclave was gone then only Chinon would remain free and that would soon fall. They had no scouts out and they halted at the edge of the deeper water to allow their horses to drink. There was laughter. Men took out wineskins and food. They had made the ford. It was the middle of the afternoon and they would reach the bridge, unseen, after dark. In their minds it was a perfect plan.

I waited until the first riders had forded the deep part and were heading towards the other bank before I spurred Dragon. My men had been watching me and their horses were just a heartbeat behind. The river was just a hundred and ten paces from us. In the time it took to cover that distance the first four riders had clambered to the bank and the majority were still in the river. I pulled my arm back and punched my spear at the surprised French lord. I twisted and pulled after my spear head had entered his body. The other three were taken by my knights and squires. Dragon slithered down the slippery slope to the water. I almost lost my balance but I managed to hold on to my spear and it rammed into the face of a knight who turned to look at the mass of men descending towards him. I was lucky the spear held.

Once Dragon was in the water the going was easier. The French knights and men at arms had drawn swords. We held the advantage for my men all had spears. I hit one knight in the shoulder. He had good mail and the head did not penetrate but I caught him sideways on and he fell into the deep water. His mail was heavy and he did not surface. Horses milled around and all was confusion but we had hit them hard.

One French knight, still on the other bank shouted, "Back! Fall back!" The men at arms needed no urging. I noticed that they had held back. They turned and fled. Those were not yet in the middle turned and rode up the muddy bank. The ones close to us were in deep water and they had no option. They could fight or die. Had they been fighting knights alone they might had had the option of surrender. My men at arms would not benefit as much from ransom. They killed knowing that the treasure on the dead would be theirs. In just a few strokes it was over.

The Battle of La Lude

Chapter 6

"Robert, take ten men and make sure that they do not regroup. Gather the horses. We will cross to the other side."

I left my men to claim the mail, coins and weapons from the twenty dead knights. Another fifteen men at arms were slain too. We had twenty good horses. Sixteen of them were that most valuable of commodities, war horses. I knew that we had been lucky catching them too full of confidence. Had they been prepared then it might have gone ill for us. As it was three of our men at arms had fallen. Four others had wounds. Gregor of Burgundy was wounded. I turned to him, "Take the wounded, our dead and the horses back to La Flèche."

"Lord, it is a scratch."

"It is a wound. I need the horses and dead to be taken back and I cannot afford to send a whole warrior. Obey me."

"Aye lord."

When Robert came back and said that the survivors of our attack had headed towards the French camp I gathered my knights and captains. We now had a chance to break the hearts of the French and I would do so. Robert had told me of their camp and an idea crept into my head.

Sir Henry was ebullient, "We trounced them! We barely lost a man!"

The words they had had still rankled with Sir Edward. He had been born a commoner and, for him, arguments were settled with fists and not words. His words were not spoken gently, "That is because we follow a good leader who plans well. We used spears against men who were in a ford and lax. We were lucky."

"Enough bickering." I could see that there was now a rift between my knights and I had to repair it. "Rest men and horses but keep a good watch. Tonight, when it is dark, we walk our horses to the French camp. I would have their sentries slain. Then we mount and ride through the camp causing as many casualties and as much disruption as we can. If we can drive horses away then all the better. When Fótr sounds my horn three times we withdraw. We pull back to the ford. We do not have enough men to be reckless."

Sir Richard asked, "And what will the attack achieve, lord? We risk men when we do not need to."

"They have such overwhelming numbers that they feel safe. We hurt them. When they attack La Lude, they will have a shock for there are now more archers within those walls than they have ever seen. Sir William has made good defences. We will watch and I will choose the moment when we break French hearts. Now go tell your men what we do. Put out sentries and rest."

I joined Fótr at the horses. "I have a fresh spear for you, lord. The other appeared in good condition but you never know." I nodded. He lowered his voice. "I have never heard your knights argue before."

"I know and it is my fault. I did not speak my heart to them often enough. Sir Edward has known me the longest. Sir Richard and Sir Henry fled England to find sanctuary with me. They have both had more success than they could have dreamed. I can see why they see their future here. The fealty they will owe to their new king will be worth it. They have to bow the knee to someone and there is little to choose between John and Phillip." I smiled, "Do not worry Fótr, when I have truly made up my mind then I will tell you and you can make your choice."

He grinned as he took off Dragon's saddle, "Oh I made my decision a long time ago, lord. Where you go so do I!" His loyalty lifted my spirits.

I drank some wine and ate some stale bread and salted ham. I had, perhaps, been less than truthful with Fótr. I had almost made my mind up already. If Phillip granted my manors to my three knights then I would return to England. I battled only to bring the King himself to speak with me. I would not bargain with some Count or Prince. I had fought and beaten them too many times to expect fair treatment.

I managed to sleep for a short while. I was woken by Fótr. "It is almost time, lord."

"Any trouble?"

"None lord. I have fed, watered and saddled Dragon. He is eager for war."

After I had made water I hung my shield and helmet from my cantle and slipped my arming cap from my head. I needed to be able to hear. Taking Dragon's reins, I said, "Let us go. Robert de La Flèche, you lead."

We headed south for the camp. We were two miles from the French. When we were just a mile away we stopped. I nodded to Ridley and he waved to the ten men who would slip silently ahead and slit the throats of the sentries. While we waited we mounted. We would ride our horses at the walk for the next one thousand paces. My men were spread out in a large half circle. I had organized my knights so that they led their own men. It was reassuring to have Ridley the Giant, Godwin and Godfrey flanking Fótr and me. I had no need to worry that our horses' hooves would alert the enemy. They were in high spirits despite our attack. Gathered around their camp fires they were drinking and eating. They were joking and they were gambling. It was ever thus in an ill-trained army.

Timing would be all. I decided to risk leaving my shield hanging from my cantle. It would protect my left leg. I also left my helmet hanging there too. I needed to be able to see and hear. We passed the first dead sentry and Roger rose like a wraith to climb on to the horse brought by Godwin. I would see the shadows of the men by the fires some three hundred paces from us. I raised my spear. My men raised their weapons. When I was satisfied that all were ready I spurred Dragon.

Fótr was right, he was eager. He leapt ahead of my men at arms and Fótr. Even though our hooves thundered I had covered thirty paces before the men around the fires reacted. Their weapons were at their tents. A few had swords about their waists. They drew them. I leaned forward, pulled back my arm and rammed the spear into the middle of a man at arms. Dragon was a powerful horse and his speed meant that the falling body slid from my weapon. I barely had time to bring it up before I saw my next victim. He was a brave man who stood before Dragon with a swinging sword. I could not risk injury to my horse and I jerked back on the reins as I thrust the spear into his neck. He fell backwards. Another ran at me with a small wood hatchet. I punched with my spear. He managed to block the blow with his weapon but the force of my strike knocked him backwards towards the fire. His hands grasped the spear and tore it from my grasp. He screamed as the fire ignited his hair. I drew my sword. The man stepped from the fire but his clothes had caught fire. He ran, screaming into the camp.

I looked around. The French had seen the threat and men were racing from their tents with weapons in their hands. The sight of the burning man must have terrified them. We had done enough. Around the closest three fires I saw twenty bodies of men dead, dying or wounded. "Fótr, sound the horn!"

Three men at arms ran at me with swords and axes. I stood in the stirrups and pulled on Dragon's reins. He reared. Two of the men showed discretion and stepped back. Perhaps the other thought he could avoid the flailing hooves. Whatever was in mind Dragon's mighty hooves crushed the man's skull. As pieces of bone and brain splattered the other two I slashed down and my sword went through the skull of one of them. Fótr's spear took the other.

"Lord. the men are retiring!"

I nodded and dragged Dragon's head around. We thundered back towards the river. I saw, from the way they hung over their saddles that some of my men were wounded. I saw some empty saddles. We had lost men. Eight French horses without saddles also galloped with us. Horses do that. They follow the herd. I was one of the last to reach the river. I saw that all of my knights had survived as had their squires. Ridley the Giant and my other veterans had also survived. That was the way of war. I saw that four of the men who were not with us had been the recent arrivals. War on the border was brutal. You either learned quickly or you were dead!

"Back to the woods. Ridley, appoint two sentries to watch here. The wounded can take the horses back to La Flèche."

We had now suffered losses which would make a difference. We had no spare spears but we had hurt them. While our horses were tended to by our squires I spoke with my knights and Ridley. "Did we hurt them?"

No one man had a true picture but by discovering how many men each knight and his conroi had killed I estimated that they had lost upwards of fifty men. Some men had been trampled as they lay asleep around the fires others had fallen to spears and swords. Satisfied I said, "We rest. If they attack tomorrow then we will have to fight again. If not, we rest too." Dawn was breaking as I lay my head down.

I was awoken at noon. Fótr pointed to the west. Gregor of Burgundy led fifteen men on horses. As they approached Fótr said, "The French have stayed within their camp save for those men at arms they sent to recapture their horses. Our scouts reported that they are cutting down trees to make a ram."

"Good." That was what I had hoped. A ram meant a slow and steady approach. My archers would decimate the attackers.

Gregor had brought not only welcome reinforcements but food and my men organised fires. The hot food and the wine they had brought would revitalise weary bodies. I knew that the French would expect us to attack again. They would have dug ditches. Stakes would have been planted and one in three of their men would be on guard. They would be waiting for the thundering hooves. We would rest. The French would watch and become tired. Weary men made mistakes. When they assaulted La Lude, those mistakes would cost lives.

We ate well. Men who had slept now kept watch. Our scouts were changed. We knew where the enemy were. They kept their scouts close to home. They did not know that my archers were in La Lude. They thought it was my famous archers who were scouting!

Ridley the Giant woke me and it was still dark. "Lord, they are on the move. We heard them break camp."

I nodded and stretched. "Let the men sleep. Wake Fótr. The three of us will be enough to investigate."

I did not take Dragon. I rode Skuld. She was better for such work. She had senses which I did not understand. We crossed the river and headed to where the French camp had been. Ridley led us to a small stand of scrubby bushes and old apple trees. There we saw Robert de La Flèche. We took shelter and spied the breaking of the camp. The tents were already down and they were being packed on to the back of sumpters. The parts of the rams were loaded on to wagons. The neigh of horses told us where they were being saddled. As the sun rose over our left shoulders I saw that men at arms and the levy were already heading west to La Lude. Two lines of mounted men at arms flanked them. The knights stayed together. They still had over sixty of them.

I glanced east. There was no sign of reinforcements. They had taken a couple of citadels and would need to garrison them. King Phillip was around Alençon and William des Roches in Angers. They had limited numbers of men. "How many men do you think we face?"

Robert pointed, "I counted banners, lord. Sixty-six knights lord including those with their lord. A couple of hundred men at arms. There were forty crossbows. They left early. I guess they want them in position before dawn. The levy? More than a hundred and fifty. They guard the rams, carts and baggage."

"We will watch and follow at a distance. They kept no scouts out?"

"No lord, but they had many men guarding their lines." He chuckled. "They must have spent a long time digging ditches."

65

We waited until the last of the levy, escorted by ten men at arms, left and followed the column of men snaking west. They were easy to keep in view and we appeared to go unnoticed. We were four hundred paces behind them. We had the river to our right and if they sent men to chase us away we could easily reach it before they did. I was confident. I wanted to see their approach. We had thwarted their original plan. They could no longer guarantee taking the bridge. That meant they would attack the softer side, the south east. William had dug a good ditch and it had been filled with river water. It would be an unpleasant crossing for the French but one I felt they would risk. William had a bridge over his ditch. He had not yet built a removable one. That would be where they would use the ram.

The lords and the knights stopped five hundred paces from the walls of La Lude. They respected my archers. I saw that the crossbowmen who had arrived in the night were behind willow pavise. They were in arrow range. The men at arms, led by ten knights, were forming lines and walking to support the crossbows. The men of the levy were assembling the rams under the supervision of a knight. I saw arms being waved and a knight led twenty men at arms towards the river. They were going to risk swimming it to prevent the bridge being used by Sir William. If we had to then we could remove them. I was happy for Sulpice d'Ambroise to spread his men out. An idea was forming in my mind.

Twenty knights and twenty men at arms along with forty of the levy headed south. They were going to cut off the castle from the south. Only half of the knights remained around the standards. I saw that they had priests with them. Men were erecting tents. They were here to stay. I observed that the first ram was almost built. I saw that there was an exchange of missiles between the crossbows and the bows. David of Wales was too crafty to show his hand. He would have his men target the crossbows. He would make them think we did not have many archers in the castle. He would save the shock of the arrow storm for the assault.

"I have seen enough. We can return to the camp. This has given me an appetite."

We smelled the food cooking as we approached our camp. My men looked up. Edward asked, "Do we eat or fight?"

"We eat first. Then we watch and, when the time is right, we fight."

It was the middle of the afternoon when we moved off. We left four men with the spare horses and our supplies. We now had fresh spears. I led my men back to the stand of trees where we had met Robert. My plan was to approach from the direction they would least expect: the east. If they saw horsemen they would assume it was reinforcements. The last thing they would expect would be an attack by me!

We used the natural folds in the land to approach discreetly. We had no banners. We heard the sound of battle even as we approached. A small ridge hid the battle from us. I dismounted and with Edward and Fótr, crawled towards the ridge. The French tents were less than five hundred paces from us. Sulpice and his knights were dismounted and viewing the battle. There was no point in using horsemen against walls. When the walls fell and the defenders fled then they would be used.

Almost a thousand paces away I could see that they had the ram across the ditch and it was lumbering up towards the gate. It was hard to see but it seemed to me that there were many bodies lying alongside it. It looked as though David of Wales had won the battle of the missiles! There were fewer men at arms now. Even as we looked I saw a few of the levy leaving. They were doing so surreptitiously. They sneaked away from the slaughter at the bridge. I wondered if they had been used in the attack. If so it was an error of judgement. You used the levy to defend or to exploit a victory.

We slid down the slope. "We take the standards."

Edward laughed, "You would attack their leader and his knights?"

"They are not mounted and they are just five hundred paces from us. If we can drive them from the field then we can destroy their camp. It is a risk worth taking." We reached my men. "We are going to attack Sulpice d'Ambroise. He is surrounded by knights but they are not mounted." My men at arms looked delighted. There was nothing they liked more than attacking knights. They had the confidence to believe that they could win and they also knew that victory brought rewards which would make them rich men for the rest of their lives. All were acutely aware that when King Phillip arrived the situation would change. We had to make hay while the sun shone! "We go in in one line. Ignore the levy. They will run. Those on the walls are close to breaching the wall. We take the standards and the victory will be ours! We will snatch it from them."

This time I donned my helmet and took the spear proffered by Fótr. "Stay close behind me. If you get the chance then take their standard and throw it to the ground!"

"Aye lord."

I made sure we were in a line and then, raising my spear, led my men forward. We were in dead ground for the first forty paces after that we broke cover. Even then we were not immediately spied. All attention was on the walls and I could hear the boom as the ram struck Sir William's gate. We were less than two hundred paces when the shout went up. The knights ran for weapons. The men of the levy who were still erecting tents, fled. I saw Sulpice d'Ambroise and some of his knights running towards the eight horses which were nearby. Those close to the walls knew nothing about it. They were clambering over the ditch to join the ram. Even as we rode I saw David of Wales archers knock down waves of French men. If they took the walls it would be at great cost.

I pulled back my arm as a knight held his shield and sword before him. There was little for me to hit. I thrust below his shield at his knee. He fell writhing to the ground. Some of the French lords had mounted. The standard was with Sulpice. I thrust my spear again into the chest of one of the knights who, with two others, tried to bar our way. Dragon contemptuously knocked them to the ground. My men at arms would deal with them. Dragon had the scent of battle in her nostrils. She was eating up the ground. The eight men we were chasing looked over their shoulders. The last two turned. They were going to try to stop me.

"Fótr, take the standard!" I still had my spear and the two men did not. They came at me from both sides. I pulled my shield tighter to me and thrust at the knight to my right. I caught his shield square on and he tumbled from the saddle. I felt my left arm shiver and shake as the sword smashed into it. I wheeled Dragon around. I could not afford to leave a knight behind me. I thrust my spear at him. It struck him but caught in his surcoat and mail. As it was torn from my grip I saw blood on the surcoat. I had a hit. Drawing my sword, I managed to block his blow. He had managed to turn very quickly. Sparks flew as our blades struck.

I saw that Ridley the Giant was with Fótr. My squire was not alone. Many of the knights had managed to get to their horses. Instead of fighting us they were following the standard. I stood in my stirrups to bring a blow down on the brave knight whom I fought. He blocked it but I saw that his sword bent a little. He realised it was useless as a weapon. He threw it at me as he wheeled his horse around. I had to block the thrown sword with my shield and, when I looked, he was heading after the other knights. Dragon would not catch them.

I reined in and looked to La Lude. The sight of the standard leaving the field followed by the knights had ended the battle. Men at arms and the levy fled south and east. Even as I watched I saw David of Wales' archers bring down more of them. Looking towards the fleeing French I saw that Fótr and Ridley had stopped. Then Fótr triumphantly raised the French standard. He had managed to take it! Victory was ours! We had won.

King Phillip

Chapter 7

We could not leave for home for some time. We had captured knights and we had bodies to remove. This was our land. We would not pollute it with enemy dead. After taking what we needed from the tents, the dead, the chests and the captives, we made a pyre and burned the enemy bodies and their ram. We stayed the night in La Lude and the next night too. I wanted to make certain that the French had gone. Sir William led his own horsemen to follow the French. The trail was easy to find. Some of their wounded had died and others had discarded weapons. They followed them back to the outskirts of Tours.

Before we left I said to my knights. "I do not think they will send a small army next time. It will be the whole French army. None of you have a castle strong enough to withstand them. When you spy them approach then flee to my castle." They looked at each other as though they doubted the wisdom of my words. "Do you have ransom you can pay?" They shook their heads. "Then listen to me and I will teach you how to play this game. Flee to La Flèche! When King Phillip comes then I will talk for you all. I have not served you ill thus far. Trust me for a little while I beg you."

Sir Edward said, "Of course they will!" he turned and glared at the three of them. "Sir Thomas knows his business." He shook his head. "All of you have what you have because of one man, Sir Thomas! Act like men!"

His scornful words had the desired effect. They all nodded. We headed to our castles. We had left good men in the churchyard at La Lude but we returned home in good spirits for we had won and my men at arms were rich!

My wife was just relieved that I was well and my men had not been hurt. Sir Richard had lost a few of his men and I could see that it had disturbed him.

He ate with his new squire and his men in the bastion. It meant I ate with my wife, squire and son.

My wife said, "The *'Swan of Stockton'* docked this morning. I think the captain has a letter for you."

I was desperate to read it but it would have to wait until the morning. My wife and my son needed me there. Alfred was keen to hear all of the details of the battles. I was in no mood to do so and I let Fótr take over the task. He was a good storyteller and Alfred was engrossed.

My wife knew me well and she remembered the late-night conversation we had had. "Did the battle change your mind, my love?"

"The opposite; it confirmed what I had already thought. There is more. I no longer lead knights who are all of one mind. I cannot lead knights who do not believe in me. I owe it to them to secure their future and that will not be easy."

"We could just leave for England, my love."

"I have never run away from conflict in my life and I will not begin now. It is not just my knights that I worry about. They are, if anything, the least of my problems. It is the men who chose to join me and the people who live in the four manors. No, I will have to think my way out of this problem but I can still make plans. In the morning I will speak with our captain. Then I can begin to make plans. We will need more than one ship. I will ask him to find other ships for me."

"And when do we leave?"

"That is out of my hands and depends upon King Phillip. If he does not come soon then we have time to prepare. We use the time well. We will need money in England. I will see Geoffrey and make sure that we have coin we can take back. We have other goods we can take back or sell. I know not what Whorlton will yield in terms of income."

My wife was perceptive. "And which men will you take with you?" She had got to the heart of it.

"I would take them all but I suspect that many, especially those with local wives, will want to stay. Ridley and those who married Swedes will come. Sir Edward has already made his choice. I will have to speak with them but first I will make certain that we have ships and we have the means to leave." I hesitated. "I must go in secret to Angers. I must speak with William des Roches. He promised me once that he would repay me for the favour I did him. I will now call in that favour."

71

I was up early and made my way to the docks. Henry, son of William was watching his men replace one of the sails. He looked relieved to see me, "Lord, I heard that there was a battle to the east of here. I am pleased that you survived."

I nodded. "We need to talk privately."

"Of course. Come to my cabin. It is a little small but we cannot be overheard."

Small was an understatement. There was a table and a chair and that was all. "You sleep here?"

He laughed and pointed to a large metal hook screwed into the side of the cabin, "I have a piece of canvas which is slung between these two hooks. It is restful." He opened his chest and took out a letter. "I will give you this before I forget."

I put the letter inside my surcoat. "My family and I will be leaving this land but I know not when."

He nodded, "When I took Sir Ralph back to England I gathered as much. It was a long voyage and he told me what was likely to happen. And you would take your men and horses?"

"As many men as I could take and the best of my horses."

"Then *'Swan'* will not be sufficient."

"No, can you find me more ships?"

"You have gold and that guarantees that someone will take you. You need it to be someone you can trust. The men on this river and the Loire know you. I will sail to Angers and make discreet enquiries."

"Once you have secured their services then I would need you close to hand. Would you be able just to take short voyages?"

"Of course. I know the river well and now that the French own most of Anjou it is easier to navigate. There is plenty of trade between here and Nantes."

I gave him some coins to secure the services of other captains and I returned to my home. I summoned Margaret. I wanted her to be there when I read the letter.

Thomas,

I can now address you as such. Sir Ralph came here before he went to Whorlton and delivered your letter. He allowed me to see the parchment. This is joyous news! When do you return?

72

I pray that it is soon for my husband, William, is not well. He has the coughing sickness. I know not my position if he dies! We also need you for the Scots are becoming tiresome again. We have cattle raids and slave raids. My husband does his best but the Bishop of Durham is a weak man who spends his time in London and allows his nephew to rule Durham for him. The Sheriffs are more concerned with collecting taxes than defending the land.

Sir Ralph seems a pleasant knight but he will have his work cut out at Whorlton. It has long been abandoned. The village is run down and over taxed.

I pray you have a safe journey home and that we are all still here when you arrive.

Your Aunt,

Ruth

My aunt had been indiscreet. If the letter had fallen into King John's hands then we both might be in trouble. I handed the letter to my wife. She smiled when she read it. "Then we can go to your family home?"

"I will leave, tomorrow, to visit with William des Roches. He may help me make up my mind."

I did not choose Ridley to go with Fótr and me. He stood out too much. I took Padraig the Wanderer. He had the kind of face you forgot in an instant and yet he had served many lords and was a true survivor. We did not wear surcoats and we took no mail. If possible, I wanted to be invisible if I could. I did not ride Skuld. I chose an older palfrey. Perhaps I would be noticed but I hoped not. I planned on arriving early on market day where we could blend in with the others going to make purchases.

We dismounted a mile from the town walls. We walked our horses. All three of us had the hoods of our cloaks up. It helped that it was raining. I noticed the damage to the walls and the gate from the siege. William des Roches knew his business. He had taken the citadel easily. He knew how to war and I hoped I would not have to fight him. I wondered what had happened to Brice the Chamberlain. Perhaps he was in the dungeon. He would receive better treatment than the Bretons King John had had him starve to death.

73

We managed to slip through because there was a wagon ahead of us which was running contraband weapons to the Cathars. With the seaways blocked the Cathar heretics were desperate for weapons. The sentries ignored us and we slipped silently into the town and headed for my house. I had decided that, even when I left Anjou, I would keep the house. Who knew when I might need it? Old Jean and his wife Anna had lived in La Flèche all of their lives. They would have lived there still if their son, Henry had not killed a man in a fight in the inn. He had been put to death by the family of the murdered man. It had happened when I had been away at war. Henry had been wild but he had been their only son. The family of the murdered man had made their lives unpleasant. I had had to speak to them on a number of occasions. When Geoffrey had suggested them as housekeepers I thought it a perfect arrangement.

Anna kept the house immaculate. I paid them a wage each week and they lived better than they had in La Flèche. Jean stabled the horses. "Will you want food, lord?"

"No, we will eat in inns. I would speak with you both."

Anna looked worried, "Have we done something wrong, lord?"

"Of course not. It is just that if King Phillip takes over this land then I must return with my family to England." They gripped each other's hands. Were they to be evicted? I smiled, "Fear not. I will continue to pay you and keep the house. When Henry, my captain, calls, he will bring you more money. He may even stay here." I looked at them. "Can you write?" They shook their heads. "It is no matter. When Captain Henry comes I would have you give him all the news from Angers and La Flèche. It may be many years until I return but I promise that one day I shall. You two will be my eyes and ears here in Anjou."

They were both delighted with the arrangement. I felt slightly guilty, using them as spies, but I had paid for the service with the fine house and a pension which would last for the rest of their lives. We ate in a local inn on the river and listened to the talk of the war. It would soon be over. King John was trapped close by Rouen and Peter de Preaux was leading the French forces to take that mighty castle. It was John's last bastion in Normandy. In two years he had lost Brittany, Anjou and now Normandy. We heard of a crusade, not in the Holy Land but here, in France. The Cathars of Carcassonne were being persecuted. Many swords were heading there. The only bright spot for the Plantagenet family was Aquitaine and Poitou. Aquitaine wanted nothing to do with Phillip and the men of Poitou were still loyal. It was nothing to do with John and all to do with his mother.

Fótr and I went, the next day to the citadel. I sent Padraig to check on ships which might augment those found by Henry. When we were admitted into the Great Hall, William des Roches roared with laughter. "By God but you make me smile! You are the thorn who pricked John and now irritates the rump of my new King and yet you are able to sneak through my walls as though you are a ghost." He clasped my arm. "Welcome Thomas!"

"I was not sure of my reception after La Lude."

He nodded. "Sulpice d'Ambroise is no friend of yours but it was a masterful display of horses and archers. You did not come here to seek praise, did you?" I shook my head. "Then on with it."

"I am no fool. King Phillip will soon come and either squash us like a river insect or tell me that I must bend the knee."

"And that you will never do."

"No."

"Then what?"

"I would leave this land and return to England."

"Then do so. I told you once that you were free to use the river. It was a heavy hint which you chose to ignore."

"It is not as easy as that. Not all of my people would choose to leave. They have families and I would leave La Flèche in the hands of someone I could trust."

"You are in no position to bargain."

I sighed, "You once said that you were in my debt. I am calling in that favour. I would have you plead my case to King Phillip. I would leave La Flèche in the hands of Sir Richard, La Lude with Sir William and Bazouges with Sir Henry." I saw him shift uncomfortably. "They will bend the knee. They will be loyal. How many other barons would you trust with such a key town and castles?"

He stood and wandered over to the fire. The rain of the last few days had made this normally warm part of the land feel cold and damp. "There is merit in what you say and I like the three knights but what of you? Do you give up all claims to manors in this land?"

I nodded. "Eleanor of Aquitaine gave me a manor in England. More importantly she acquired a document for me which means I can travel in England and live there. King John may not be happy about it but he swore on a Bible."

"I would not lay too much faith in that but I admire your optimism." He looked at me thoughtfully, as though weighing me up. "Very well. I will do so."

He smiled. "There must be something of the soothsayer in you, Thomas. King Phillip is on his way here even as we speak. He left Paris yesterday. He will want to see you! I will ride north to meet him."

"Then I will return home and prepare."

Padraig was at my Angers' house when I arrived. "Wasted trip, lord."

I was disappointed, "No ships then?"

He smiled, "Oh no sir but Captain Henry had already spoken to them. Depending upon when we sail we could have six ships; if we need them."

"Come let us sit outside on Jean's bench and watch the river. I would talk." I picked up the jug of wine Jean had placed on the table and nodded towards the goblets. Fótr picked them up. When we were seated I poured us each a goblet. I raised mine and said, "To La Flèche."

"To La Flèche."

"Padraig, when we return to my home I intend to ask my men and my archers their intentions. I would know if they wish to risk following me to an uncertain future in England or to stay here and become subject to King Phillip."

"I will follow you to England, lord." He laughed, "It is in my name, Padraig the Wanderer."

"Good."

"But you wish to have an idea of who else will follow?" I nodded and sipped my wine. "That is a hard question. Some names are easy: Ridley, David of Wales, Mordaf, Godwin, Godfrey. All of those would follow without a moment's hesitation. My own shield brother, Richard Red Leg, he would come. There are some who have married girls from La Flèche. They would be torn. They would wish to be loyal but they have roots here too." He emptied his goblet. "I cannot be more accurate than that but I will say that all would wish to follow you! No matter which lord they serve at the moment they all regard themselves as Sir Thomas' men. Even if they stay part of them will still be owned by you."

Fótr poured Padraig some more wine and asked, "And why is that?"

"Because most of them came here when they had nowhere else to go. Many had been abandoned or rejected and yet Sir Thomas took them all in and made them welcome. He made them safe and that buys loyalty that no gold can."

He had given me much to think and made the meeting with my men even more urgent.

We headed back the next morning. My talk with Padraig and Fótr had cleared my mind. After speaking with Margaret and warning her that we would leaving sooner rather than later I gathered every man at arms and warrior. I left my walls empty, save for Fótr and Padraig, and gathered them in my Great Hall. From Padraig I knew that they were all expecting me to leave. That made it easier.

"All of you are my warriors and will always be my warriors. However, I cannot serve King Phillip. He comes here soon and, when he does, then I shall leave with my family for a small manor in England. I freely give you all a choice. You may stay here, with my blessing, or you may come with me to England. For those of you with families my offer extends to your families. Sir Richard, Sir William and Sir Henry will be staying here. I have hopes that they will be confirmed as lords of their manors." There was a murmur of conversation and I held up my hands. "I do not need the answer yet. You will need to talk to your shield and arrow brothers as well as your families. Tomorrow I shall be here in my hall and you can tell me your answer then. To those who choose to stay, and that may be all of you, can I say that I will always remember your courage and resolution when we have fought our foes. A lord never led better men."

I stood and left. The men drifted out. I saw a couple approach me. I held up my hand, "Tomorrow. This is not a trivial decision. I would have all of you give thought to it. Besides I have four more visits to make."

With the walls manned once more Fótr and I rode first, north to Saint-Jean-de-la-Motte to speak with the garrison there. Then I went to Bazouges and across to La Lude. After I had spoken with the garrison I spent some time speaking with Sir William.

"You know that my heart wishes to come, lord. Marguerite and I have been with you a long time. We remember Sweden."

"I know."

He pointed to his three children who were playing in the bailey. His eldest, Robert, was a year and a half older than Alfred. "I have roots. Had you asked me while I was still at La Flèche then I would probably have come but building the walls of La Lude and getting to know the farmers and those who live in the village, well it has tied me to them. I am torn. I cannot abandon my people."

"And I understand. England will not be easy. From what I can gather Whorlton is run down and poor. Staying here is the right decision for you but I know that I will miss you."

"I will always be your knight, lord."

"And that gives me great comfort."

My last visit, just before dusk was to the bastion. As we took the ferry across the river Fótr said, "The knights have not changed their minds then?"

"No, Fótr. Sir Edward comes with us but the others stay. Each have their own reasons. Sir Richard is the one I understand the least for his nephew is in England. He is his only living relative and I would not be parted from Alfred for the world. Before I leave I must speak with him privately."

The arrangement I had made with the bastion and the three castles was that they would tell their lord and he would send the names of those who wished to travel with me with his squire. I confess that I was filled with trepidation when I sat in my hall. Father Abelard had agreed to act as my clerk and he would write down the names of those who would come. We had barely sat down when what seemed like all of my men entered. As the parchment was filled I felt humbled. When the hall was emptied I said, "Father Abelard, four squires will come to add names to the list."

He nodded, "Lord, you have not asked me yet, if I wish to follow."

I looked at him in surprise. "You would come?"

He smiled, "I have ambitions too, lord, just as any of your warriors. If I stay here I will be Father James' assistant. You have no priest and besides, I would see England. I have read much about the times of the Romans. If you would have me then I would follow."

"Then you are my priest and welcome!"

As I stepped outside some of my more senior warriors were waiting for me. None had been in the hall. I looked at them: Robert of La Flèche, Hamlin the archer, Griff Jameson' Tom Robertson, Rafe and Tom son of Tom. I smiled, "You are here to tell me why you stay. You have no need to."

Griff nodded, "I know, lord, but we owe you an answer. For Tom Robertson and for me we were born in this land. Our mothers, aunts and uncles live here too. As much as we wish to follow you to the land where our sires of old were born our feet are embedded in this land."

I nodded.

Tom son of Tom said, "And we have all families now. I have land which I till. My wife is from Angers and she does not wish to go to a cold and wet land like England."

I held up my hand, "I understand and I am honoured that you have been torn." I patted my breast, "All of you will be in here."

There were no more words for we were men and could not trust ourselves. Having spoken to Father Abelard I realised that I had others with whom I needed

78

to speak. Geoffrey was like Griff and the others. He wished to follow but he had ties. I was pleased that I had made the offer. I went to the town and summoned the council. They needed to know my decision. There was a mixture of relief at not having to fight King Phillip and genuine regret that I was leaving.

Alain of La Flèche stood, "I speak for all the council when I say that you have been a strong lord and we will miss you. When your ship comes here to trade know that our special relationship will continue. We will not forget you."

By late afternoon Father Abelard had his list. Thirty of my men at arms would come with me and thirty-five archers. The whole of the garrison from Saint-Jean-de-la-Motte followed Sir Edward's lead and chose my path. As I had expected few from La Lude chose to come. Until Alfred grew Sir William was as close to a son as I had and I took it as a compliment that they chose to stay with him. There would be enough men to garrison La Flèche and Bazouges but the Bastion would only be able to have a night watch.

My wife had also spoken with her ladies and some of those who worked as servants. Eight wished to come with us. When Henry of Stockton arrived the next morning, we had a list of the number of ships we would need.

"And when would you need them lord?"

"I will stay until I have spoken with King Phillip but there is no reason why our goods should not be loaded and our horses can be gathered at the quay ready for loading."

"Then I will see the captains." He smiled. "We barely have enough ships." He looked up at me, "And the coin will be paid when we reach England?"

I shook my head, "No Henry. We will do this properly. See Father Abelard and he will give you the coin you require."

"Father Abelard?"

"Until we get to England he has agreed to act as my steward."

At noon the next day I was surprised to see wagons and men heading from the north. It was Sir Edward. When he was sighted I left the keep and headed for the town gate. He dismounted in the square. "Is there trouble? You have left your castle."

He smiled, "I did not think you would wish me to fight with King Phillip. He comes south with his army. I was ready packed when my scouts saw him." He smiled. "I left my gates closed. It will give him something to ponder."

I pointed to the ships. "Your men can load your goods on the ships and your horses. You are the first here and you can be the first to board."

"What if King Phillip does not agree to your proposal?"

"Then we take to the walls and have a glorious end! You had better send a ferry for Sir Richard. He will need to be in attendance and send a rider to Sir Henry and Sir William."

After warning my wife that we would soon have royal guests I went to my tower and saw the French army as it snaked its way down the road from Saint-Jean-de-la-Motte. As soon as they took the western road I went with Fótr and ten men at arms to the town's west gate. We stood outside the gate as King Phillip and William des Roches appeared at the head of their army. There had to be more than two thousand men.

King Phillip frowned and looked at William des Roches. "What is this Sir Thomas? You asked me to bring the King and I have done so. Now you bar our passage!"

I shook my head. "No, lord, I am here to escort the King and his senior lords to my Great Hall. My town is small and this army would fill the folk with fear." I smiled, "That is all."

The King frowned and then dismounted. Smiling he said, "You have a stiff neck Sir Thomas but you are a strong leader. Had your King John been made of such stuff then things might have gone differently. Lead on." He looked up at Ridley the Giant. "I can see that I will be able to walk in the shade!"

As we walked through the town I saw my people bowing to their new lord. It appeared to please the King. I also saw him taking in the defences. We walked through my gate and headed towards my keep.

"I can see why this was so hard to take. When my lords told me that it was a rock I wondered for Chateau Galliard fell to me and my men but La Flèche remained a thorn."

My wife greeted us at the door to the hall and led us inside. Food and drink were laid out and servants were ready to serve. I waited until King Phillip and William des Roches were seated before I joined them. Water was provided for the King to wash his hands. Father Abelard came and blessed the food and drink. When the servants poured the wine, the King looked pointedly at me. I smiled and drank, "Your Majesty does me a disservice. I have never killed a man I did not face with a sword in my hand."

William des Roches shook his head, "You really do steer your own course, Sir Thomas!"

The King drank and said, "I apologise for my mistrust but after the death of Duke Arthur at the hands of your King John I began to wonder at the motives of Englishmen."

I nodded, "And after the attempts on my life by Templars and hired assassins you can understand my mistrust of French Kings."

King Phillip flashed me an angry look and then turned it into a smile and nodded. "We will never be friends."

"No and that is why I will leave this land, with your permission."

"And if I do not grant you permission.?"

"Then this beautiful manor will be covered in the blood of many of your men and all of mine for I will never bow the knee to you."

I saw the shock on the faces of his lords. Only the King and William des Roches appeared unsurprised, "Then what do you propose?"

At that moment Sir Richard entered. "Three of my knights do not wish to leave this land. This is one of them, Sir Richard of East Harlsey. I would have him as lord of La Flèche. He is a good knight and he will bow the knee to you."

I saw the King look at William des Roches who nodded. "I will speak with your knight after you have departed. If his answers satisfy me then I may well accede to your request." He smiled. "It sounds so much better than demand. This is good wine. Now that this is my manor I can enjoy a better cellar. Now what about the other castles?"

"The three of them did not exist before we came. The one you have passed is empty and is my gift to you!"

He laughed, "You give me what I could take. Very generous."

I smiled, "We could have burned it but we did not. La Lude and Bazouges also have lords who would serve you. Both are doughty warriors and would keep this land safe for you." I lowered my voice. "There are many rebellious barons in this land. I can assure you, lord, that if my knights swear an oath to you, they will keep it."

Sir Henry arrived. "This is another of your knights?"

"It is."

"And the last will be on his way?"

"Even as we speak."

"Then, in principle I agree to your proposal. When I have spoken with my knights you may return." He nodded, "I am guessing you have ships to load!"

I rose. "I have and I am pleased that we did not have to fight. It would have been a pity if royal blood had been spilled."

He laughed, "Defiant to the end. I pray that all my knights defend their land with your fervour Sir Thomas!"

81

The Trials of the Sea

Chapter 8

My three knights all met with the King's approval. They were all good knights but I am certain that William des Roches' word and support helped. His new title was *seneschal of Angers, Loudun, Saumur, Brissac, Beaufort, and 'all the land of Anjou' at the King's pleasure.* My knights swore oaths of fealty as did the town council. I was not present. King Phillip sent me from my own hall. I was not certain why. Part of me thought it a cruel act but another part wondered if William des Roches had thought it might be easier for me. It mattered not for I had much to do.

I was selfish. I had my family and my horses Dragon and Skuld aboard *'Swan of Stockton'*. Fótr's two horses were also loaded aboard. We had most of the treasure and the precious items Margaret could not live without. Her ladies boarded with us. I would take no servants. I knew that there would be many in England whom I could hire. I spread my men at arms and archers amongst all of the ships. I had ten archers and four men at arms with me.

I was on the quay when King Phillip and his knights emerged. He walked over to speak with me. "It has been an interesting experience, Sir Thomas but I pray that our paths never cross again. I am not certain who would come off best." He nodded to his seneschal, "You have a fine advocate here. You owe him much."

William des Roches shook his head, "No, Majesty, I owe Sir Thomas more than I could ever pay and he did something I could not. He remained faithful to a cause even when it was obvious to all that it was lost. That is a rare trait. King John had best look to his laurels. Once Sir Thomas gets his teeth into a problem he does not let go."

I clasped his hand, "I know not about that, my lord, but I have enjoyed our friendship and despite the war that will come twixt our lands I hope that we can remain friends."

King Phillip shot me a sudden glance, "Are you prescient or do you have spies at my court?"

I laughed as I shook my head, "Neither, Your Majesty. It is just that there are two bulls in the field and there is room for but one."

As they headed for the gate King Phillip looked confused and William said, "I shall miss you Thomas!"

It was dark when we finished loading and low water. We would have to leave at high water which was during the middle of the night. In many ways it was better. I would be able to slip away and not see my home disappear. I had not thought that I would end my days there but I had thought to have seen my son grow a little more in this Angevin sanctuary. We ate our last meal in the hall. My knights and their families joined us. Lady Marguerite and my wife wept much. They had both travelled from the Baltic with me. They had endured much together.

As they wept at some other memory they had shared I said, "My ship will still call here. I have negotiated good deals with the wine merchants and when I have worked out what we can send back there will be a healthy trade. I invite you both to visit." I spread an arm around the table. "I invite you all."

I turned to Sir Richard and led him to one side as the good humour returned, "What I cannot understand, Sir Richard is why you did not wish to return to be with your nephew."

He emptied the goblet of wine, "That was the hardest decision I ever had to make. I fear the death of my son had the biggest influence. He lies in the graveyard. It gives me comfort that I can be with him. However, there is another reason. I feared that his uncle's sins would return to haunt him."

"Sins? You were the victim of the Sherriff and King John."

He shook his head, "Ralph believes that his father was innocent of treason. He was not and neither was I. We plotted with other barons against the King. We were betrayed. If I return then your parchment will not help me and, worse, it may condemn Ralph. I love him like a son. This is the best outcome. I can try to live up to your high standards and you, I know, will guide Ralph and make him a better knight than his uncle. You can trust me with your manor, lord."

"I never doubted it and now that you have spoken from your heart then I understand your decision better. I hope that we never have to fight each other."

"Why should we lord?" He looked confused.

"While William des Roches is seneschal then there is no reason you should but if your liege lord ordered you to war against England you would have no choice."

"War with England?"

"King Phillip is ambitious and he has defeated King John and gained all that King Henry ruled. He will not be content with just that. He will see a new empire and it will include England, Wales and Ireland."

"I pray it will not come to that lord. I would not like to fight against my homeland and you."

Despite my hopes that we would leave quietly more people came down to the quay than I expected. All of my merchants were there. Alain of La Flèche had told me that they admired the way I had sacrificed myself for the good of the town and they would never forget me. My knights too and their families were tearful. When we sailed west it was unlikely that they would ever see me again. They would talk of visiting but they would not.

"Cast off Captain Henry!" Now that the time had come I was keen to leave quickly. Long goodbyes were not part of me.

I put one arm around my wife who held Rebekah in her arms and waved goodbye to my home. For my wife and many of my people it was as though we were going to a foreign country.

We slipped through Angers just before dawn. The river was swift and the winds favoured us. The rest of my people were asleep. My wife and our children had the captain's cabin. He had rigged a second hanging bed for Alfred and he thought it wonderful. Despite her misgivings my wife soon slept and the babe was as safe in the canvas as in her cot in La Flèche. I stood with Fótr and watched Anjou and then Brittany slip by.

"How long to reach Whorlton, lord?"

"I confess I do not know. I must speak with the captain when we are at sea. It could take more than half a month to reach the north east coast of England but it is not as simple as that. Whorlton is many miles from the sea. We have three choices. We can land at York and travel north. That is not a long journey but we would have to speak with the Sherriff of York and I would avoid that if we could. Whitby is not far away but the journey would be hard for the ladies. Then there is Stockton."

"You wish to land there, lord?"

"I wish to land there. However, I would not put my aunt and her husband in jeopardy. Captain Henry will know better than I." I looked at my squire as he yawned. "You need not stay awake just for me. I cannot sleep and I have much to think on."

"Thank you, lord. I am tired." With that he curled up in a ball in the corner of the deck and was soon asleep.

He was right. If I could then I would land at Stockton. I wanted to see my aunt and to learn as much as I could before I headed south. The letters she had sent were highlights only. There was more I needed to know. We had too many people for such a small manor as Whorlton. I would not put Sir Ralph out. I had enough treasure to buy a manor. Of course, once I spent my coin, I would not be able to easily replace it. England was at peace. I had warriors I needed to pay and no wars to pay them.

Captain Henry had slept while we were in the river but as we passed Nantes in the third hour of the day the first mate awoke him. I listened to the interchange. "Are the other ships keeping station?"

"Aye captain, the lantern at the stern helped. We made good time for the river was high and the winds favoured us."

"Have a good sleep."

As the mate went below I left the gunwale. "Could I speak with you, Captain Henry?"

"Aye, just let me look at the compass." He went to the tiller and looked down. Seemingly satisfied he looked to the north and the south. "Good, Jack has kept us in the right channel. What can I do for you my lord?"

"I asked you to take me to England. Where should I land? I ask your advice for you know my homeland better than I. I have spent too many years beyond her borders. I value your words."

"You wish to travel to Whorlton?" I nodded. "Then Stockton would be the port I would choose."

"Will that not put my aunt in danger?"

"She is a tough lady, although her husband was ill on our last visit but the Bishop of Durham does not bother with Stockton. All of his trade goes through Hartness. I am one of the few ships who ply the Tees. It takes longer to reach the sea than it does from La Flèche! There are too many twists and turns in the river." I laughed at the look on Henry's face. "The port is not what it was in my father's time. The Scots have more interest in it than either the Bishop or the

86

Sherriff. People have been leaving as trade dries up. I am the only ship which regularly puts in at the port. Your coin, spent there, would help the people."

That decided me. "Then Stockton it is." He made an adjustment to take us further west. We continued along the safe channel. Soon we would be in the ocean and then there would be danger. I knew that the last remnants of England, the Channel Islands, could be the graveyard of careless captains. "Tell me Captain, as a seafarer, is there any way to speed up the journey from the sea to Stockton?"

"Aye lord. There is huge loop by Norton. The gap between the two bends is but two hundred paces and yet the river loops for over a mile. The wind is always against you at some point for it is almost a circle. If you were to dig a cut then you could easily take a mile of river from the voyage." He rubbed his beard as he thought it through, "And when the land was drained it would be very fertile."

"When we reach England, I will suggest it to Sir William." We sailed north and west for many miles until we had to make a turn. Henry checked that the other ships were on station as we headed closer to the last remnants of English rule for many miles; the Channel Islands. The wind was favourable and we were making better time than we could have hoped. I pointed to Guernsey which lay like a shadow to the north. The Breton coast lay menacingly close. "I don't envy them. They are surrounded by enemies."

"Don't waste your sympathy on them, my lord. Most of them are pirates. If we had a decent King he would have put a constable in charge who would defend the seaways."

"Who is the constable now?"

"I know not. He is based in Jersey but there is a lord on each of the islands."

My men began to rouse themselves. Most went to the leeward side to make water or to empty their bowels. David of Wales waved, "I will get some food organized, lord." I waved my acknowledgement.

I heard a baby crying. It had to be Rebekah. "I will go and see how my wife fared."

Henry smiled, "Don't worry sir, she would have been as snug as a bug in the canvas. It is restful."

I went into the cabin and saw what he meant. My wife's weight had pulled the canvas tight about her. The baby would have been safe and she would have been rocked to sleep. Alfred was still asleep. I saw that she was nursing the baby.

She smiled at me, "I would have one of these in my home save that it only fits one and needs the motion of the ship to work. I have never had such a comfortable night's sleep and Alfred never murmured once."

"Good. I will get some food organised."

As I went on deck I heard, from the mast head, "Sail ho!"

"Where away?"

"Nor by east, Captain."

"Can you see any flag?"

"Not yet but I think she has come from the islands. She looks English built."

I wandered to Henry, "Trouble?"

"Could be, although we have the wind. If they are pirates then they would have to sail into the wind."

The lookout shouted, "Captain there are three of them and they have oars too." We had a strong wind behind us and it was taking us closer and closer to the three ships. I knew enough about ships to know that if we turned then we would lose some of the speed for the wind would not be as favourable.

Captain Henry was decisive, "Let us get some sea room. Alf, go and signal the other ships that I am taking us further west. They should have Sir Thomas' men stand to."

I looked at him, "Pirates?"

"I hope not but let us err on the side of caution eh, my lord?"

"David of Wales, have the men stand to. We may need your bows!"

I went to the cabin and picked up my sword. Margaret said, calmly, "Trouble?"

Could be. Better get dressed and wake Alfred." I grinned, "He will be unhappy if he misses this battle too!"

By the time I was on deck we had made the course correction. The wind was not as favourable from that quarter. I could not make out the ships. "Will son of Robin you have good eyes. Climb the forestay and identify the standard."

He swarmed up and reached the crosspiece. He stared and then shouted, "Red flag with yellow crosses, no, they are axes." He looked down. "It is Brice the Chamberlain, lord."

I shouted, "Captain Henry, it is worse than pirates. It is English men I have defeated who wish me harm!"

88

There was no point in donning mail. If this came to close quarters then we were dead men. This battle would be won by the skill of my captain and by my archers. I hoped that the other captains were as good as Henry. As the other ships joined us in heading north and west it soon became clear that the three ships were heading for our ship. They knew the *'Swan of Stockton'* and that it was my vessel. For Brice the Chamberlain this was personal.

Alfred came from the cabin. He had his dagger strapped to his young body. He would not be called on to use it but his little face showed me that he was enjoying standing with his father's warriors.

"David, get your men into the rigging. They will have better targets. If they can kill the men steering we might escape."

"Aye lord. Right lads, up the rigging!"

I turned to Ridley the Giant. "I hope they won't board but, if they do, then we will have to beat them back quickly. There are too few of us for a sustained battle."

"Aye lord."

As we were heading more west than north the wind, from the south by south west, was not as much help as it might have been. The three ships had their oars out and their sails down. They were closing with us. I went to the stern. Captain Henry looked up at the sail and then east to the three ships. "We should outrun them, my lord. Men cannot row for hours. The days of the Viking raider are long gone. The attack may add half a day to our voyage but better that than losing our ship and our lives." He glanced astern, "The others are also heading further west. We will evade them."

We might have done for, as time passed, I saw two of the oar driven ships begin to fall back and a gap opened. Then disaster struck. *'Rose'* was astern of us and suddenly she almost stopped in the water. Worse, her bow slewed around. One of the crew shouted, "Captain! *'Rose'* has lost her tiller. The withies must had frayed and snapped."

Captain Henry cursed, "Damn!"

"Can they repair it?"

"Aye lord but the nearest galley will be upon her before she does."

"Then we must turn and fight them!" He looked at me as though I was mad. "Captain I have the finest archers anywhere. If you can close with them then my bow men can do so much damage that the galleys will be unable to continue." I pointed astern. "I cannot let those people fall into the hands of Brice the Chamberlain!"

"You are the lord. We will do as you command. Come about!"

I turned and saw Margaret with Rebekah, she had come on deck and was holding her hand on Alfred's shoulder. She smiled at me. "You are a good man, husband. Alfred, come and have something to eat."

"But the battle!"

"Will wait until you have eaten and besides the ship's crew do not need a small boy beneath their feet." He obeyed.

As soon as we turned then the wind caught us and the *'Swan'* flew. The stricken *'Rose'* had given the rowers on the three ships renewed energy and they had changed course to go to her. Only Brice's ship appeared to be the danger. Our sudden manoeuvre had taken them by surprise and we were now much closer to them than they were to *'Rose'*.

"Captain can you take us by their stern and around her?"

He shook his head. "We would lose way, lord. We would be sailing into the wind."

I nodded, "Then the other alternative is to sail before her bows and up across her stern. We will still have the wind."

"That would work, lord but my crew would have to be nippy and your men swift."

"Do not worry about my men!"

As the captain gave his orders I shouted up to the archers, "We will sail across her bows. Kill as many of the crew as you can. Then we sail around her stern. I would have all there killed!"

David's voice drifted down, "Aye lord, Young Dick died at the hand of these men. They shall pay."

We appeared to be closing alarmingly quickly. Suddenly Captain Henry threw the tiller over and we almost stopped. The bows of the galley seemed to be aiming at our midships and then he put the tiller over again and the wind caught us. Arrows flew from my archers and I saw the lookout pitch to the deck from the mast. The wind caught us and we flew. We were so close that I could see, at the stern, Brice the Chamberlain. He shouted orders but, even as the men grabbed crossbows, they fell. The oars became ragged as my archers slew the oarsmen.

Captain Henry shouted, "Hold on archers! We come about!" He turned us so that we passed between the leading ship and her consorts some eight lengths away. They were rowing for all their might as we passed by the stern of Brice the Chamberlain's ship. David of Wales and his archers were few in number and they were precariously perched but they knew their business and the crew at the stern were killed to a man. The exception was Brice the Chamberlain. He hid beneath his shield and was protected by his armour. Even so, as we turned to head north and west once more I saw two arrows sticking from his leg. Our arrows had done the damage. The ship slewed to face south as the sailor steering fell. My archers kept up a withering rate and oarsmen fell. We watched as the other two ships slowed. They would not catch us.

I saw *'Rose'* resume her course. The other ships were further west. Their captains had looked to themselves. I turned and saw a grinning Alfred with Fótr standing protectively close. He had seen the effect of my archers for the first time. It was a lesson for the future. When he became a knight he would know how to use the skills of such men.

It took most of the day for us to regain our formation. As we passed *'Rose'* Sir Edward and the crew of that ship cheered and waved as we passed. Their captain shouted, "The tiller is repaired!"

Captain Henry murmured, "It should never have broken in the first place. You can tell when a rope is frayed!"

We sailed north and east under reefed sails for it was night time and Captain Henry did not want us to risk losing one of the fleet. We were far from land. The coast of Cornwall lay many leagues to the north and our flight had taken us well to the west of Guernsey. It did mean that we had sea room.

I was tired enough to need sleep more than food or wine. I shared one of the hanging canvas beds with Alfred. My wife was correct, it was cosy and soporific. I could have closed my eyes and been asleep instantly. Alfred, however, had other ideas and he chattered away with questions about the battle and my archers until, eventually, his mother said, "Alfred if you wake your sister I will make you sleep outside on the deck! Go to sleep! Your father needs it even if you do not!" It worked. He was silent and I slept.

Dawn saw us approaching the busy waterways between Flanders and England. After I had made water and taken some of the cheese and ham from Ridley the Giant I joined Captain Henry at the stern. He smiled, "We are all in formation and making good time. The other captains have realised the benefits of staying close to us or perhaps your men aboard them have chivvied the captains. I have never seen such close sailing."

"And is that the dangerous part over?"

"In terms of human enemies, yes, but it will take us half a day to reach the headland of Dover. We will be lucky to have cleared the Thames estuary by dark. I am afraid the waters there are crowded. However, I am happier that we travel these waters in daylight. There is less chance of collision. We will have to crawl north. Tomorrow we will make better time. Our course to escape the galleys proved a blessing. The winds we found have made this one of the quickest voyages I can remember. Perhaps the Good Lord wishes to hasten your arrival in Stockton!"

"Perhaps."

He was right. The journey took longer than I had expected to reach Dover. Ships sailed across our bows as they headed to the ports on the south coast. We had to negotiate fleets of fishing ships. There were other ships heading south and, to take advantage of the wind, their course oft times meant that we had to slow to avoid a collision. Once we passed the busy waterways we had a sea which was almost empty. Any ships we saw were many miles away and there was no danger of collision.

Two days later we saw the cliffs of the Yorkshire coast. Once we had passed the Fens the number of ships we passed diminished and we could use more sail. Only a handful of my men had ever seen this part of the world and they were with Edward astern of us. The rest lined the sides of the ship as they looked at the abbey of Whitby rising high above the cliffs and the small fishing ports nestled in tiny inlets along the coast.

My wife had left our sleeping daughter with a servant and she joined me. Alfred was with Fótr and both were too busy looking landward to bother us. "I will be glad when this voyage is over, husband. I must smell foul."

I nuzzled her head and kissed her hair. "You smell fine to me!"

She shook her head, "I am sorry, husband, but as you smell worse than a stable I doubt your judgement. And I will be pleased to be spared the indignity of making water on a ship!"

I had much sympathy with her. The arrangements were primitive. For modesty's sake Captain Henry had rigged a canvas in the leeward side of the bows but, even so, the ladies had to sit with their rears hung over the water. They had learned to do what they had to in pairs.

"And food! Salted ham and cheese! I will be happy if I never eat them again! I yearn for something cooked. I am desperate for bread!" She suddenly looked at me, "Will your aunt be able to cope with the sudden influx of people?"

I nodded, "From what I have been told our coin will be more than welcome. I will not impose upon my aunt and her husband. I will buy what we need from Stockton. We left La Flèche rich. I would use that coin to make our life here in England comfortable."

When we turned west at the river the journey slowed. The wind was now against us and we had to use the crew and my men to man the sweeps and row us down the river. For the ladies the sight of the seals basking on the sands and wild birds soaring as we passed, kept them entertained but it took a whole day and night for us to crawl the few miles to Stockton. I would suggest to Sir William that we make a cut in the river. The journey was intolerable.

When we reached Stockton the rest of the passengers were relieved and pleased. I felt sad for I saw the desolation of King John. The castle had gone and all that remained was the hall. I saw that Sir William had fortified it with a fighting platform and a small tower. Thornaby castle had also gone. All that remained was the church. This was not the river and home I had left to follow my father and King Richard to the crusades but this time, at least, I was coming home. I would not have to flee to Sweden and I could begin my life anew. On my last visit there had been despair and anger. I had a family and I had followers; there was now hope.

Home to England

Chapter 9

We docked at the quay. Our approach had been so slow that I had expected my aunt and her husband to greet us. They did not. Instead we were greeted by a small, neat man, "Are you Sir Thomas?"

"I am."

"I am Edgar my lord's steward. Lady Ruth begs your forgiveness for not greeting you personally. She would have been here to meet you but Sir William is close to death."

I nodded, "Fótr, see to the unloading. I must go to Sir William!"

"Aye lord!"

The days when we would have had to negotiate the gatehouse were gone. It was open bare ground before the halls, stables, store rooms, bakery and the kitchen. I hurried after the steward. Everything was as I remembered it from my last visit but it looked a little more run down and decrepit. The Great Hall was easily recognisable and Edgar took me up the stairs in the south tower to the master chamber. When I entered there was the smell of death. It was as familiar as the smell of my horse. I had sat with enough dying men to recognise it. Sir William lay propped up on the bed and my aunt sat holding his hand. He looked like a skeleton. He was gaunt and thin. A tendril of blood was wiped away from his mouth by my aunt even as I entered. A priest stood close by chanting prayers.

Lady Ruth rose and came to hug me, "God has given you wings. Had you been an hour later then he would have passed away. My husband has clung on to life for he knew you were coming." She shook her head, "I know not how. Come he would speak with you."

I went to the bed. The priest made to leave but Sir William said, "Father Richard I beg you to stay. I wish you to attest to the words which I now say to Sir Thomas."

He nodded.

Sir William took my hand, "I have followed your exploits from afar. If I had had a son then he would have been just like you. I am dying. It is not a warrior's death. I have not long. Are you listening, Father Roger?"

"I am, lord."

"This manor was granted to me and my heirs. My wife is a woman and the Bishop of Durham has made it clear that a woman cannot inherit. The Church is both mean and petty. The Bishop, or his nephew, at least, knows I have no children. I therefore adopt Sir Thomas of La Flèche as my heir. I give him the manor and the right to protect the people. I ask him to watch over his aunt, as I know he will. To my wife I leave my treasure, little though it is."

Ruth squeezed his hand, "My treasure lord, is the time I have spent with you. You have given me a life I could not have expected."

He nodded. "You heard that priest?"

"I did lord."

"Then go now and write it down quickly. I would not have clerks and clerics rob this warrior of the home he deserves!"

He scurried away and Sir William closed his eyes. The effort had been too much for him. My aunt took a jug and poured wine into a goblet. She held it to his lips. She whispered to me, "The healers have put a drug in here. It numbs the pain. He hoped that you would come before the end." I saw tears in her eyes. "He is a good man and wonderful companion. I will miss him."

"I should leave you alone."

She shook her head. "When he passes I would have you here with me. It will comfort me much."

Sir William coughed a little as the wine was poured into his mouth. He opened his eyes. "You have brought all your people?"

"I have."

"Good. I feel sleepy. I shall just rest my eyes for a while." His breathing was so shallow that I feared he might be dead already.

My aunt held her husband's hand and mine. I wondered if he would just slip away in his sleep. He was barely breathing. My aunt looked at me and gave me a wan smile. To break the silence I said, "Sir William barely knows me. I met him just a few times and yet he gives me that which my heart most desires, Stockton."

She patted my hand, "He knew your quality the moment he met you. He said you had something about you. In you was every distillation of the true knight. All of your actions from the moment you left us confirmed it. With each letter and deed his admiration grew."

"Even the death of the Bishop?"

"In many ways that marked you as a knight with ideals. The Bishop had done wrong and it was right that he was punished. Sir William may not have approved of your method but he said that it took courage to do as you did."

I took those words in and looked at the old knight I had barely known. I am not sure how long we sat there. Time seemed to stop. The only sound we heard was his laboured breathing. Suddenly he opened his eyes and looked at his wife, "My love you are still here."

She leaned forward and kissed his brow. "Where else would I be lord save at the side of the man I have loved more than life itself?"

"And for me I just regret that I did not meet you sooner. We were meant to be together and I am just sorry for whatever sin I committed which has caused this disease."

"You committed no sin. Now rest. Perhaps Sir Thomas' arrival has helped you begin to heal."

It was a vain hope. His body shook in a final paroxysm of pain and he forced a smile, "Farewell my love I…"

The old knight lay still. His breathing had ceased. We sat there for a moment and then my aunt prostrated herself on his body. I stood and left the chamber. Outside were the priest and my wife. The priest looked at me. I said, simply, "It is over."

He nodded, "I will go and say prayers for his soul and prepare for his burial. This is a sad time but welcome to the manor, Lord Thomas."

Margaret hugged me and then, as she pulled away said, "Lord of the manor?"

I nodded, "Strange is it not? He adopted me and made me his heir before he died. The priest attested to the arrangement. This is our new home." I looked around, "The children?"

"They are in bed. The housekeeper and the steward were kind. We have fine rooms. My women watch them."

The door opened and Lady Ruth appeared. Wiping a tear from her eye she smiled, "You must be Margaret. My nephew has told me much about you in his letters. You are even more beautiful than I imagined. I cannot wait to see the children. I will move from my rooms tomorrow. You are lady of the manor."

Before I could say anything, my wife shook her head, "No, Lady Ruth. We are grateful for a roof. We would not dream of putting you from your room."

"Come then, we will drink wine and toast Sir William. We do not grieve for he is not in pain any longer and he was glad that Sir Thomas returned. This is a time for celebration and joy. We will bury him on the morrow and then we can hold a feast to welcome your people. Stockton needs this influx of new blood. Between them the Bishop's nephew and King John were like leeches sucking the life from this town." She raised her goblet, "To Sir William, a good knight and a better husband."

"Sir William."

We drank and each of us was silent. Lady Ruth thought of her husband and I thought of the tricks fate plays. I think my wife was taking in the change in our circumstances.

Lady Ruth smiled and broke the silence, "Did you have a good voyage?" We told her of the attack and our experience.

"You poor dears! That must have been awful for you." She smiled, "Although I suspect Alfred might well have enjoyed the experience." Margaret yawned and Lady Ruth said, "Go to bed. I have work to do. My husband must be prepared for burial."

She would not allow us to help her and so we went to bed. We had been given the room which I had occupied whilst growing up. It seemed smaller somehow.

The next day was not the first day I had envisaged. Instead of taking my son and my men to explore the town and the manor we crammed into the tiny church to say goodbye to Sir William. Most of my men had to wait outside. Sir William had, apparently, planned his own funeral. He was to be buried outside the church and not with my family. It was the mark of the man. He did not wish to intrude, even in death. The stonemason had already made the stone which would lay on top of it and we stood around the grave in silence.

My wife and her ladies stood with Lady Ruth. They comforted her. As Sir Edward and I led my men to return to the hall, David of Wales said, "Lord what is this?" He pointed to a stone in the graveyard.

my in he

> **In memory of Sir Richard of Stockton, Captain Dick.**
>
> **He was the finest of archers, the most loyal of friends and the noblest of warriors. Those who pause and look remember a great man who died that you might live in peace.**

"Dick was great grandfather's archer. If you speak with those the town they still remember his name. He came with the Warlord when a young man. He had been an outlaw in Sherwood."

David nodded, "And yet is buried here amongst the great and the good."

I nodded, "And he was knighted although the great man did not use his title."

David of Wales nodded, "The great men never do, lord. It is only the weak and the venal who hide behind titles." He looked around. "Lord, this is a fine manor. I take it that this will be our new home?"

"It will."

Ridley the Giant had been standing nearby and he joined us. "Then we need a new hall lord. Last night we slept in the stables. They were large enough but we cannot use those as our quarters."

I had not known and he was right. "Then our first task is to build a hall." I looked around. There had once been a mighty gatehouse facing the north. That had been the focus of many Scottish attacks. I led the two of them to the ground where it had stood. Using my dagger, I scraped away the top soil. The blade rang on stone. "It is as I thought, the foundations remain. As I remember this was a gatehouse with double gates. We have good foundations. There is no reason why we cannot build a hall with two floors; one for the archers and one for the men at arms. We can build it with a fighting platform and a door which emerges from the second floor."

Ridley frowned, "Why not build it with crenulations and towers? We could make it a second keep."

"I have yet to visit the Bishop of Durham but I do not think he will allow us to build what amounts to a castle. We will have to be clever about this." I smiled, "What think you, David of Wales, should we dig a ditch around it to the river? It will drain away the water for this ground will flood in winter."

He smiled, "Of course, lord and we can build a bridge. That way we could remove the bridge if we had to."

I nodded, "Precisely. There is a mason in the town, or there was. His sire, William, helped to build the castle. I will ask my aunt."

"And the stone?"

I looked around. There was some but nowhere near enough. "There is a quarry west of here. Do you remember, Edward?"

"Aye lord it lies between Piercebridge and Barton."

"Then ask Captain Henry to take you and some men thence. I will give you coin to buy the stone."

He nodded and looked around, "Lord when I left to join you I thought that Stockton had fallen far. This is even worse than I thought. I do not think it can go much lower. There is precious little money in this town. How will you earn an income?"

"I know not but my great grandfather came with less and you know what he managed to build up." He nodded. "Ridley, leave Godwin in command of the men. Have them begin work on the hall. I want you and David to ride with me to Whorlton. I must speak with Sir Ralph. We have much to tell him."

"The horses are still unsteady after the journey lord."

"I will take Skuld. She is hardy. Choose the best of the rest. It is not far."

When I reached the hall Fótr hurried off to prepare my mail. I knew not what lay between Stockton and Sir Ralph's manor. Lady Ruth and my wife entered. Alfred was holding his great aunt's hand. She smiled, "Your son is a delight, Thomas. Sir William would have loved him."

"He has his moments. Aunt I have asked my men to begin to build a hall for them. I would use the old gatehouse. Do we have a mason?"

"Leofric. He is the grandson of William. He is the one who carved Sir William's grave but there is precious little stone left. It was taken away when the castle was dismantled."

"I am sending Sir Edward to the quarries by Barton. He will buy some. I go to Whorlton with Fótr, David and Ridley."

Alfred shouted, "Can I come?"

"No, my son for with Edward and me away I need you to watch the ladies. Besides you need to explore your new home."

He nodded. I saw my aunt smile. Alfred would be as close to a grandchild as she would ever have. He would replace her dead husband. He would not want for fuss. When I was dressed I went to the quayside to pay off the other captains. As they headed downstream I handed over more coin to Sir Edward. The small chest Fótr had carried was now empty. Edward said, "Soon, lord, your coffers will be empty."

"Then, Sir Edward, we will find some way of filling them. When I return, tomorrow, from Sir Ralph, I will have a better idea of our finances."

As we crossed the river on the ferry I wondered about Wulfestun. My aunt had held that manor. I wondered if she still did or would that be another argument I might have with the Bishop of Durham? The three men with whom I rode had never seen this land. To me it was familiar. We passed Thornaby. The church remained but Sir Wulfric's castle was gone. My aunt had told me that the manor was so poor that it was not a lord who held it but a reeve. He was a man who ran a manor for a lord. I would need to speak to him.

The ride was but eighteen miles. We passed through the manors of Maltby and Hutton. Both had churches but I saw that there were no castles. When my father had been lord of Stockton there had been no need for castles here. His castle stopped any attacks from the north. As we passed through them I could not help notice that the villagers appeared thin and gaunt. Life was not easy in this land which was mismanaged by King John and his Sherriffs.

We had passed through Hutton after watering our horses in the Leven and Ridley asked, "Who is lord of this land?"

I shrugged, "No one of importance else there would be a fine hall or a castle. The Sheriff of York is King John's man." I could see that the three of them were confused. "Sherriffs were a useful tool in times past. They helped the King to manage the many manors in this land. Under old King Henry they were dispensers of justice. When King Richard went to war and John became Regent, they changed. King John used them as a way to increase his power. He could do little about the barons directly but by appointing the Sherriffs he was able to control them indirectly. He uses taxes as a weapon. The Sherriff has a garrison of men at arms. If barons oppose the Sherriff then they oppose the King."

They nodded and then Fótr, who had grown more thoughtful as he grew older, said, "What if the barons rebelled?"

I reined in Skuld, "This must go no further. I would not have Sir Ralph know this but the barons did rebel. The difference was that it was not like Normandy. They did not combine. It was minor acts of defiance. It is what got Sir Ralph's father killed and why Sir Richard remains in Anjou."

I saw the scales fall from their eyes as all became clear.

"I will remain silent on the matter, lord."

Whorlton was well named. The hill upon which the village and castle stood was on a whirling hill at the edge of the moors. The land below was fertile while the moors were desolate. Patches of forest and woodland dotted the west facing hills. Sir Ralph had done well in the short time he had been here. There was a wooden castle. It looked like Sir Ralph had recently deepened the ditch and improved the defences. The Dowager Queen had told me that permission had been granted to build a castle. This looked like the original one. It would need to be built of stone. We had been spied from afar and were greeted at the gate. "My lord. It is good to see you." He looked around. "Where are the rest of the men and your family?"

I dismounted, "I have much to tell you. First let me walk the walls of your castle and you can tell me of your situation."

As we walked he confirmed that the manor was run down. There was a fine church with an avenue of yew trees and there were a dozen or so crude houses but the people were poor. It seemed they eked out a living growing little more than what they needed. We looked east to the moors. "That is part of the manor, is it not?"

"Aye lord and we hunt in the woods and use the timber but that provides little."

"What about sheep?"

"Sheep, lord?"

"They are hardy creatures and require little more than that for grazing. We could export the wool to La Flèche. There is a market there. If we built a few walls to enclose them it would provide an income. They just need a shepherd and would use land which is otherwise wasted."

"That is a good idea, lord." He turned to look at me. "Then you do not return here with your family, lord?"

"I will tell you more when we eat. Now about these wooden walls. We can make them of stone. To the south the nearest stone castle is Helmsley and to the north, Durham! I cannot build a stone castle at Stockton." He gave me a surprised look. "I will tell you all later. If this is made of stone then we can control a larger area." My aunt, when we had been watching Sir William die, had told me of the many incursions from the Scots. Now that the manor of Stockton had no castle they often ravaged the valley. Hartburn, Elton, even Norton had all been ransacked. "The Scots will raid south of the river if they can for the Bishop of Durham is indolent. You can spy their raiding parties from here. You can see all the way to the Tees."

"My men have but six horses and two of those are poor."

"Then you will find or breed more. Horses are the key to controlling this land and to beating the Scottish raiders."

"Where will I get stone, lord?" he hesitated, "And how will I pay for it?"

I swept my arm around me. "Unlike the Loir and the Tees this is not a river valley with clay. You have rocks all around you. Hew rocks from close by and use those. This needs not be a pretty castle. It needs to be a rock. You remember how we built the towers at La Lude?" He nodded. "Then use the same technique. The better stones on the outside. Large stones on the inside and then infill with whatever waste stone you have."

Ridley said, "Lord, you can plaster your walls on the inside and that will cover much of the roughness."

Sir Ralph smiled, "I confess lord, I thought that I was caretaker for you. Now that I know this is to be my home I can have a better idea of how to build."

I nodded, "And build for a wife and family, Ralph. You are a bachelor knight now but will not always be so. I need you to make new knights whom my son can lead."

The next day, as we left I could see that I had given him much to think on. "Thank you, lord, for your advice. It is sage. I just wish my uncle was here. I miss him."

"I do not think he will visit. There are many reasons. I will be sending my ship there regularly. Write him letters and I will send them."

When we reached Stockton, I could see that my men had cleared the soil from the foundations. There was no sign of my ship. I did not expect to see it. It would take time to bring the stone from the quarry to the river and then to load it.

102

That evening I told my aunt and my wife of my plans. "You will need to speak with the Bishop of Durham. You will need to take Father Roger with you."

"What about Father Abelard? Will he have a position here?"

I looked at my wife. I had forgotten my priest. "I have had much on my mind, wife. I will think about him when I have time. Aunt what about Wulfestun? Is there still a hall there?"

"There is. It still belongs to me for I bought it. I have a couple of retainers who keep it for me. The last Scottish raid killed the men there and took the women and girls as slaves. Why? Do you wish me to return thence?"

I shook my head, "No, my lady. That is the last thing on my mind. I have brought many men with me and Wulfestun lies north of here. I thought to put Sir Edward there. He can be our sentinel who watches for the Scots when they come."

"That is a wonderful idea."

"Then Sir Edward can build a church and Father Abelard can be the priest there."

My wife beamed, "You are a clever man, husband!"

"And I thought to have him and his men help mine to make a cut in the Tees. If we link the two bends close to Norton and Billingham we can speed the journey to the sea for our ships and increase the ground we can farm. My captain believes that a shorter journey will increase trade. If we can get sheep for Sir Ralph then we can send the wool to Anjou. We need trade through our port!"

She patted my hand. "You are so much like my father. He was always looking to better the lives of his people. When I think of where we were and now this nadir…" Her eyes welled with tears and she shook her head.

My wife smiled and held Lady Ruth's hand. "My husband is resourceful but he works too hard. We will barely see him until Whorlton is built, the cut is made and we are secure." Lady Ruth nodded. She was unable to speak.

"I needs must visit the Bishop and I will have to travel to York. Other than that, my love, I will be a home bird until our nest is built."

She smiled, "Good for we have another chick which will be here in six months."

"You are with child?"

"I am!"

My aunt rose and kissed my wife on the cheek. Joy returned to her face. "Then it will take an army to take me hence. It will make me young to see three children growing up in this hall."

103

Scottish Raid

Chapter 10

I was too busy during the next month to make either visit. York and Durham would have to wait. To be truthful I was reluctant to go. There would be confrontation and I feared, despite the presence of Father Roger, that my title would be rejected. We began to build the walls of the new warrior hall and when they were as high as a man I sent Sir Edward and his men, along with Father Abelard to begin work on Wulfestun. I had sent Captain Henry back to La Flèche with hides. The manor still produced a good quantity and they would fetch a higher price in Anjou. There were other items which we were able to send to trade. We had iron from the Eston Hills and we had seal skins taken from the basking seals. It was little enough but it was trade and I was keen to maintain the links. The cut in the Tees would have to wait until we had a hall and another church.

Most of my men were put to work on the moat around the hall. We called it a ditch but it was a moat. With arrow slits in the walls and a fighting platform it would be a tower which housed warriors. I would have liked a curtain wall but that might be deemed to make my hall a castle. We extended the moat around the hall. It helped to drain it and we used a bridge across it. Instead of a curtain wall I put the burghers to work repairing the town wall. It had fallen into disrepair. To be fair the decay had begun when I was a child but that had been because the town wall was unnecessary so long as the castle stood. Without the castle it became a necessity. My aunt showed me the buildings which had been destroyed in the last Scottish raid.

"Aunt, are these raiders brigands or are they led by lords?"

"A mixture. Knights lead large warbands." She smiled, "That was a word my grandfather, the Warlord, used and it fits. They sweep down from the north using the high ground to the west. They take cattle and sheep. We are a large town and with no castle we invite danger for they take the young girls."

"Young girls?"

"Brides or whores; they do not seem to differentiate their function. It is why the town has far fewer people. Many fled south of the river. The fords are much further west and when they attack we anchor the ferry on the south bank. They were not strong enough to attack the hall."

My aunt was not a warrior but that told me much about the men who came south. They were brigands masquerading beneath a Scottish standard. They were old fashioned raiders. If they were anything else then the hall would have fallen. We needed warning and if they were a warband they would not have discipline. My aunt told me that refugees fleeing south gave them warning of raiders. The next time they came they would have a shock. I had sixty-five warriors ready to greet them. Our problem was horses. We only had thirty horses. I could not mount my archers. Horses were a priority. Luckily Sir William's horses were available for breeding and I had the stable master, Ethelred, begin to breed them. When we had coin, I would buy horses. Until then I would have to make do with what we had.

Alfred was growing and although we did not have enough full-size horses we had many ponies and as he was big enough now I gave him his own and we took to riding my land. I showed him where there had been castles when I was young and where there had been halls. It saddened him that all we saw were a few houses and spaces where the halls had been destroyed by a vindictive Hugh de Puiset.

"Do we get to build them again?"

I shook my head. "In the time of the Warlord things were different. Now the Bishop of Durham decides where the castles may be built. It will make life hard for us but we will prevail.

Winter was approaching and the work on the hall became urgent. By the time we had had the bone fire the outside of the hall and the church were finished. The first, early snow came at the beginning of November. We had to make the roofs quickly or all our work on the interior would have been in vain.

To those who had not been with me in the Baltic the snows came as something of a shock. Luckily the snow did not remain on the ground but it was a warning.

My ship returned with much needed money and two barrels of wine. They were a gift from my former burghers. Captain Henry left to make profit for himself. The Tees froze during harsh winters and we would not see him again until the spring. It made us feel even more isolated.

I was toying with the idea of visiting Durham before Christmas hoping to find the Bishop in a charitable mood when a rider came from Sir Edward, "Lord we have refugees from Fissebourne. The Scots are raiding!"

"Tell Sir Edward that we come!"

My aunt's face showed the pain of the memory of the other raids. She said, "Thomas our people have suffered enough."

"And they will suffer no more. Fótr fetch Ridley and David of Wales and then saddle Skuld." I went to my chamber to don my hauberk. Since my return I had reinstituted the Sunday archery practice. Sir William had not maintained the training. David of Wales had been appalled at the poor standard. It was improving but now, at least, there would be burghers on the walls with bows to defend themselves. By the time I reached the hall armed and mailed, my captains of archers and men at arms were there.

"David of Wales, I charge you with the defence of my hall and town. Had we more horses then I would have taken some of you with me. As it is we will have to do with men at arms."

"Fear not lord all will be safe with us."

"Ridley, I want every man at arms mounted."

"Aye lord, they are already saddling their horses. Whither do we ride?"

"North to Wulfestun first. Fissebourne is twelve miles from here. I suspect they will raid Wulfestun when they are finished at Fissebourne. With Sir Edward there they are in for a shock."

Fótr had spears ready and he handed me a spear, my shield and my helmet. This would be the first time my gryphon would be seen in England for some time. I would make the Scots rue their foray south.

Edward only had six mounted men. When we reached him, there were just four of them ready with Sir Edward. "I have sent two of my more experienced men north to the Durham Road to scout out the Scots."

"How many Scots are there?"

He shook his head, "The twenty people who fled here were terrified. According to them there were hundreds but I know that is an exaggeration. They said there were knights. They had big horses and wore mail. They said there were five and I am inclined to believe that number."

I dismounted. "There is no point in tiring out our horses and we can do nothing until we know where they are." My men all dismounted as did Sir Edward and his men. When I swung from leg from my saddle I saw that he had dug a ditch around the hall and the huts of the villagers. It would not stop an attack but it would make an assault more difficult. I said, "You need a banner."

He shook his head, "Lord, I was a man at arms and I need no standard."

"You do and you need one which will mark you as my knight. I have just two of you to command and one is many miles south. The Scots are intimidated by our banners. Have a banner made."

He looked mystified. "But I wear your surcoat!"

"You have a manor. Whatever we take from these raiders, use it to have a surcoat and banner made. Your men need to be identified on the field and by our foes. I want them to fear us."

He looked confused still but he nodded, "Aye lord, but it seems a waste of good coin."

"You will learn."

His two men rode in a little after noon. Richard Tallboy reined in and pointed north. "They are heading down the Durham road. They have left some of their men south of Fissebourne with the animals and captives. There are four knights and their squires. They ride palfreys and not warhorses. They have sixty or so men. They are not mailed and few have helmets. If I was to speak the truth lord they look like bandits. They have no scouts out. They ride confidently as though this is their land."

To many other warriors the odds would have seemed high but my men were all mailed. We were experienced and knew how each of our shield brothers fought. The fact that we were mounted also gave us an advantage. I turned to Edward, "They will be coming here. Where is the best place to stop them?"

"Two miles north of here, lord, the road passes through land which undulates. There are woods on both side of the road. I know a place where we could use the undergrowth and the trees for cover. As they came up the road we could hit them. Or we could split our forces and send some behind them."

I shook my head. "We are too few in number. We hit their knights and then fall upon the men on foot. If Richard is correct and they have neither mail nor helmets then all of our blows should hurt them. I will follow you!"

Edward mounted and shouted, "Jack! You command the men I leave. Use the men from the village to fight!"

Jack son of John nodded, "Aye lord. Your hall will still be here when you return! This time they will not find it unguarded."

We rode in a column of twos. My men followed Edward's. His squire, Gilles rode behind Edward. All of the men I led wore my surcoat and followed my standard. That would have to change."

I shouted over my shoulder as we rode. "Fótr you, Ridley and Godwin of Battle will flank me. We will wait below the crest of the road and when we hear them we will ride to draw them on. The rest of you will be spread out on both sides of the road and remain hidden. When they come for us you will attack from their flanks. Pass the word."

"Aye lord."

I counted on the fact that the Scots did not know that there was a new lord. They would expect it to be old Sir William. They had raided with impunity before. The recent cold weather and early warning of snow had made them decide to use our valley to supply themselves. Further north, closer to their own homes, there were too many castles: Norham, Morpeth, Warkworth, Alnwick. All had good garrisons and would stop any incursions. That was why they had come from the north west. The high, bleak ground would hide them.

We dropped down one gentle slope and I saw woods to the left and right of the road ahead. There was a crest. Sir Edward reined in, "That is the spot I had in mind."

"Good then you and Godfrey take our men and spread them out on both sides of the road. You need not me to teach you how to ambush. When they approach give a treble whistle. We four will appear and draw them to us."

"Will they attack?"

"This time they will for they will see four men. They know not me. I have never fought the Scots. It has been more than twenty years since my father rode these roads. We will be forgotten. After today then things may well be different."

"Aye lord."

I dismounted and the other three followed suit. We walked to just below the crest. I handed my reins to Fótr and walked to spy out the land. Edward was right. It was perfect. There was a steep slope and the road curved just three hundred paces from us. They would turn the bend and then they would begin to climb the slope. When Edward whistled we would move towards the crest. We had plenty of time to walk our horses to the crest. I saw that my men were disappearing into the trees. Edward and Godfrey knew their business. They walked them there so as to minimise the disturbance and damage to the trees. When they had disappeared, I walked back to the horses and my men.

"And now we wait."

Ridley had some dried venison. He cut a piece off and offered it to me, "Dried meat, lord?"

"Aye. It will moisten my mouth." I chewed. We had found that chewing made us less thirsty. I did not understand it for the meat had been dried but it worked and the act of chewing had a calming effect. "Wait for my command to charge. Fótr, today you try to kill a knight. There is no point in seeking ransom. If they are raiding for slaves and cattle with brigands then they will not have enough coin to pay ransom. Their mail, helmets and horses are more valuable. Do not get carried away. Edward, Godfrey and the rest can deal with the bulk of their men. I have chosen the best to be with me for I wish us to win."

Fótr nodded, "And the captives and the animals, lord?"

"If we succeed then we rescue them next!"

Edward's whistle came a short time later. We donned our helmets and we mounted. We could hear the noise of hooves and the chatter and laughter of men who had yet to lose a man. This was a warband which had enjoyed the freedom to kill, steal and rape. They were in for a shock. When we were all mounted I nodded and, with my spear in my right hand and my shield pulled up we walked to the crest. I saw them. They were a third of the way up. The horsemen were at the fore and the rest were spread out in an untidy tangle.

As soon as we were spied there was a commotion amongst the Scots. They saw four mailed men. The leading knight drew his sword and urged his men forward. Despite the fact that the knights and squires were mounted the men on foot kept very close to the horsemen for the first thirty or so paces as they hurried to get at us before we could flee. That suited us. Edward and Godfrey would have more success if the enemy were packed together and unable to use their weapons effectively. I did not move and that would worry the knights. They would ask themselves why? Doubt and indecision never helped a warrior. You had to be committed. The four knights filled the road and the squires rode behind. When they were just a hundred paces from us I spurred Skuld.

I had my spear across my cantle and I chose the leading knight as my target. He had been the one to shout commands. He had an old fashioned open face helmet. His mail was made of overlapping scales. His sword was shorter than mine. His shield was not as long as that which we used. It did not cover his lower leg as mine did. I took all of that in as we charged towards each other. I moved my spear to the right. I saw him switch his horse so that he would take the spear on his shield. I watched, as we closed, and saw him begin to move his shield up for he thought I would go for his head or his chest. I pulled my arm back for we were barely twenty paces from each other. He was, obligingly, standing in his stirrups with his sword raised. He intended to strike down on me as I extended my arm to spear him. I thrust, not at his chest, as he expected, but at his unprotected thigh. My spear head tore through his chausses and into his saddle. The impact broke off the head.

As his squire approached with a sword ready to hack at me I rammed the broken end of the spear at his face. It tore into his eye and then into his skull. Ahead of me I saw my men as they ripped into the Scots. I glanced over my shoulder and saw that Fótr was struggling to deal with the knight who faced him. However, before I could get to him I had a second squire to deal with. He was fast and he was keen. He wore no mail beneath his surcoat. It was leather. I barely blocked his strike as I drew my sword but the action drove his blade into the air. I stood and punched him in the head with my shield. He tumbled from the saddle.

Using my knees to guide Skuld I rode at the knight who was in danger of defeating Fótr. These were raiders. This was not a battle. There was no honour in the combat. I brought my sword across his back. I felt it grate along his spine. His back arced and the sword and shield fell from his lifeless limbs. He tumbled over the back of his horse.

The other two knights were dead. I saw the last two squires look at each other and, wheeling their horses, fled the field. As they ploughed through their own men they added to the confusion of the attack on their flanks. As their horses trampled some of their own men so others joined the two squires in flight. I turned Skuld and headed down the road to help Edward and Godfrey slay as many as we could. A sweep with my sword at head height took one man in the head. I swung my sword from on high to bite into the shoulder of a second. It did not take much for the rest to flee. Fighting farmers with bill hooks and scythes was one thing, facing mailed men with good swords was entirely something else. They fled. My men pursued them.

I saw that Edward and Godfrey had survived. I turned to see how Fótr fared. Godwin had taken my squire's helmet from him and there was blood. Godwin said, "The young master was lucky, lord. He has a well-made helmet and that saved him."

I nodded, "Collect the horses." I saw that the knight I had hit with my spear had bled to death. I had struck something vital.

"Aye lord."

"Ridley, search the knights and squires. See what they have on them. I would know who they are."

Fótr shook his head, "I am sorry lord. I am not yet ready to face a knight."

"It was wrong of me to ask you. You acquitted yourself well. Practice with Godwin and Godfrey. You will improve." I turned. I could not see my men and so I said, "Fótr, sound the horn. We still have some captives to recover."

The horn sounded three times. Sir Edward and Godfrey had not joined the others in the pursuit. They had ensured that none of those lying on the field was feigning death. "Did we lose any?"

Sir Edward shook his head. "We surprised them and we wore mail. There are four who have wounds."

"Then send them back to your hall with the horses. The ones you left there can join us."

"We go on?"

"There are English captives at Fissebourne. We go to their aid. When the men are back have them water the horses. We have a short rest and then we head north."

Ridley had returned with the coins, rings and seals. "You know, lord, that the squires will have warned them."

"Perhaps but if you were the Scots would you wish to return empty handed? They cannot outrun us for we are mounted. They will take the best of what they have and hope that we delay the pursuit. We will not!"

We headed north at a steady pace. I had Fótr at the rear. Although his helmet had taken the force of the knight's sword I was concerned. I hoped that we would not need him to fight. I did not have scouts out. Until Edward's other men joined us there would be too few of us to split our forces. Sir Edward rode with me.

"These were wild men, lord. Most of them had tattooed bodies. Six of them fought bare chested! Bare chested in this weather! They must be desperate."

I shook my head, "It is an easier life to take from others than produce yourself. Scotland is a poor country. They think that they can raid here with impunity. The lords of Northumbria have shown us the way. They have strong

111

castles and knights who are ready to use their weapons. When time allows I will ride north to speak with them."

As we rode down the road we saw some of the Scots who had succumbed to their wounds. Edward was right. Some were bare chested and barefoot. Richard had said that the Scots had been camped at the River Skerne. We saw where they had left the road. Their trail led across fields. We were getting close and so I drew my sword.

"Spread out. Our priority is the recapture of the captives!"

I spied a hedgerow ahead and saw a gate. The trail led to the gate. I headed for it and saw below me the animals they had abandoned. Just a mile away and heading north west were the remnants of the warband. There looked to be thirty or so Scots. They had more than sixty captives. They were mainly women and children. Even as they saw us the Scots began to run, driving the captives before them. It was futile.

"After them. Fótr, take three men and protect the captives!"

"Aye lord!"

Skuld opened hr legs. I saw the Scots beating the captives with the flat of their swords. It was to no avail and the Scots pushed them to the ground and ran. My men had their blood up. The sight of the warband hitting women and children with their swords was too much. Even as we chased the men on foot I realised that there were no horses with them. Where had the squires gone? The released captives huddled together as we thundered by. I could rely on Fótr. The captives would be cared for.

I swung my sword to hack into the skull of the Scotsman who had no idea how close I was. The second one did hear me and he crouched low. It was to no avail. I leaned from the side of my saddle and brought my sword across his side. Ahead of me I saw a Scot turn. He had a spear and he was thrusting it at me. I rose and, jerking Skuld to the right, I stood in the saddle and took the top of his head as his spear hit my shield and slid off. I reined in for Skuld was tiring. She was not as young as she once was. There was little point in damaging her for bandits.

My men slew those within sight and then, like me, reined in. I saw that the men we had killed had little with them. Perhaps their lords intended to pay them when they returned north. They would now have nothing. I reined in when I reached the captives. As I dismounted a priest abased himself, "Lord, you have saved us. Did the Bishop send you?"

"No, I came from Stockton. What happened to the Lord of Fissebourne?"

The priest shook his head, "We have had no lord for these last three years. The Bishop sends each year for his taxes and that is all that we know."

"And all these are from Fissebourne?"

"No, lord, some came from Kelloe. It is not far north of here."

"There are none from Bishop Middleham?"

"No lord. There are armed men there for it is a residence of the Bishop."

"Then I leave you to ensure that the rightful animals are returned to their owners."

"You leave us lord?"

"Fear not, my men will ensure that the Scots do not return. As for me I have to go back to Stockton. I will be back here in two days' time and then I would have you come with me to Durham. Would you be willing to do that?"

"Of course, lord."

Aimeric of Durham

Chapter 11

Leaving Edward and the bulk of my men to ensure that the captives were safe, I returned with Fótr and Henry Youngblood. We passed the men who had come from Wulfestun on the road and I sent them to aid their lord. We picked up two horses from Wulfestun. We reached home after dark.

"Where are the rest of the men, lord?"

"Do not fear, David of Wales, they are all safe and we have scoured the land of Scots. I returned for Father Roger and to speak with my aunt."

"That evening, as we ate, I told my wife and aunt of the skirmish. Alfred's eyes were wide. He wished he had been there. Then I questioned my aunt about what she knew of the area north of Wulfestun and about the Bishop of Durham. Satisfied that I knew all that she did I told them my plans. I was happy that they met with my aunt's approval. I had learned that she was a shrewd woman.

With Father Roger and two of my archers we headed north for Fissebourne. We reached it before dark and we stayed in what had been the hall of the lord of the manor. I gathered that the priest had been using it. It was poorly furnished and decaying. The villagers showed their gratitude by cooking for us. My men found supplies which had been left by the Scots. I realised that they must have raided further north. Sir Edward told me what they had discovered.

"Many of the men fled." I raised my eyebrows. He nodded, "I know lord it seems cowardly but look at it from their point of view. Had they stayed they would have died. The Scots do not take prisoners. During the night they returned. Their wives and mothers gave them the sharp edge of their tongues. When we took the captives back to Kelloe we found it was the same story.

Kelloe never had a lord of the manor. The Steward of Bishop Middleham dealt with the running of the village. I think it was just seen as a source of income."

Ridley the Giant shook his head, "I cannot understand it, lord. Even in Anjou the lords did not abandon their people."

I nodded, "Welcome to the Palatinate. I had a long talk with my aunt and now understand the situation. Tomorrow we take the priest…" I looked at Edward.

"Father Michael."

"And Father Roger. We will visit the Bishop although, from what I have heard, he is in London. Still we can speak with the one who is supposed to be in charge, his nephew. From what my aunt tells me he is the source of the problem. This may work out better for us. We shall see."

I drank some of the ale which the priest had produced. It was not good. I guessed that they did not have enough of the ingredients. The manor appeared to exemplify all that was wrong with England. From the King down, they took from those below them. The ones we had rescued were at the bottom. They were the ones who were providing those above them with the food and the comfortable life. My aunt had told me of barons whom I could trust. They were the ones who were opposed to King John and his ways: John FitzRobert de Clavering, Eustace de Vesci and Richard de Percy were three. De Percy was related to the royal family and, as such, he appeared to be in greater danger than the others. As Arthur and the Fair Maid of Brittany discovered to their cost, it did not pay to be in any way an heir to the throne.

I felt happier now that I had two archers with me. They could scout and they afforded all of us better protection. I needed more such archers but the ones I had brought were all that I could afford and it took time to train men up to be archers. Had the Lord of Fissebourne trained the men of the manor each Sunday then perhaps the outcome might have been different.

The two priests walked. Neither felt comfortable on a horse. It meant the journey took longer than it should. The ten miles which should have taken a couple of hours took us half a day. We arrived at noon and it was market day which meant that the gates were open. Even so we were stopped.

"Who are you, my lord and what business do you have here?"

"I am Sir Thomas of La Flèche and my business is for the ears of the Bishop."

"He is not here, lord. His nephew Aimeric commands."

"Then it is him that I need to see."

The two sentries looked at me and the men I led. Ridley the Giant was behind me and I saw the fear in the sentry's eyes. Father Michael said, "These are good men, my son and mean no harm."

Reluctantly we were admitted. Taking just Sir Edward and the two priests we were admitted to the Bishop's chambers. The last time I had been here I had killed the Bishop. It felt strange to be returning. Much had happened in the intervening years.

The priest who asked us to wait outside gave me a strange look. I could see him trying to work out how he knew me. The last time I had been here I had been younger and with a skin burned by the sun. I had changed. He seemed reassured by the two priests who accompanied me. He said, "If you wait here my lords I will find out when Lord Aimeric can see you."

We had to wait an inordinately long time. I guessed it was to increase the man's feeling of self-importance. That was confirmed when we were admitted. Aimeric was young. I had him at no more than twenty-two summers. He had a neatly trimmed beard and he smelled like some of the lords I had known in the Holy Land.

"How may I help you? I am a busy man. My uncle, Philip of Poitou, Bishop of Durham, is in London and he expects me to run the Palatinate in his absence. It is a great responsibility."

I nodded, "I understand, and I would not have come were my business also of great importance."

"You are Sir Thomas of La Flèche?" I nodded. "That is close to Angers is it not?" Again, I nodded. "What business can Anjou have here in Durham?"

"I have been given the manor of Whorlton. However, since my return I have been adopted and left the manor of Stockton."

"The manor of Stockton? How can that be? Sir William was childless!"

"I was adopted by him. Father Roger can attest to the fact."

Father Roger stepped forward, "Yes lord, all was done properly. Sir Thomas was adopted by Sir William and bequeathed the manor on his death bed."

Just then the priest who had taken us in recoiled and pointed an accusing finger at me. "You are the Bishop killer! Sir Thomas of Stockton!"

Aimeric had heard of me and he too recoiled. "What is this? Murder?"

I smiled and took out the parchment. "Yes, I killed Hugh de Puiset but I have done my penance and been forgiven... by King John. Read this document and all will become clear."

116

He read it; three times as though he was trying to find a flaw. He could not. "I find this distasteful. You are stripped of your manor and by this," he waved the parchment, "you regain your land!"

"Nonetheless it is legal."

"Very well. Is that all?"

"No for I was called upon to help rid the Palatinate of Scottish raiders and recover the animals and the captives they had taken. This is Father Michael. He was their priest."

"It is true my lord. If it were not for his lordship then we would all be captives."

"Then I thank you. Have a safe journey home."

"I have not finished. The Bishop is responsible for this land. There is no lord at Fissebourne. There was once; Sir John of Stockton kept it free from raiders. When he fell at Arsuf, fighting for King Richard, his heirs were dispossessed. We need a lord at Fissebourne."

He was lost for words. "It is for my uncle to make the appointment."

"Then until he does I will take responsibility for ensuring the safety of the manor."

"That is kind."

"Kind but not generous. You have been milking the manor of Stockton. Until you appoint a new lord then Stockton will be as Sadberge and we will have a Liberty."

"You pay no taxes?"

"That seems fair. Who else will protect the land from Scottish incursions? You? What is required is the appointment of a lord of the manor and a tightening up of the borders of the land. Had I not intervened then Wulfestun would have been destroyed... for a second time and Stockton, which no longer has a castle, would have been attacked. These are the responsibilities of the Bishop of Durham. The rights are that when we pay taxes we should have his protection."

I saw smiles playing about the lips of the two priests I had brought. Aimeric looked bereft of words. He nodded, "I accept this document and the word of your priest but I am not the Bishop. When my uncle returns then he will make a decision. I will write to him this day."

As we left the castle Father Michael said, "You have an interesting way with you, my lord. You look young but your words are sage. Did you mean what you said?"

"That I will protect you?" He nodded. "Yes. Sir Edward here will send men each day to visit your village. If your people can keep watch for danger then there will be men at arms who could be at your village in half a day."

"Half a day may be too long, lord."

"I believe it is written that the lord helps those that help themselves. If your men trained each Sunday after church with the bow then they would not need to run away. If you put up a palisade and dig a ditch then the Scots would struggle to overcome you so quickly. They raid you because they can. They do not raid Bishop Middleham. There, they have a wall and they defend themselves. Until you cease to be sheep then you will continue to be shorn."

Father Roger nodded, "Sir Thomas is right. You must be the shepherd to your flock and help his lordship to protect them. Trust me, he will."

It was after dark when we returned home. My men were glad to be back in their unfinished hall for it had a roof and they had hot food. They had good ale and they had warm fires for the winter had returned. The Christmas would be a white one and that meant that the Scots would be unlikely to return. They had raided when they did to gather supplies for the winter. They had failed. They would return but it would not be until the new grass grew.

My aunt was delighted with the result but she was, generally, in a good humour. Christmas was coming and, for the first time in her life, she would have children around her. She would have a family and she threw herself into the preparations. She used her own coin to buy what we needed to make it a memorable feast. We were lucky. When we had come from Anjou we had brought dried exotic fruits and spices. The puddings and cakes we would enjoy promised to be the finest ever.

My wife had had time to make our quarters more to her liking. The goods we had brought made it feel like La Flèche. The married men I had brought with me had been able to take over abandoned huts and houses. Before the winter had set in they had improved them. Stockton was filled, once more, with the sound of children for many of my men had families. Ridley the Giant had the largest family. Seven of his children had survived. Soon the eldest, Petr, would be ready to serve as a warrior.

I said to Ridley. "If you wished I could train him as a squire. Fótr will soon be ready for his spurs and I have need of a second squire."

"Lord, that would be a dream for me. When I joined you, I thought to end my days as a man at arms but I see that my son has the chance to be elevated. Sir

Edward has shown me that. My son is a good lad and he is keen to learn. He is strong and has skills with a sword."

"Good. Can he read?"

Ridley hung his head, "No lord."

"No matter. My wife and Fótr can teach him. He will be my squire!"

Sir Ralph sent messages that although the snow had been severe the preparations they had made meant that neither the garrison nor the village would suffer. I had yet to find the sheep for the moors but I would. The taxes I would save would pay for them and for more cattle. The Scottish raids over the years had depleted the herds which my father and grandfather had built up. We were starting with nothing. Whatever we produced would be our work. We were still short of horses. We also needed more archers but we had survived our first few months and I was hopeful that we could continue to make our lives better over the winter.

Christmas was joyful. I invited Sir Edward and Sir Ralph to join me. Sir Ralph declined. I admired him for that. It showed he was serious about being a true lord of the manor. Sir Edward came with Gilles, his squire. Gilles was now fully grown and a handsome man. Like Fótr he would need a bride soon but there were precious few women of the right age for them. The Scottish raids had seen to that.

I invited my captains too and their families. The rest were happy to organize their own festivities in the newly completed hall. They were all single men and I think that some of the unattached women from the town were invited. It would not be seemly for my wife or Lady Ruth to witness what went on.

I had never seen my aunt as happy as that Christmas day. She bounced Rebekah on her knee. Now that she was older she could understand much more and Aunt Ruth sang silly songs and danced with her. Alfred was bemused but jealous enough to ask to be part of it too. That delighted my father's sister. I sat back and watched. Sir Edward also enjoyed himself. It was a night without responsibilities for him and he drank heavily. He could always hold his ale but he was still drunk enough to require David of Wales and Ridley the giant to carry him to bed. When everyone else had retired there was just Lady Ruth and me left.

I could tell that she was reluctant to go to bed. "You enjoyed this night?"

She nodded, barely able to speak, "My sadness is that William was not here to witness it but I am certain he looks down from heaven and feels what I feel."

"And what is that?"

119

"I feel complete. I never had children of my own but this one night has shown me what I have missed. I will try to make each day like Christmas for Alfred and Rebekah and when your new child is born then that will be even more joyous. I am so happy that you have returned."

"As am I."

She suddenly became serious, "Thomas... Tom, I have to warn you that while things have gone well hitherto there will be storms to face. I cannot see the Sherriff being happy at your return and you have tweaked the Bishop's nose. I hope that does not come to haunt you."

"I must be myself. I cannot be another. I have accepted that John is King. I am not happy but I accept it. However, I will not accept they he should not be questioned. He should be accountable. He has lost Normandy, Anjou and Maine. Phillip is greedy and John is in danger of losing England. I will make this land safe and secure and then find other barons who are of the same mind."

"Take care, my nephew. You are precious to me." She hugged me.

I helped her up the stairs for she had drunk well. I was up early the next morning. I had not indulged as some of the others had. I ate well. I ate alone. I was surprised when Edward appeared at the door. "I thought you would have been sleeping off the drink."

He shook his head, "I enjoyed the ale but it did not make me drunk. I was just happy."

I laughed, "Tell others that, Edward son of Edgar, but I know you better."

He tucked into the food and, when he had finished said, "I think I will go and find where the ale came from. I would have a barrel or two at Wulfestun."

"I believe it was Maud the alewife."

He frowned, "Maud? I knew a Maud once. It cannot be the same one for this one married a farmer from Yarm. She was a comely wench."

"Maud is a common name."

"Aye lord. So it is."

Fótr joined me when Edward had gone. "And what will you do on this St. Stephen's Day?"

"Godwin said he would help me to practise." He smiled, "I did not drink much last night and he did. I hope it will make my task easier."

"Think again, Fótr, Godwin can fight well drunk or sober!"

When my wife joined me with my children she was also in good humour. "Staying up late means that I get more sleep in the morning. With this one," she patted her tummy, "I need all the rest I can get for he is never still."

Alfred joined us. He had a platter filled with meat. "Can you eat all of that, son?"

He nodded, "Aye father. I would be as big as Ridley the Giant and then I will be able to defeat every warrior I meet!"

When Lady Ruth joined us, the atmosphere became even more festive. I was not certain that I would be able to cope with such celebrations until twelfth night. I had hoped for time to go hunting and riding with Alfred and Fótr.

It was noon when Edward returned and he had a silly expression on his face. "You have been a long time buying ale!"

He looked at me blankly, "Ale? I forgot."

I was puzzled. This was not like Edward. "Then where have you been?"

"I spoke with Father Abelard. I am to be wed!"

"Wed. Do you not need a woman for that?"

My wife said, "Husband!"

Edward smiled, "His lordship is right. It does seem strange but when I went to buy the ale I found that Maud was the same comely girl from my youth. Her husband died and the farm failed. She is now the ale wife and I asked her to marry me. She said yes. Father Abelard said that we can marry at Michaelmas!"

Lady Ruth was the most delighted of all, "A wedding! On top of Christmas!" She looked up to heaven. "Thank you, Lord!"

We laughed.

The wedding was held in our church in Stockton. Sir Edward's was too small. Even my church could not accommodate all of my men and many were outside. It was later, when we were toasting the bride and the groom that I realised this was the first marriage, since my own that I had witnessed. Most of my men had just taken women and become husband and wife. It seemed momentous. Maud became Lady Maud and was a little over awed by it all. My wife and Lady Ruth took her to one side to put her at her ease. I stood with Ridley and Edward. Fótr, Gilles and Petr were close by. Our two older squires were as interested in the marriage as any. They were lusty young men and seeing an older knight like Edward marry made them both think about their future. They could not marry while still a squire but they could become betrothed. The trouble was there were no young women for them.

"Soon, Edward, you will have children like Ridley here."

"Maud is not young lord. I am not certain." His words belied the hope that was in his eyes.

121

All was well and we looked forward to a new year which would be as hopeful as the old one had ended.

.

Sherriff of York

Chapter 12

My plans to visit York were delayed. It was not procrastination on my part merely that we had problems in the valley which needed my attention. When the snows melted in February it was followed by unusually heavy rains. There was flooding. Thanks to the ditches dug by my men Stockton remained largely undamaged but the lands around Norton and Hartburn were inundated. We had to house the refugees in Stockton. When the rains abated I decided to put in place the digging of the cut in the Tees. It would prevent flooding. Every man from my garrisons and every man in the valley was involved. I was entitled to call upon each man for forty days a year. It was supposed to be in times of war. I used five of those days for a war against the river!

It was messy work and it was hard work but it brought every man and warrior together. Sir Edward and our squires worked in kyrtles and seal skin boots alongside pig farmers, herdsmen and tanners. The levy returned to their homes after five days and my men and I finished off the work. Father Abelard had joined us in the labour. He had a clever mind and his advice helped to save us from catastrophic mistakes. He wisely suggested building up the banks to prevent flooding and, some years later, during the great flood of 1212, we were saved the devastation which destroyed whole settlements further upstream.

By the time we had finished I had to hold my first assizes. In England they tended to be more regular than in Anjou. It helped me to get to know the people of my manor. I discovered the good and the innocent as well as the rogues and the chancers. Dispensing justice was a great responsibility. The Sunday morning training had yielded results. The men were much better with their bows. None could compete with my own archers but David of Wales identified four young men who could be trained to be archers.

Sir Edward and his bride made Wulfestun more secure and comfortable. Although his wife had seen thirty summers she soon fell pregnant much to Edward's delight. A practical woman, she had the women who lived at Wulfestun turn the bolts of cloth Edward had bought into surcoats for his men at arms. He took as his sign the hawk, for his father had been a hawker.

The arrival of my son, William, also delayed my departure for York. He came at the beginning of May. Having held my assizes, I had contemplated leaving for York when the hall was filled with women racing around as my son entered the world. For my Aunt Ruth this was a wondrous moment. She would be present at the birth of a child. She regarded my children as her grandchildren. Alfred and Rebekah both called her Nanna. As I waited I sent Fótr to Whorlton to inform Sir Ralph that I would need him when I visited York. He lived within the land controlled by the Sherriff of York. He would need to visit with the King's representative.

The birth was more difficult than the other two had been but the child was born healthy and my wife, although tired, was well. I stayed at home during the rest of May. The final delay was the arrival of *'Swan of Stockton'*. She had wintered in the Loir for her hull needed cleaning. She had a cargo of wine. We would sell it. Captain Henry had made money for himself with short journeys down the Loire and the Maine. He was happy. We loaded his cargo of iron and hides. I asked him to bring back as many horses as Sir Richard and my other knights could spare.

I had collected the taxes just after the assizes. It meant I had coin. I had confirmed Sir William's steward, Edgar of Hartburn, as my own and I left him with half of the coins. That would be a reserve in case we needed it. The Scottish knights had yielded us some coin which Edward and I had shared. We were not as badly off as we might have been. The rest I took with me. I took just six men at arms and four archers. The land to the south was at peace. Sir Edward had ensured that the north was also free from danger. We had bought a breathing space with our defeat of the raiders. They would return.

As we had some money to spare and the hall was becoming crowded I set my mason to building an annex to the hall. It would mean that visitors could be accommodated and yet the ditch would still protect the halls. The alternative was to tear down my hall and rebuild. That was impractical. An annex would suffice. With three children, Lady Ruth's women and my wife's it would be hard to put up Sir Ralph and his squire if they came to stay. When I was happy that the mason knew my thoughts, we left.

When I reached Whorlton I saw that Sir Ralph and James Broadsword had improved the castle over the winter. When the floods had devastated the valley, they had left Sir Ralph's lofty perch untouched. He now had a stone keep and the gatehouse was under construction. I also saw that he had a squire.

"Who is this, Sir Ralph?"

"This is John of Swainby. His father has the largest farm in Swainby. He wished his son to be a warrior." He lowered his voice. "He paid for his horse and mail, lord and, to speak truly, he is a keen youth. James is training him."

"I have the same with Ridley's son, Petr. They will both become, in time, good squires."

"Did you collect your taxes?"

"Your taxes lord." I nodded. "I did and the Sherriff's man collected them. He was surprised that there was a lord here but pleased for he had more taxes than in other years."

"How so?"

"This land is free from Scottish raids but thanks to the injustice of King John and the Sherriff's rule, there are many bandits and brigands. I have scoured my forests of them. I left their heads on spears and we have had no repetition. The people were able to work harder and produce more."

"Good. Bring your surplus coin with you. We shall leave for York on the morrow. If we ride hard we can do it in a day. It is but thirty-eight miles and we have good horses."

Sir Ralph brought just his squire. He left his men toiling on the new gatehouse. Our three squires chatted and I rode with Sir Ralph. "I asked you to bring coin to see if we can buy some sheep." I tapped his surcoat, "And you still have my surcoat."

"I am proud to wear it lord!"

"Thank you for that but, like Sir Edward I would have you wear your own. There may come a time when associating with me may harm you."

"But this is your manor!"

"Perhaps, but one of the reasons I am visiting the Sherriff is to ensure that we hold on to it. Now that I am lord of Stockton there may be a problem. And there is something else, you need a wife. I would have my knights produce children. Sir Edward is to be a father."

"There are precious few young ladies close to me. The nearest lord appears to be at Helmsley and I have yet to meet him or his family."

I now saw why Whorlton had been neglected for so many years. It was isolated and poor. The purchase of sheep might transform it into something which would yield Sir Ralph enough money to hire more men at arms. He had a small garrison.

"Tell me, lord, what do you know of the Sherriff? I know little."

"I met him when I was on crusade. He may remember my name if not me. That is my hope. He is close to King John and that is why he is High Sherriff. He was given Pontefract Castle which is a powerful and important stronghold. He is also High Sherriff of Cumberland. In truth, Ralph, I am not certain that we shall see him but I have to present my parchment for your protection."

As we were clearly knights we were allowed free entry to the walled city of York. We entered through the old Roman gate. The walls were Roman and made York the greatest fortress in the county. I headed for the river. There was an inn there my father had used. It was called *'The Saddle'*. He used it for it had a stable and, in his time, had served good food.

I dismounted and the innkeeper came out. He bowed when he saw my surcoat. "You must be the Earl of Stockton!"

I shook my head, "That was my father. I am Sir Thomas, his son."

"The squire who saved King Richard! The hero of Arsuf. You are welcome, lord. Tab, see to the lords' horses. Fetch their baggage!"

Our rooms were adequate. Petr and Fótr would have to sleep on the floor but they did not mind. It was too late for any business and so we ate in the inn. The innkeeper, Edgar, proved to be a mine of information. He told us of the Sherriff and the men who were powerful in York.

"The Sherriff is rarely here, lord. His son, Sir John acts as Constable. It is he that you will need to see."

I could tell that he was keeping information from me. He told me of the markets and where we could buy cloth. He told me the best place to purchase sheep but when I pressed him about Sir John he was evasive. I realised that I was being unfair. Edgar had to live in York. I would be wary when I met the Constable.

We left our men to wander the town and we took our squires to the keep. It was a circular one and looked, to me, to be impregnable. The river protected one side and the mound was one of the biggest I had ever seen. We were asked to wait in an ante chamber while we were announced.

John de Lacy was a little younger than I was. I could see that he liked to impress his guests for, while he was a short man, he had a large chair on a dais which meant that even when seated he was at eye level. If I had brought Ridley the Giant he might have had to look up. A clerk hovered nearby and there were two men at arms behind him. We stood there like penitents while he read the parchment I had given to the clerk.

He nodded, "So you are the lord at Whorlton, Sir Thomas?"

Unsure of the correct form of address I said, "No Constable. Sir Ralph here acts as castellan for me. I have inherited Stockton manor."

He frowned and turned to the clerk. They whispered. "I thought your family was disinherited. They lost the manor!"

I nodded, "They did but Sir William, who was the incumbent, died but, before he did, I was adopted as his heir. I have presented the testimony to the Bishop of Durham."

"Then you are indeed a fortunate man. To have murdered a bishop and offended a king would not normally garner such rewards."

I smiled a thin smile, "Perhaps that is because I was unjustly treated."

He leaned back and put the fingers of his hands together. "My father, the Sherriff, has spoken of you. He was at Arsuf that day. He was with King Richard. He admired you for what you did. For that reason and that reason only, I will allow you to continue to have Sir Ralph as your castellan." He turned to the clerk. "Have it so noted, Cedric."

"Aye lord."

"However, as you failed to inform me of your arrival I fine you and your lord ten gold pieces."

I saw now why the innkeeper had been so circumspect. John de Lacey was lining his purse while his father was absent. This was little short of extortion. I saw Sir Ralph open his mouth and I shook my head. I reached into my purse and took out ten coins. It would hurt our finances. I placed them, one by one, on the table. I took the parchment and rolled it. "And this means that all debts are paid? There will be no further… requests for payment save the annual taxes?"

He smiled, "If Sir Ralph obeys all of the laws of this land then that will be so."

I nodded, "We would appreciate a copy of those laws, lord for we have recently come from Anjou and there the law is a little less murky!"

He coloured. "Of course. Return in the morning and Cedric will have a copy ready for you."

"And a copy of the judgment on Sir Ralph."

"Of course."

"You are a careful man Sir Thomas."

"I have learned to be so in the Holy Land, Durham, Sweden and, latterly, Anjou. I have learned to adapt."

When we left Sir Ralph said, "I am sorry my lord. This is my fault. I should have presented the parchment as soon as I arrived but I was so busy…"

"Peace Sir Ralph. This was robbery pure and simple. The fact that it was legal does not change what it was. Now I see why the barons are unhappy. There appears to be no redress from King John's officers and they exist only at his favour. We will have to be more careful."

I spent some of the coins I had left making purchases for my wife. She needed fine cloth so that she and her ladies could make clothes for my children. We met up with my men at arms and archers in the inn. The food was good and, unlike the Constable, Edgar did not rob us.

"What did you learn?"

Godfrey shook his head ruefully, "That York is the most expensive town I have visited. We called in at an inn by the cathedral. The ale was twice the price it is here. We found a smithy selling weapons. I could have bought five swords in Angers for the same price as one in York."

Edgar had been listening, "That, my lord, is a local tax. A tenth is added to every bill and sent to the Sherriff. It is his son's idea. Most of the inns charge more just to make a profit. Here, I cannot afford to. My customers are, generally, sailors and they are careful with their coin."

The next morning, we collected our documents and headed for Northallerton. There was a sheep market there. It was a thirty miles journey. There was a lord at Northallerton. Sir Hugh Fitzwaller was known to me. I had met him in Angers once for he had a cousin who had a manor in Poitou. He was happy to accommodate us. He was particularly friendly because of my great grandfather and his role in the battle of the standard. Sir Hugh was old fashioned and was still loyal to the memory of the Warlord and Archbishop Thurston.

We sat at his table with his wife, his two sons and his daughter. They were of an age with Fótr and Ralph. They chatted happily. His daughter, Isabel, was stunning and I could see both Fótr, Gilles and Sir Ralph, vying for her favour. Sir Hugh obviously wanted to speak. He did so furtively. "I am pleased that there is a lord at Whorlton. I liked not the empty manor but even more important I am happy that a descendant of the Warlord is at Stockton. You will be a barrier to the Scots."

I shook my head, "I have no castle. I have a hall which has a fighting platform. I can hold off a warband but not an army with siege engines."

"The King has much to answer for." He sipped his wine. "I can speak to you in confidence? You are a true and honourable knight?"

"Of course."

"Then know this, there are barons here in the north; they are more powerful than I. These barons are unhappy about King John and his malignant rule."

"Rebellion?"

He shook his head, "No Sir Thomas, a different kind of war. They use alliances and wish to bring the King to account for his actions. He uses *'ira et malevolentia'* to those who do not do as he wishes."

I had heard of this anger and ill will. Thomas Becket had been killed as a result of this.

"The latest to suffer is William Marshall."

I could not contain my shock, "But he is the greatest knight in the land. He took over as adviser to the King after my great grandfather passed away. He is renowned as the most loyal of knights."

"Then that should tell you the strength of feeling. I have heard the de Lacey family may be the next to suffer *'ira et malevolentia'*. He fears their power."

I leaned back and sipped my wine. Now I saw that John de Lacey was not necessarily acting with the best interests of his father in mind. He was lining his own purse. It was his father who would suffer if the mismanagement of the County came to light.

"With your permission, Sir Thomas, I will tell the barons who are unhappy that they may speak with you."

I nodded, absent mindedly. Had I left one baron's war to walk into another?

"Richard de Percy is the most vociferous. You will like him. He hates the Scots for King William constantly petitions King John for the return of the title of Earl of Northumberland!"

His wife leaned over, "Husband, must you be so indiscreet! You know that there are spies everywhere."

He patted his wife's hand. "I know my love but this is not one of them. He brings hope to this land but you are right I will curb my tongue." He turned back to me, "And what brings you to my manor? Had you gone to Whorlton from York then you would have been there already."

I nodded, "You have a sheep market tomorrow."

"Aye. The new lambs will be sold."

"We would use the high land to the east of Whorlton and Swainby for sheep. It will give Sir Ralph an income."

Sir Hugh nodded, "He looks like a fine young man. Is he married yet?"

"He is still a bachelor knight, why do you ask?"

Sir Hugh smiled, "There are few eligible knights in the county. I am inordinately fond of my daughter. I could marry her off to someone who lives many miles away but I would miss her. The two seem to get on. I would give a substantial dowry. And it would strengthen the bonds which bind us."

I thought back to my wife. She had almost been made to marry a man she hated and I would not inflict that upon either Isabel or Sir Ralph. "If the couple are in agreement then you have mine too."

"I will speak to them both in the morning." There was a sudden burst of laughter from the young people. He smiled, "Now is not the time."

The castle was large enough for me to have a chamber to myself and I could not sleep. I had too much racing through my mind. If Sir Ralph could be married and if we could buy lambs for his future flocks then that would make that manor secure. The conspiracy with the barons was more dangerous. I had a young family. Would I be putting them in jeopardy? I was running out of countries to which I could flee. I would have to tread carefully. I would have to, in light of the King's treatment of William Marshal, do something I had never done before. I would have to put on a false smile for a King I despised!

The young couple were more than happy at Sir Hugh's suggestion. The disappointed one was Fótr. I do not think he dreamed that he might marry Isabel. However, he still had the half heart locket from Eleanor, Fair Maid of Brittany. We had heard that THE King had moved her from Brough to Bristol. That was too far for us to visit. Fótr was most unhappy. Sir Ralph's joy made his heart ache more. Leaving them to arrange the details I went with Sir Ralph's coin and his squire to the market. Despite the snow it had been a good year for lambs. There were many twins. I spent all of Ralph's gold, for he would be getting more from Sir Hugh when he received the dowry.

As they were penned for us Godfrey said, "My lord, forgive the impertinence but have you not forgotten something?"

"I do not think so."

He smiled, "Perhaps a shepherd. I know not about these matters but what I know about sheep is limited to a good mutton stew!"

The man who had organised the sale had been listening. "Lord if you wish a shepherd they gather outside the inn called *'The Standard'*. You may find one who needs a master."

Leaving my squires and archers to watch the lambs I led my men to the inn. We saw the shepherds. They had dogs and crooks. The dogs did not socialize with each other. Each shepherd's sheepdogs kept apart although the shepherds were quite garrulous and chatted with each other. I suppose they lived a solitary life and when they gathered they made up for that. There was one exception. A youth who stood alone with his dogs.

I stood before them. "I need a shepherd."

One, an old man with a grey beard said, "Where is the farm, lord?"

"The manor of Whorlton." I pointed east.

The old man shook his head, "Not for me lord. I am a lowland shepherd. I have never heard of sheep up yonder."

"No this would be the first." I looked at their faces. All the ones with experience looked away. "Will none of you consider it?"

The youngest of them, the one who had been alone, raised his hand, "I will lord!"

The others all laughed and the greybeard said, "Lord, do not listen to Gabriel! He has never had his own flock. Those dogs are his father's and he died in the winter."

I saw the young shepherd colour. "Is this true?"

"Aye lord."

"Yet you still think you can do it?"

"Lord these dogs, Scout and Shep, are the best pair of sheepdogs you will ever see. Even old Brian there will agree." The greybeard gave a reluctant nod. "As for inexperience; well lord I have worked with my father for eighteen summers. I know sheep. I will not let you down."

I took out a silver coin. "Then you are hired. I will take you to the sheep and then your lord."

"Who is my lord?"

"Sir Ralph of Whorlton."

"Is he your son, lord?"

I laughed, "No, Gabriel and I must look older than I am. I am Sir Thomas of Stockton."

The greybeard suddenly dropped to a knee. "I am sorry, Sir Thomas. I meant no disrespect. I did not recognise your livery."

"Rise, Brian. I took no offence. The day an Englishman cannot speak his mind will be a sad one for England."

The looks on their faces showed that they thought that day had already arrived.

Brigands in the Valley

Chapter 13

I reached Stockton two days later. There had been much to do. My wife was delighted when I told her our news. I was about to go to view the work on the new hall when Ridley accosted me. "Lord, there are bandits in the valley."

"How do you know?"

"Ethelbert the forester found the old charcoal burners in the woods to the west of Elton. They were dead and their hut ransacked. He found the remains of a butchered deer. The charcoal burners would have sought permission."

"Charcoal burners could not have had much."

"No, lord, save food and ale. Ethelbert thinks they spent some time in the hut for the two bodies had been left outside and attacked by animals yet the ashes in the fire were still warm."

"When did you discover this?"

"Yesterday. David of Wales sent out his men but they found no tracks."

I nodded. This was where Edward's local knowledge would have come in handy. "Have four archers and six men at arms mounted. Skuld has ridden far, saddle me another horse."

"Aye lord, "Petr and Fótr; we hunt bandits."

Petr said, "I will fetch our helmets."

"You will need neither helmets nor mail. We hunt human animals!"

Margaret shook her head, "Must it be you?"

"I know the land. I think I know where they will have gone. We may have to stay out overnight. Do not worry."

Once mounted Ridley said, "Where do you think they will be, lord?"

"By the river between Prestune Farm and Eggles' Nook." I led them along the river. There was a trail there.

"Why there, Sir Thomas?"

"Because, Petr, they can always flee across the river if men come. They can use the river to fish. They can even capture one of the smaller craft which ply the river but, most importantly, because they can remain hidden. When we had a castle at Thornaby then that was impossible. The river was in plain view of the castle walls. Without a castle and a lord they can raid the isolated farms of Elton and Hartburn. There are fewer of them now but they would be attractive to bandits."

King John had much to answer for. His scouring of the valley had taken the lord of the manor from Yarm. With the castle destroyed it was now a farmer who controlled the land for the Sherriff. The same was true of both Appleton and the village of Wiske. My men at arms were the only ones who could patrol this land. The road west was used by travellers who did not wish to use the ferry. The bandits could have rich pickings.

"Ethelbert thought that they were Scots, lord."

"How did he deduce that?"

"Some of them were barefoot and there was a piece of material such as the Scots use to make a cloak."

I nodded and said, "Silence now for we enter the forest. Dick One Arrow and Cedric Warbow, take the higher ground in case we flush them. We will take the river trail."

"Aye lord." They took the fork and followed the path which climbed up the valley side. Gruffyd and Mordaf rode just ahead of me with bows strung and an arrow held in their hands. They had noses like good hunting hounds.

The ground was bare but was still moist from recent rains. It deadened the sound of our horses. Since we had put the cut in the river it had flowed faster upstream and had begun to eat into the bank. The river would readjust. Consequently, we found that it had burst its old banks and spilled over the path. Mordaf suddenly stopped and leapt from his horse. He waved me forward. I saw that where the river had flooded over and then seeped away there were two pairs of footprints in the mud. One of them was barefoot. They headed up the slope. I signalled for my men to dismount. I pointed to Petr to watch the horses. He almost objected but his father glowered at him and he nodded. He tied them to the trees and then drew his sword.

134

With the two archers on our flanks I led Fótr and my men at arms with weapons drawn up the slope. We followed the path left by the footprints. On the harder ground they disappeared but we were able to pick them up again where there was an open patch of ground which was wetter. We heard squealing from ahead. It was not the sound of animal squeals; there were wild boar in the forest. It was a human squeal of pain. It came from our left and so we left the trail we had been following and, placing our feet carefully, headed up the slope. The noise grew louder and I could smell wood smoke. Their camp was close.

I heard a Scottish voice. I did not understand the words for they were in Gaelic but they told me that they were near. In many ways I was glad that Petr was not with us. The men I led had done this before. They would not panic nor would they react to whatever they saw. They were disciplined and Petr was young. Mordaf and Gruffyd each nocked an arrow. They used the cover of the trees to move closer to the crackling sound of the fire and the sound of girls in pain. It was now obvious that there were at least two girls.

"Please, no! Do not hurt my sister!"

A Scot shouted, "Then lie still and it will hurt less!"

There was a great temptation to rush but that might have ended disastrously for the two girls. I used the cover of the trees and the bramble bushes to approach the camp. It was a big one. There were at least twenty men. Two of them were astride two young girls. Neither looked to be older than thirteen summers. I trusted my two archers. They would target the rapists. The others would be taken by my men at arms and my squire. I saw that my men were in position. We were twenty paces from the camp. I raised my sword and ran towards the camp.

I heard the sound of two bow strings and the rapists were thrown back. The girls screamed, "Fótr! See to the girls!"

I swung my sword at a huge warrior who had picked up a two-handed axe. He had been quick and the axe came towards my head. Had it connected then I would be dead but an axe, once it had begun its swing cannot deviate. I ducked and slashed at the same time. The axe head almost shaved my hair but my sword ripped across his gut and disembowelled him. He fell writhing and twitching to the ground.

My men set about slaughtering the brigands with ruthless efficiency. They despised those who abused women and children. The fact that they were Scots merely exacerbated their cold anger. Two of them ran towards Fótr. My squire stood between them and the girls who clung to his legs. I leapt across the dying

135

giant and brought my sword down the right-hand side of the nearest one. My sword tore down his arm and shoulder. His squeal sounded like that of a stuck pig. As the other looked to his right Fótr showed his new-found skill and brought his sword across the neck of the brigand. He fell, his blood spurting and choking his life away.

Cedric and Dick appeared on the ridge above us and they began, with the Tomas brothers, to pick off the bandits with their arrows. One dropped his sword and yelled, "Mercy!"

Ridley the Giant glanced over at the girls and took the man's head in one blow.

"Are there any left alive?"

Cedric Warbow shook his head. There were two sentries at the ridge line. They are dead."

"Mordaf, Gruffyd, fetch the horses. Put these bodies on the fire. We will burn them." I wandered over to the girls. They were shaking and still clung to Fótr. Although now was not the time for detailed questions I needed to know whence they came. I said, as quietly and calmly as I could, "Where is your home?"

The elder of the two, the one who had shouted to protect her sister, said, "By the river." She pointed upstream. I remembered that there was a flat piece of land. I could not remember a hut or a house but it had been almost twenty years since I had been here.

"Cedric and Dick, ride upstream. Keep to the path. There is a flat piece of ground a mile or so away. See what you can find."

Ridley threw the last of the bodies on the fire and my men put more wood on the pyre. The air was filled with the smell of burning hair and clothes. Soon it would be the smell of human flesh but, by then, we would be on the way back to my hall.

Ridley said, "Most were Scots but, from their appearance, some were English or perhaps Danish."

I nodded. When we had attacked the Scots, we could not have been certain that they did not have more parties further south. Vikings still raided this coast. It seemed that all that was bad sank to the bottom of the pond and congregated there. When the horses were brought back I said, "Let us mount and get these girls to my wife and my aunt. They will know what to do. Petr, Fótr, put them on your horses. Let them sit sideways and you lead them.

136

They nodded and Fótr said quietly to Petr, "Talk to them gently about anything. Idle chatter might keep this horror from their heads."

I knew it would not. They would wake screaming in the night. They would recoil at a man's touch. It was why I had Fótr and my young squire with them. My men and I looked too much like the bandits. I had seen the fear in their eyes when I had approached. As we headed back I said, "Mordaf, were there any more signs of bandits?"

"I think not, lord."

"Nonetheless I would have you take out all of my garrison tomorrow, Ridley. Ride the borders of my manor. Visit the woods and look for anything untoward. These animals have destroyed at least one family, perhaps more. I am now lord of the manor and this is my fault."

Ridley said, gently, "Lord you were away. It is not down to you."

I shook my head. I would not make excuses for my failing. "I should have had you all patrolling."

"Then we would have exhausted horses for we are still perilously short of them, lord."

That was my dilemma. I was used to Anjou where every man had two horses. Those horses were still in Anjou. Captain Henry might take a month to return with horses; if they were available! I had much to think on. I sent Mordaf ahead to warn my wife so that when we approached the hall the women of the hall were ready.

My squires gently helped the girls down. The elder of the two took Fótr's hand and squeezed it, "Thank you, master. You risked your life for us and we will not forget it."

I could see that Fótr was touched. My wife and lady Ruth whisked them away. We had just unsaddled our horses when my two archers, Cedric and Dick, grim faced, rode in. Their hands were soiled and they both looked solemn. "Well?"

"We found the house. It was a family. Two small boys had been butchered. The man had put up a fight but he had been cut up. We could not find his head. The woman…" Dick One Arrow could not speak more.

Cedric said, "These were not men, they were animals. We buried the family lord. That is to say, what we could find we buried. It looked like the family fished the river. There were fish traps and a small boat." He had seen much death in his life but the deaths of that small family affected him more than any.

"Thank you. We will scour the land for any that we missed. For now, wash the stink of death from you. You have all earned your coin this day."

I had no appetite and I picked at my food. My wife and my aunt had still to return and my two children wondered at my silence. "Father, what happened to those girls?"

I looked at Alfred, "They fell into the clutches of bad men, evil men.. We punished them."

"They are dead?"

"They are and they died without confession. They will now be burning in hell!"

When my wife and my aunt returned they were both drawn. My wife said, "Come children, it is time for bed." Alfred thought to object but one look at my face convinced him to obey.

Lady Ruth did not touch the food. She poured herself a large goblet of wine and drank it in one. "Those poor bairns. They are called Ada and Agnetha. Their mother is…, was, Norse. The younger one has not uttered a word and when I saw what they had done." She put down the goblet, threw her arms around me and sobbed uncontrollably. I had never seen my aunt react like this. Even the death of her husband had not brought on such tears. I held her until she pulled away. "Thank you." She dabbed her eyes, "You must think me foolish."

"No aunt. I saw the girls and I saw what they had suffered. They will recover…?" It was a question.

"I confess I do not know. I brought Father Roger to look at them but the younger one hid. She is terrified of men. Your wife will ask Brigid the midwife to examine them. She knows about such things." She took my hand, "We will keep them here, will we not?"

I nodded, "Do you have to ask? And tomorrow we will search for any other such vermin as those that did this. I will ride to Wulfestun and warn Edward too."

My wife came down stairs. She was nursing William. She sat before the fire. When she spoke, it was though she was speaking to the air rather than to us. "When William becomes a man, I pray that he will behave as a man and not as an animal."

I sat next to her and held her hand. "We will bring both our sons up to understand the difference between right and wrong. You do not have to be a lord to know such things." My aunt slipped away. I think she went to the church to pray. It was a sombre night.

I took my squires with me when I rode to Wulfestun. The rest of my men were abroad seeking more felons. As we rode Petr asked, "Lord, when will I be able to fight alongside you?"

"When I think you can do so without risk of dying."

"Surely, lord, all men can die in battle."

"They can but as Fótr will tell you a good squire stands close to his lord holding his banner and watching how men fight and how men die before they draw sword themselves. Those animals we slew yesterday were desperate creatures. They were not worth the life of one of my men. Had you gone against them you would be dead."

Fótr said, "When I cannot beat you in practise then you may be ready. It is only recently that I have fought alongside my lord and I have nearly come to grief."

That seemed to satisfy Petr who looked up to Fótr.

I saw that Maud was heavy with child when we reached the manor. As I expected Edward was close to home. It was a hot June day and we retired into the cool of the hall for some of Maud's ale. It was perfect for the weather. She took herself off to allow me to talk and so I was able to be explicit with Sir Edward. He was a warrior who had seen much but I saw him angry. Perhaps it was the prospect of becoming a father soon.

"I know you keep watch for raiders. You need to watch for bandits too."

He nodded, "The Bishop has returned."

"Ah, then I can expect either a visit or a summons."

I then told him what I had learned in York and Northallerton. He looked worried, "Lord, I fear for you. This sounds like treason."

I shook my head, "When these northern barons come I will speak with them. I am not a fool, Edward. I will not commit but we have legitimate grievances. I need to build a wall around my hall. I need towers but I am forbidden yet Stockton is all that stands between Scottish ambition and the heart of northern England. But I will be careful"

We found no sign of more bandits but we maintained our vigilance. We took on two more men at arms who arrived on a small ship which came from Flanders. It seemed they had served an English lord. He had died of a plague in the fever filled islands of the Frisian coast. They had taken ship and worked their passage for they had heard of my return. I did not hire them blindly. Ridley and David of Wales interrogated them while I spoke with the captain to arrange for cargo. He had brought, speculatively, some lace and fine cloth from Flanders. It was not cheap but I bought it for two reasons: it pleased my wife and it was another ship which would trade with us. We sold him some hides and some iron. It was the beginning of an influx of ships. The new cut made the river more attractive to ships.

The summer passed. Crops grew, animals were fattened and life went on. I heard from Sir Ralph. He was now a married man and he sent a chest of gold to me from his dowry. He had not needed to do it but, as his letter told me, he now prospered. The Lord of Northallerton was a friend and that increased trade.

The two girls improved. The elder, Ada, was a lively chatty thing but Agnetha remained silent and fey. My aunt took her under her wing. While Ada looked after Rebekah my aunt trained Agnetha to be her maid. I heard her talking to her one day as I passed her chamber, "Now you do not need to speak to be a good maid but if you do then it will make life easier." There was a long silence. "We have time enough to talk. Now here is my brush. Let me see if you can brush this grey hair of mine." Another silence followed. "Well done. I can see I have made a good choice."

It reminded me of Sir Edward's father, Edgar, when he had been schooling a particularly skittish horse. After a month Agnetha actually smiled. Six weeks later and I heard her laugh. As my aunt told us, it was a beginning. And then the '*Swan*' arrived with twelve horses. It was a great gift and it swelled our numbers dramatically. We would now be able to field over thirty mounted riders. With the horses we were breeding when Alfred had seen ten summers in a year or so we might actually have a surplus.

When Edward's son, Edgar was born it was cause for great celebration. Preceding the best harvest, we had ever had it was a sign that God smiled, once more, on our valley.

Conspiracy

Chapter 14

It was October when a rider came from Wulfestun to warn me that lords were approaching. He said that they had ten men at arms with them. My wife and Lady Ruth went into action to prepare. The small hall for guests had been recently finished

This would be the first time we had used it. Edward's rider had just said five lords. We had no idea how many others were with them. I changed into a clean surcoat. Petr and Fótr did the same. I set my servants sweeping up by the stable and had the stable master prepare stalls. Thanks to the horses sent by Sir Richard we would soon need more stables. Some of those used by my father had fallen into disrepair. Horses had not been a priority for Sir William in the dark years when I was away.

I recognised the standard of the Bishop of Durham, and I saw, with him, his nephew Aimeric. I did not recognise the other three lords. They did not look like clerics. Six of the men at arms wore the livery of Durham. The other four and the knights all wore the same livery. They dismounted and Aimeric said, "Uncle this is Sir Thomas. Sir Thomas this is the Bishop of Durham." The Bishop held his hand for me to kiss the ring. I bowed and did so. It was a deliberate act from the Bishop to put me in my place.

"You are welcome, Bishop Philip, to my hall."

One of the knights stepped forward. His surcoat had five golden fusils on blue background. "I am Richard de Percy. I am Baron of Topcliffe and Hexham. These are Sir Roger and Sir Robert. They are my household knights."

"Come, my wife is in my hall." I pointed to the newly finished hall. "There is accommodation for you there."

Aimeric shook his head, "His Grace and I will ride back with our people. We will return to Durham when our business is completed."

Baron Richard said, "We will take you up on the offer for we are far from home. Roger, see to the baggage."

"Aye lord."

As I led them into my hall I made certain deductions. This would be a very brief visit. Sir Richard was not with the Bishop. His lands were beyond the Palatinate and I wondered why they were together. I had many questions racing through my head. My wife and Lady Ruth awaited us at the door to my hall and I introduced them. With food and my best wine on the table we waited until the Bishop was seated and then we sat. It gave me a chance to view Philip of Poitou. He was much older than the rest of us. He had a stern face and in all the time I knew him I do not think that I ever saw him smile. He had the look of a cleric. Hugh de Puiset had been a bishop who liked good food and wine. When Philip of Poitou ate and drank it was like a bird. He pecked at his food and sipped at his wine.

I waited for the Bishop to speak. He had invited himself. There was an uncomfortable silence. I could see that my wife found it hard. Lady Ruth saw that I was not initiating a conversation and she smiled. There would be no small talk. Whatever the Bishop had to say he would need to raise himself. He looked at his nephew who spoke, "My uncle has been apprised of the document you were given by the king and the testimony of the priest."

I merely nodded.

Philip of Poitou had expected me to respond in some way. When I did not he was forced to speak. "My nephew tells me that you withheld your taxes!"

"Yes, Your Grace, for I have had to use my men to keep the lordless land of Fissebourne safe. Has Your Grace appointed a lord?" My voice was calm but I lifted the end of the sentence.

The Bishop said, "That has nothing to do with the matter. Stockton belongs to the Palatinate and you owe me taxes."

"That is true and it is part of my responsibility but part of the responsibility of the Palatinate is to keep the people safe. Kelloe and Fissebourne suffered because there was no lord to protect them."

"You would lecture me?"

I smiled, "I have spent the last fifteen years fighting to keep people safe. I am not certain that you have."

My aunt said, "There was a time, Bishop, when the Lord of Fissebourne was a strong lord. Your predecessor used his position to remove the lord's family from that land and destroy the castle. That was not your fault, Bishop but surely you can see that you cannot let the people of the manor go unprotected. My nephew is willing to continue to protect them until you provide a lord. Is not the loss of taxes worth it?"

The Bishop played with the rings on his left hand. "I will seek a lord but I like not this, my lord. It reeks of extortion."

"It is not. Thanks to Hugh de Puiset, Stockton is not the town it was. The castle was torn down and the town was over taxed. I intend to make it rich once more but that will take time."

He jabbed a finger at me. "I will have no castle in Stockton! I will not have my power threatened!"

"And I have not asked to build one."

Aimeric said, "Yet you have built a moat and there are arrow slits in the walls of your hall."

"The ditch drains the water when we flood. Had we not had the ditch then we would have been inundated in last year's floods. As for the arrow slits… my men and I hunted down Scottish raiders and bandits from my land. They had come south and killed my people. Would you have me make it easy for a Scottish army to destroy my home?"

The Bishop said, "There may be raiding warbands but the Scottish King will not attack!"

Sir Richard shook his head, "I disagree, Bishop. I have visited Alnwick and Warkworth. The lords there tell me that the Scots plan just that."

"My lord at Norham has not spoken of danger."

"Then perhaps they attack further south. I would suggest, Your Grace, that you look to your own position."

"Sir Richard, I have been assured by King William himself, that the Palatinate will be safe from any Scottish army. He is a pious man." He rose. "I will appoint a lord but when the taxes are due, Sir Thomas, you will pay them!"

We escorted the two men to their horses and watched them ride away. Sir Richard smiled, "My lord that was a masterful display! Now that he is gone we can talk more openly. Perhaps you could show me what was once the bane of the Scots, Stockton Castle."

He wanted to be alone. I nodded. "Of course, we will begin at St. John's well for it is a holy place." The well was close to my church and, as such, quiet.

143

When we reached there and there was no danger of us being overheard, he spoke. "I have spoken with Sir Hugh of Northallerton." He was obviously one of the conspirators. "Now that your knight has married his daughter then you are one of our number."

"I speak no treason, Sir Richard. If that is your intent then I ask you to leave. I am hanging on to this manor by my fingertips."

"I know and you should not be. The Bishop's actions are symptomatic of this King. Where are the rights of the lords? Where are the rights of the people? We live a parlous existence up here at the edge of the realm. We have poorer land than in the south and yet we are taxed as heavily. Do you agree that we should have more rights as barons?"

I could not argue with that. "Perhaps, but I will not rebel against the King. When last that happened the Scots took Northumbria. My grandfather and his father had to retake it. Would you wish that?"

"No, Sir Thomas and we are all grateful to your family. That is why we need you on our side. Baron de Clavering and Baron de Vesci are both powerful barons. We would petition the King to adopt a fairer policy. That is not treason."

"He might regard it as such."

"We would keep our swords sheathed."

"Then, I am sympathetic to that cause and I would support it... peacefully."

"That is all that we ask."

"And what of this Scottish threat? Was that to put fear into the heart of the Bishop?"

"No, Sir Thomas, that is a genuine threat. King William is allowing the barons on the border to prepare a raid on Northumbria. King John is beleaguered. The Pope and he are at loggerheads. He has lost Normandy and seeks to hold on to Poitou. What better time to take Northumbria? He will not be part of it so that, if it fails, then he can deny responsibility."

"Northumbria is far from here."

"Yet if we lose then there is nought to stop the Scots razing the valley for you no longer have a castle. Besides we would appreciate having the hero of Arsuf with us. We all know how you helped to conquer the Estonians and you were one of the few lords to emerge from the Norman Baron's War with any honour."

"I do not have many men."

"Yet the ones you lead are worth five or six of a Scottish led army."

144

He was right. If the Northumbrian barons could not hold the Scots on the Tyne then there was nothing to stop them from flooding the land. The Bishop's words had told me that there was an agreement between the Bishop and the King of the Scots. Durham would be safe but all else was not.

I nodded, "Very well. It will take a day for us to reach the Tyne."

"We hope to stop them further north than that. I will send riders to you." He smiled. "Their men may raid in winter but their lords will not. It is almost the time of the snows. They will not come until March. That gives us all four months to prepare."

That would give me the breathing space I needed.

He and his knights were courteous and polite as we ate. My son was fascinated by them for these were three new knights. We discovered that they were on their way south. Sir Richard said he was going to Topcliffe but I suspected he was going further south than that. There were other lords whom the conspirators needed. They left early the next morning and I was left with much to ponder.

Petr needed more training. His weapon skills were improving but there was more to being a squire and, ultimately, a knight than just being able to use a sword and shield. Alfred was older now and bigger. Since he had been given a pony he thought himself a squire in training. I decided that he should train alongside Petr. Fótr was almost ready to be a knight. It was only Petr's lack of skill which had prevented me from doing so. I called Alfred and my two squires together. "There will be a war coming and you, Petr, are not yet ready to carry my banner. Fótr, I want you to spend the next month making him so."

"Yes lord."

"And Alfred can also be trained." My son's eyes widened in delight. "Not that he will be going to war but when Petr is proficient enough then you shall be knighted and Petr can continue to train Alfred." I had given Fótr an incentive. He wished to be a knight with all the benefits that would bring. He would train him.

Petr said, "Will I need a hauberk, lord?"

I shook my head, "If Fótr has an old one which will fit then use that but you are growing too much. A hauberk is expensive and you do not need it. The leather jerkin will have to suffice."

He nodded.

Alfred looked disappointed, "Then I will not have one either?"

"Not until you have seen fourteen summers. But the two of you can have a helmet. In your case, Alfred, it will be leather. Now go, you have much to teach them, Fótr." He picked up the wooden swords and small bucklers. He led them off to a quiet corner where they would not be observed by the sentries on the fighting platform of my hall.

David of Wales and Ridley the Giant had been waiting close by. I waved them over as Fótr began to teach the two boys how to swing their swords and block with their shields. I saw Ridley smile as his son took a blow to the wrist from Fótr. He knew that such blows were the best teacher.

"Baron Richard warned me of a danger from Scotland. They will attack Northumbria. I know it is far from here but I would rather fight in their lands than in the valley."

Ridley nodded, "Besides, lord, there is more chance of booty!"

"There is that. We are still short of horses. We will need sumpters if we are to campaign north of the Tyne. David, I would have you and three of your archers ride around the manors close by and see if you can purchase horses. They may not know of the forthcoming war and so we may be able to get them cheaper." As soon as there was a hint of war then the price of horses doubled. Warriors needed them and merchants were keen to have a beast which could take them away from danger quickly.

"Aye lord. I will leave Cedric Warbow to continue working with the new archers. They are improving but they are still below the standard I expect."

He left us and I said to Ridley, "We will need to leave men to guard our home when we go. I leave the choice of men to you. Jack the blacksmith appears to know his trade. I want every hauberk to be perfect. Check each man's sword. We need no defective blades. I would rather spend coin to get good swords and mail." I smiled. "The Bishop wants his taxes next year!"

I left him to organize the men and I rode to Wulfestun. If my men had known I went alone they would have been worried. I did not tell them. If I could not ride the land of Stockton then I had no right to be a lord of the manor. I rode close to Norton. It had been a greater manor than Stockton at one time. The church was older than mine. It was beginning to grow again for there was more land for farming. The Bishop had yet to appoint a lord of the manor. I had a mind to ask him to appoint Fótr. If he could not find one for Fissebourne then I doubted that he would find one for such a poor manor as Norton.

I waved to the farmers. They did not know me well, yet, but the Reeve, Walter of Norton had told me that they were happier with my men riding their

146

manor. When I reached Wulfestun I discovered that Edward's son had been named after me. I was honoured. Maud was nursing him as I arrived. She scurried away. She was ever shy around me. Sir Edward and Gilles were working with their men to construct a stone tower attached to the hall.

I dismounted and Gilles took Skuld to water her. I said, "Are you becoming a fortune teller, Edward?" He looked puzzled. "The new tower."

He pointed to the hall. "Now that I have a wife and a son I need somewhere they find sanctuary if bandits come. It is an old-fashioned sort of tower. The entrance is on the first floor. It can only be accessed through the hall."

"And it may prove useful."

He came closer. "There is danger?"

"There may be." I told him of my visit and the dangers which had been mentioned.

"You know, lord, that I will not have a great number of men to bring. I do not have many horses and I need my family protecting."

"I know. The conroi I lead will not be the largest I have ever commanded. There will be but three knights and I doubt that we will have more than thirty or forty men at arms and, perhaps twenty or thirty archers. It will have to do. It will be February or March when I shall need you."

He looked relieved. "Good for that gives me time to train the men of the manor. They are better than they were but…"

I nodded, "And you might invite the men of Norton. It is closer to you than Stockton. They do not have a castle but they have a wall."

"Aye lord."

I returned a different way. I rode towards Hartburn. Sir Harold had once been lord of the manor there. He had never had a castle but the hall, which had been built by Wulfstan, had been burned during a raid. It was now a blackened pile of timbers. We had neither the men nor the coin to build it but one day I would have a lord of the manor there too. My horse drank from the beck and then I turned and rode to the Oxbridge. This was the start of my manor and the pig farmers who lived there had prospered in the time I had been back. The sight of the pigs snuffling in the muddy ground by the beck was reassuring.

Over the next weeks, as the weather deteriorated, we did not stop. Fótr worked with Alfred and Petr. When it was too wet for horse work they practised with swords and when the nights drew in and it became too dark he worked with them on the reading, writing and courtly skills. For Petr this was the hardest task.

Fótr hit on the novel idea of using Rebekah to act as a lady. She thought it a wonderful game and Alfred and Petr were able to learn how to address a lady, how to bow and, most importantly how to speak. One skill that was hard to teach was singing. Fótr had a beautiful voice. Others, in Anjou, had said that he could have made a living as a troubadour. I had never needed the skill but my father had insisted that I learn. It was part of being a knight. He could play the rote well. It was not an easy instrument to play. Alfred found the rote easier to play but Petr was a more confident singer.

As the nights lengthened and the days grew colder we prepared both for winter and for war. Cedric Warbow had managed to buy two palfreys, three rouncys and six sumpters. He had done well. It was also reassuring to hear that the land to the south of us was at peace. Just before Christmas I went with my three squires and two men at arms to Whorlton. It would be the first time I had seen Ralph since his marriage. I had deliberately left him alone. His life had changed dramatically. I also intended to speak with Sir Hugh.

Isabel was with child and Sir Ralph was no longer the youth who had served me in Anjou. He was a man grown. He had broadened out. As I said, when we inspected his impressive defences, "Being lord of the manor suits you."

"Thank you, lord. I owe all to you. We are more prosperous and when our ewes lamb I will return some of the coin I was loaned by you."

I waved a dismissive hand, "The coin can wait but I will need you, your squire, four men at arms and four archers in March. We go north of the Tyne."

"That is when my child is due."

"Nonetheless I will need you."

He nodded, grimly, "Then I will be there."

We rode to speak with Sir Hugh the next day. As luck would have it we could not have picked a better day. When we arrived at the castle he was speaking with ten men. I waited in the shadows of the gatehouse and I listened.

"I am sorry but I have no need of men at arms. The land is at peace and my warrior hall is full. You might try Sir Ralph at Whorlton. He may need one or two of you."

The leader knuckled his forehead, "Thank you, lord."

I nudged Skuld forward, "What is your name?"

He bowed, "William of Lincoln, lord. I lead these men. We were in Poitou when King Phillip's men captured our lord. The ransom was paid for him but we were left bereft. We worked our passage on a ship to York but the Constable there called us vagrants and had us thrown from the city."

That confirmed my decision. If de Lacey did not want them then I did. "I am Sir Thomas of Stockton. I was lord of La Flèche." I could see that they had heard of me. "I can give you a home and pay if you would serve me?"

They all nodded vigorously and William said, "Aye lord! We have heard of you and it would be an honour."

I tossed a couple of silver sixpences to him. "Here is money for food. Stockton is just a day's march north. I will be there before you."

"Thank you, lord."

Sir Hugh led us to his hall. "Did Baron de Percy tell you of the Scots?"

"He did lord."

"I will need Sir Ralph and some of his men. Lady Isabel is due to give birth when I take him. You will need to help watch his lands for me."

"That I will but worry not about my daughter. She knows what is expected of her. She can stay here when she is due. My wife would like that." He lowered his voice, "And what of the Baron's proposal?"

"I tell you what I told him. I will not rebel for that will open the door to the Scots but I will support a peaceful protest. I can say no more."

He nodded, "Have you heard that King John has been excommunicated? And that there is an interdict. Priests may only baptise and hear the confessions of the dying. That will hurt the church."

I knew what he meant. Many priests became rich as a result of weddings and indulgences. King John would also suffer. Matters were coming to a head. King John had enemies at home, in France, Scotland, Ireland, Wales and in Poitou. Now, it seemed, he had made an enemy of Pope Innocent!

• Edinburgh

• Dalkeith

Berwick

• Lauder

• Norham

• Galashiels

Bamburgh

Jedburgh

• Alnwick

Warkworth•

| Durham

The New Castle

3 miles

N

The Battle on the Coquet

Chapter 15

If the last Christmas had been a good one then, with three children and the two rescued girls, this one was even better. My wife and my aunt knew that we would be leaving in three months for war with the Scots and they were determined to make it a celebration which would live long in the memory. The blanket of snow which surrounded the hall and the frozen Tees made the hall seem, somehow, cosier. My aunt and my wife spared no efforts to make the children and the two rescued girls happy. Agnetha even managed to speak with my Aunt and say. "Thank you!" It may not have seemed much to anyone outside the hall but to us, it was the best present any of us could have had. She was on the way to recovery and a damaged soul had been saved. By the time twelfth night came we were ready to go back to the preparations for war.

My son would soon be seven. Even as we left for war he would celebrate. Partly as a gift for a future squire and partly at apology for leaving him at home I gave him his first sword. It was little more than a dagger but the smith had done a good job and the hilt and the pommel were well decorated. With a fine scabbard he was able to strut around my hall like a young knight.

We had schooled the new horses and the saddler had made saddles for the horses we would ride. David and his archers had spent the winter fletching. We had plenty of arrows. The smith made us spear heads from the poor swords we had taken from the bandits. We had spare spears. Father Abelard, who was a well-read man, told us of the Roman horsemen who had had a scabbard for their javelins on their saddles. We fitted the scabbards so that my men at arms could replace broken spears. I was lucky. I had Fótr and Petr to bring me replacements.

As the days lengthened and the snow abated the preparations grew apace. Once we had passed February I was watching for the horseman from the north. When the message arrived then we would mobilise. It was not that I wanted to leave my family and go to war, it was just that I knew it was coming. I wanted it over with. It was the second week in March when the sentry on my fighting platform shouted, "Lord, two riders from the north. They wear yellow fusil on a blue background."

I knew what it meant and I shouted, "Captains, squires, to me!"

Petr was the first to reach me. "Take a horse and ride to Whorlton. Tell Sir Ralph I have need of him. Return with him. When you reach here then you will be told whence you ride."

"Aye lord." He had grown over the winter. It was a lonely ride south but I knew that he would cope.

His father arrived and shouted, "And wrap up warm!"

He grinned, "Aye father!"

"The riders approach. We will be leaving as soon as I discover our destination. I know we cannot reach the Tyne this day but we can reach Wulfestun and leave on the morrow. Go, pack and say your goodbyes."

All had known this day was coming and the goodbyes would be less tearful.

The two riders reined in, "Our lord sent us. The Scots have been seen gathering at Jesmond. It is an army. The Baron would have you join him at Otterburn. The other lords are coming to join him there."

"And the High Sherriff?"

"My lord sent to him." That was the whole of the message and I wondered if the Sherriff would appear or would he let his barons fight the war for him?

This would be a test of the character of Robert son of Roger. I had heard he was a weak man. A threat to his county would show if that was true or merely a malicious rumour. The two messengers came with us. They would need to rest their horses before returning to their lord. My forty-eight men had fifty-six horses and Dragon. The eight spare horses were laden with arrows, food and blankets. We would take no tents. My men were hardy despite having lived so long on the Loir. Baron Percy's two men slept. We helped Sir Edward and his men to prepare their own equipment.

If we left before dawn then we could stay at de Percy's hall at Hexham. The horses would need rest after that but it was a short way to Otterburn. The extra men I had taken on at Northallerton meant we had left a good garrison at

Stockton and we would be able to leave more at Wulfestun. The men I took, with the exception of Petr, were the most experienced that I had.

It was after dark when we entered the hall at Hexham. There was no castle here but there was a hall. We were all chilled to the bone and ready for food. The two messengers had warned the steward and all was prepared. I first asked about the Scots.

"There is no further news, lord. They are north of us but the melting snow means that the land is not as easy to travel." The steward was an old warrior. I saw that he only had two fingers on his left hand. "If I had been the Scots then I would have come a month since. The ground would have been harder. Still, it is the Scots. They are hard to predict."

I nodded, "And yet the Baron knew when they were coming."

"He is a wise lord. He has spies and he keeps a good watch on the border. I am lucky to serve Baron de Percy." His words spoke much about Baron de Percy.

We did not leave at first light. I still hoped that Ralph, his men and Petr would still reach us but, more importantly, I wanted the horses rested. It was not far to Otterburn and we reached it in the late afternoon after an easy ride. I saw many standards there but no sign of Robert son of Roger, the Sherriff of Newcastle. Of the Scots there was no sign. As we headed for the standard of de Percy I reflected that this would be the first time since I had left Anjou that I would not be leading men into battle. I would be following. It had been a long time since that had happened. Even in Sweden I had made the major decisions. I hoped I would not come to rue my decision.

After I dismounted de Percy clasped my arm. "You made good time. De Vesci and de Clavering are on the other side of the tower. We have sixty knights and two hundred men at arms. I brought my levy."

"And the High Sherriff?"

"He has not spoken of his intentions. I hope that his conscience will make him join us. He has sixty knights at his beck and call." He looked at my men as they unpacked the horses. "You have tents?"

"We need no tents. What about the Scots? Do we have news of them?"

"The mud slowed them down. My scouts reported that they are camped in the forest north of Byrness. They are eight miles from us."

"They will have scouts out and know where we will be. Can they get around us?"

He thought about it. "They could but they would have to go through the forest and over the ridge. If they did then they would be in the Coquet valley. Rothbury Castle might hold them up but it has but ten men guarding it. The rest are here." He suddenly looked worried. "Do you think they might do that?"

"Just because you wish them to come here does not mean that they will. If I were leading the enemy army I would do that. Why fight a battle against a waiting army when you can go around them and capture key castles?"

He nodded, "Walter."

A man at arms came over. "Aye lord?"

"Send four men to watch the Scots. If they do not come here I would know where they go."

"Aye lord."

When his man ran off the Baron said, "While you make yourself comfortable I will speak with the others. We had assumed that they would come here."

I said nothing but it showed their lack of military experience. They were better plotters than generals. They should have had men watching the enemy. We would have done. Edward had been listening and he shook his head. "We would have had scouts watching the Scots all the time."

"They will learn, Edward, they will learn."

The Baron was away for some time. It was dark before he returned. "Thank you for your suggestion, Sir Thomas. I confess we expected them to come to us."

"The Scots will avoid a battle if they can. They prefer to ransack and pillage. You have assembled an army which is large enough to intimidate them."

Just then Sir Ralph and Petr rode in. I was relieved. I now had all of my men together. My men had prepared food and we ate in the open. Baron de Percy had provided sentries but I saw that Ridley had men watching the horse lines all night. We looked after our own.

I was awoken in the middle of the night by Fótr. "Lord, it is Lord Percy. The scouts have returned."

I rose and wrapped my cloak about me. It was very cold. Although it was March it felt like the depths of winter had we been in Anjou.

Baron FitzRobert de Clavering was with him. "You were right, Sir Thomas. The Scots only pretended to make camp. They force marched and they have Rothbury under siege."

"You said it was just a small garrison."

154

Baron FitzRobert de Clavering nodded, "It is but the Scots do not know that. Baron de Vesci has marched his men to go to their aid."

I felt my temper rise. We had few enough men and you did not divide an army. "Why do we not march with them? It is a disaster to split your forces."

"I know but Rothbury falls under Alnwick and that is de Vesci's castle."

"My lord, we must follow quickly. My men are all mounted. Do you have a guide to take us to the Baron?"

"Of course."

I shouted, "Stockton! Mount! We leave!"

As we mounted our horses Fótr said, "Lord the Baron of Warkworth looks young to be commanding so many men."

I nodded. I had thought that myself. I wondered just what I had gotten myself into. We had had a good position and now we had thrown it away. I shouted to my knights, "Sir Ralph, Sir Edward, we go just to stop the Baron of Alnwick Castle being destroyed. No glory. We use our archers to hurt the Scots and withdraw. The rest of the army is following."

"Aye lord."

The guide took us on a very primitive road. It was barely wide enough for three men to ride abreast and it had an uneven surface. I rode just one horse's length behind the guide. When I spied the enemy, I would not have long to make my dispositions. We soon began to pass the tail end of the men of Alnwick. That worried me. This Baron Eustace de Vesci was so impetuous that he risked hitting a superior force piecemeal! He was not keeping the few men he had together. Knowing that we were catching up the column I spurred Skuld. Fótr and Petr had Dragon with the baggage.

I had no time for politeness, "Move to the side! A lord is coming through."

These were men on foot and they resented having to move but as I was flanked by two other knights and followed by my men at arms and archers, they complied. As dawn broke I saw the men spread out for a mile ahead. We were descending towards Rothbury which I could see perched on the hill above the river. I saw no sign of an attack. I would not have expected one. A night attack on a castle you did not know could result in disaster. When I began to catch horsemen I was more hopeful for we had yet to see the Scottish outposts. The Scots were not fools. They would have men watching for us.

I saw the banner of de Vesci ahead of me. I knew that Eustace was related to the King of Scotland. Even as I rode up to him to ask him to stop I wondered if this was some elaborate plan to deliver Northumbria to the Scots. Eustace de

Vesci reined in. "What do you want, Sir Thomas? I go to the aid of the castle of one of my knights." He gestured at a young knight who was riding next to him. "There are few men within! I will not wait for the rest of the army to catch us."

"I know, Baron, but I would not have you lose your men trying to save it. I have the rest of the army coming. Will you heed my advice?"

"I was in Palestine and met your father. I was not at Arsuf but, for the sake of that glorious day, I will listen to you but I do not promise to do as you say! This is my land!"

I sighed, "Good. Do you have archers?"

He looked confused and then waved a vague hand at the men on the road behind us. "Some of the levy do."

"No, I mean real archers. My men are just that and they are mounted. I will send my archers ahead. When they find the Scots, they will send their arrows at them. They will annoy them. They will wound and kill them and, hopefully, the Scots will decide to chase them from the field and we will be waiting here to ambush them."

The young knight said, "Sir Thomas there is a better place lower down. It is flatter and will allow us to use our horses. The river will protect our right flank."

"Good!"

Baron de Vesci said, "What if they do not come?"

"Then my men will slaughter them and we will have won. They will come for us."

He reluctantly agreed. As we moved towards the site which Baron Rothbury had suggested I rode with David of Wales. "Take four of my men at arms as horse holders. Hurt them David."

"They will follow us, lord. You have come up with a good plan and we have plenty of arrows."

When we reached the site, my men rode off. Baron de Vesci said, "What now?"

"We put the horsemen on the left. We have twenty knights and fifty men at arms. Your ten dismounted men at arms and your levy make a shield wall with their flank by the river. Those archers you spoke of can be behind the spearmen and they can rain death on the Scots."

We prepared. I mounted Dragon and Petr took Skuld to the baggage. Fótr held my standard. The men were still strung out along the road and while the horsemen were ready the four lines of men who would have to hold the Scots

156

were perilously thin. They would be reinforced as more men arrived. We had to buy them time. The castle was just a mile away and the flat ground meant that we could not see the Scots. We did see the arrows as they soared into the air. Annoyingly we did not see the effect. I kept my helmet hung over my cantle. I needed to see all. I looked again at Baron Alnwick. He did not look like a reckless young warrior and I wondered what had prompted his decision to leave the army and make a suicidal attempt on the Scots. I had no doubt that if I had not rushed after him he and his knights would not lie dead and his levy would be spread to the four corners of the land. More arrows soared and then I heard Scottish horns and the drums that they liked to use.

I knew what was coming and I shouted, "The Scots come! Stand to!"

Baron de Vesci looked at me, "How can you be so certain?"

"The horns and the drums. Besides I have seen my archers at work. They will have sent three hundred arrows at the Scots. Those who wear no mail will be hit. Two hundred men could be wounded or worse. The Scots cannot afford to take those kind of casualties. They will chase my archers from the field and David of Wales will lead them here."

"You have a great deal of confidence in your men."

I said, simply, "Of course I do. They are my men."

We heard the clamour and furore of the Scots above the hooves which thundered towards us. David of Wales would lead them to the middle of our line and move obliquely across our front to help us flank them.

I saw my archers and the four men at arms. There were no empty saddles. The danger would be a horse which might fall as they galloped over the uneven ground. Behind them I saw the Scottish knights and mounted men at arms. They also had hobelars on small horses. They were armed with javelins. The horses prevented me from seeing the men on foot but I saw the banners and standards waving as they hurried towards us. We would be outnumbered but all that we had to do was hurt them and David of Wales and my archers could begin to slaughter them once more.

I donned my helmet. "Prepare to charge!"

I had left Godwin of Battle to command the men on foot. He would hold them in line. I needed every other mounted man at arms and knight that I could. Charging in a single line I hoped to sweep the Scottish horse from their mounts and discourage them.

The Scots were two hundred paces from us. They were a whirling mob of angry men. Some of the wilder men on foot had managed to keep pace with the horses. It was time. "Charge!"

I spurred Dragon. The other knights and barons had war horses but Dragon was a seasoned mount. He had fought in France and Anjou. He was a warrior. I rested my spear on my cantle. We had caught the Scottish knights without spears and lances. They had just mounted their horses and hurtled after the archers who had caused them so much damage. I ignored the hobelars. They wore no mail and had no helmets. My archers would slaughter them and the shield wall would hold them. It was the knights we needed to destroy. The knights were the leaders. The more we killed the more of their men would leave. Despite my need for coin I was not worried about ransom. When I struck it would be to kill.

I rode towards the right-hand side of the Scottish knight with the blue shield and the white fusil. I hung my spear at my side and invited a blow from his sword. He stood in his stirrups and leaned forward. I lunged with my spear. It caught him under the arm. He was standing and I lifted him higher. He lost his balance and tumbled from his saddle. I changed my grip and held it overhand for the next knight was approaching quickly. He had a war hammer. He would not stand in his stirrups, he would swing sideways just above my horse's head. As I brought my shield across my saddle I thrust down with my spear. It went through his chausses into his thigh and stuck in his saddle. The spear was torn from my grip as his dying arm smashed his war hammer into my shield.

I saw that we had penetrated their front line and now it was time to draw them back to our archers. "Fótr, sound fall back!"

The three notes sounded and all of my men and my knights reined in, turned around their horses and galloped back. Some of de Vesci's knights kept charging and were cut down by the wild, half-naked and tattooed warriors on foot. As we rode back I saw that at least twelve Scottish knights lay on the ground. Those that were not dead already soon would be. The reckless men on foot had also been cut down. My men at arms did not miss such easy prey. There were small horses wandering the field for my archers had scythed the hobelars down. One had the rider being dragged by his heel. He did not care. He was dead.

Even as we approached I saw the arrows soar over our heads to pick off reckless horsemen who had followed us too closely. When I heard the Scottish horn sound then I knew this battle was over. Knots of Scots and Northumbrian knights, eager for glory, still fought but the majority of the warriors obeyed the horn and withdrew. I saw that Sir Edward had taken a prisoner. One of the Scots had surrendered to him. The man was lucky for Edward rarely gave them the opportunity to do so.

Baron de Vesci took off his helmet and walked his blood spattered mount towards me. I took off my helmet. "You were right Sir Thomas. They had many more men than I thought. Rothbury is lost."

"Not yet, Baron. Have you ever tried to take a castle?" He shook his head. "It is not easy and they have a problem, us. They know not if this is our whole army. When Sir John and Sir Richard arrive it will give them something to think on."

Baron Rothbury shook his head when he returned. He was leading his limping war horse. It had been badly cut and his shield was dented. "They are anmimals! Poor Sir Roger was too reckless. I have lost a knight."

"Next time, Baron, heed the horn. I sounded it for a purpose."

He flashed me an angry look. It was nothing to do with me. He was angry for his horse had been burt and he had lost a knight. "Why are you here Sir Thomas? Your manor is not even threatened."

"True but if you lose, and looking at the strategy I saw employed this day then that is likely, then my valley would be unprotected. I fight here so that my land and my people are safe."

He stared at me and then led his horse off. Baron Eustace said, "A little brutal Sir Thomas."

"The truth often is. This is not a game, Baron. Men died out there and there is little glory to be gleaned from an axe through your leg. I do not fight for honour. I fight to win."

He nodded. "And what now?"

"Have your men cut stakes and make a barrier before us. When the rest of the army comes we can make camp and then work out how best to destroy this Scottish rabble."

"Scottish rabble?"

"They are badly led. There was no order to their attack and no one took charge. They are a warband. If King William thinks they can gain him Northumbria then he is truly deluded."

After Petr had led Dragon off to be unsaddlled and cleaned, I joined Edward and Ralph at the river. We stripped off our surcoats, mail and gambesons. We stepped into the icy water. Other knights looked at us as though we were mad. We were not. The refreshing river washed away the blood and the

159

smell of death. The icy water numbed our bodies and took away the hurts. We had all taken blows. They had not bled but that did not mean that they did not cause hurt.

It was late in the afternoon when Sir Richard led the rest of the army to join us. As the men erected tents, Sir Eustace and I told him and Sir John of the action. "I believe, from what David of Wales told me, that more than a hundred of the Scots fell to arrows. Twelve of their knights died and eight squires. Thirty hobelars perished and another twenty of their men on foot. We lost two knights and six men at arms. We were lucky. Eight knights are wounded and may not be able to fight tomorrow."

Sir Richard said, "Do we have a plan?"

Baron Eustace nodded, "Aye beat the bastards!"

I was warming to the Lord of Alnwick.

They all looked to me. I suppose because I was the most experienced. "It seems to me that now that we have the knights of Warkworth and Hexham we can use them to destroy their horse. At the same time we can use our archers, behind an advancing shield wall of the levy, to break the hearts and spirits of their men on foot. The danger to the levy is the hobelars. The men at the front need long spears."

Baron Eustace said, "But your archers are much better than what we have brought."

"I will put Captain David in command. He knows how to use even the poorest of archers."

We spent some time speaking of the logisitcs. I insisted that the wounded knights be with the levy. They would give the farmers some backbone. There was little point in mounting men who could not fight on a horse.

David of Wales arranged our own sentries to watch our horses and our lines. I sat with Sir Ralph and Sir Edward. "Is there much ransom in your knight, Edward?"

"I know not. I was about to skewer him when he shouted, '*I yield*'. I thought he was going to shit himself!"

We both laughed for Edward was so serious. "I confess that I could do with ransom but I am not certain that these Scottish lords have much money."

"Some have for they have estates in England. Part of the purpose of this raid is to recapture land which was given to Scottish lords in times past."

Edward finished his ale. "The lads did well stripping the dead. The other knights were not bothered and most of their men at arms were just glad to be

160

alive. David and Ridley shared it equitably. And we have ten of the hobelar ponies and four war horses. Not bad for a skirmish. Perhaps on the morrow we may do even better."

I did not sleep well. I worried about the lords with whom I fought. If they were conspiring against King John then their performance on the battlefield did not bode well. I was glad that I had not committed my self. I woke early and went to the river to make water. Petr and Fótr joined me.

"We fight today, lord?"

"We do. Petr you will carry the standard for I need Fótr to be behind me. We are short of knights and men at arms. Are you ready, squire?"

My squire nodded, "I am, lord. I promise that I will not let you down."

"The thought never entered my head."

It was cold fare we ate. While Petr went to saddle the horses Fótr helped me don my mail. When I returned home the blacksmith would need to replace a couple of links on my hauberk. A blow from one of the Scots I had fought the previous day had broken one of them. With my arming cap and ventail hung around my neck I sought de Percy and de Vesci. They were warming themselves at the night fire the sentries had kept burning.

Baron de Percy pointed to the skies. "The men who live up here tell me that there will be a chance of rain today. The ground is already muddy. If the rain comes in the morning it will harm our attack. The horses will struggle."

"And the archers will not be as effective. There is no sign of imminent rain. We attack sooner rather than later. If I were you, lord, I would rouse the men."

I was not in command. It was down to Baron de Percy to do so or Eustace de Vesci. They looked at each other and Baron Warkworth shrugged, "Sir Thomas seems to know what he is doing and I would rather get this over with and have Rothbury safe and the Scots gone from my land."

"I would do so quietly, my lord. No horns and shouting. The Scots may well be resting after a forced march and a battle they were not expecting. If we can achieve surprise then so much the better."

I did not need to give such commands to Sir Edward and Sir Ralph. They, along with David and Ridley, were already shaking awake those who still remained alseep. Of course it was not a silent procedure. Horses neighed and the sound of jingling mail could be heard but the Scots would, I hoped, put that down to the camp rising. Horns and clamour would suggest battle. The sun rose although there was so much cloud cover that it was still gloomy.

161

Petr brought my horse. Keen to be part of the battle Petr already wore his open face helmet. He handed me Dragon's reins and gave Flame's to Fótr. He hurried back to the horse lines for his own. I saw that de Vesci had one of his men help him to mount. He was older than I was but I could never remember my grandfather, even when he was a greybeard, needing help to mount. I pulled myself into the saddle. My shield hung from my cantle. I lifted it and slipped the long strap around my shoulder and let it hang over my left leg. I hung my helmet from my cantle. Fótr offered me a spear. I shook my head. "Later. I need to see if the enemy are making their own preparations.

I nudged Dragon forward and he picked his way through the stakes. I saw a slightly higher piece of ground. The rats and vermin fled from the Scottish bodies as I passed. The slightly elevated piece of ground allowed me to see parts of the Scottish camp. They did not appear to be forming for battle. I used the viewpoint to examine the ground. It was flatter towards the river. That would help our men on foot and archers. The ground to the left of me, where I intended the horse to charge, was broken up by buildings. We would not be able to use a continous line. I frowned. De Vesci should have mentioned that. It would alter our plans.

I turned and headed back to our lines. The knights and men at arms were all mounted and gathered. They waited expectantly. "We will have to change our plans."

De Vesci snapped, "Why?"

"Because until I examined the ground over which we are to charge I did not know that it was broken up by buildings and small stands of trees."

He looked confused, "And why is that a problem?"

"Because we will not be able to charge in one line, my lord." He opened his mouth and then I saw the realisation sink in. "We charge in conroi. I will take mine in the centre. Baron de Percy you take my left and Baron de Vesci the right. Baron de Clavering you will be the reserve. If one of us hits a problem them you will go to their aid. If one of us breaks through then your fresh knights exploit it."

They nodded but Baron de Clavering said, "You have but three knights. I have more. Should you not be the reserve?"

"And have you charged an army before, my lord?"

He was so young that I knew he had not. He might have fought in a mêlée in a tournament but little more. He shook his head, "You are right." He smiled. "Your men can take the risk and my men will garner the glory."

162

I saw de Percy shake his head. De Clavering was young and more than a little arrogant. He would learn. I just hoped that his knights would not pay the price for such arrogance.

The wounded knights who could still fight were gathered with the men on foot. They were marshalling them into their lines. I waved over David of Wales. "The locals say there will be rain later. I would end this battle sooner if we can."

He looked up into the sky, "Aye I smell rain in the air." He gestured with his unstrung bow at the levy who were armed with a bow. "I have spoken with the archers I am to lead. They are keen enough but I fear we will not be able to maintain a steady stream from all. I can guarantee that our men will but these have not the strength nor the discipline."

"So long as their arrows fall and the spears stop the enemy closing then we have a chance."

I returned to the knights. The three lines of spears were ready. I nodded to Baron de Vesci. He waved his sword and the three lines moved ponderously down the valley. Although the ground was flat they would not move quickly. Their strength lay in a continuous wall of spears. They were the anvil and we were the hammer.

I joined my men and Fótr handed me my spear. Petr, behind me, unfurled the banner. I saw that he held it in his left hand and his shield hung from his left arm. Fótr had taught him that. I raised my spear and spurred Dragon. With Sir Edward and Sir Ralph flanking me we headed towards the Scottish camp. My line of horsemen just had our squires behind us. Fótr would fill in the gap if one of us fell. De Clavering and his conroi would be fifty paces behind us. We picked our way towards the Scottish camp. We still could not see it. They would, of course, see our banners before we saw them. That could not be helped. If that was their only warning then we had a chance.

I guessed they had seen us and that we were close when I heard horns rousing them. Then, as we passed around a stand of trees I saw the camp. They had not dug a ditch nor embedded stakes but they were awake and arming. I saw knights donning helmets as their horses were brought to them. The men who fought on foot had nothing to delay them and they were being forced into lines. The hobelars mounted their horses. They would be ready to meet us first.

We were three hundred paces from them and I spurred Dragon. I had to trust that the lines of spears and our archers were approaching the Scots. If we had to face the whole Scottish force then we would lose. This time the one commanding the Scots had them take spears and form some sort of line. They had learned from our skirmish. I glanced down my line and saw that we were all together. I could feel the occasional pressure from the boots of Ralph and Edward. We were in as tight a line as we could get. I spurred Dragon to go a little faster. We would hit them as three conroi. It was not ideal but it could not be helped.

The Scots had managed to mount their knights. Their hobelars, armed with javelins, charged us to give the knights the opportunity to form a line. It was brave but it was foolish. The light horsemen galloped across our front. They hurled their javelins. Those who did not close with us wasted their missiles which either bounced from our mail or fell ino the earth. The braver ones who tried to close were speared. Their riderlesss horses hurtled back towards the knights who were forming up. It would disrupt their lines further.

I reined Dragon back a little to allow our line to regain its integrity. I prepared my spear for we were less than two hundred paces from the Scots and the knights were moving towards us. Knights often prefer to fight other knights. There was more honour in that. Our three standards showed the Scots that we were the only knights who were facing them and they came for us. The rough line they had formed became an even rougher wedge as the knights jostled to hit the three English knights who faced them.

I pulled back my spear as the first Scottish lance lunged at me. It was a good strike and, as his lance was longer than my spear, he hit me first. He wore an open helmet and, as his spear splintered on my shield, his face showed the triumph he felt. My shield was a good one and I had angled it so that most of the impact went behind me. In contrast, I rammed my spear at his middle rather than his chest. The spear struck his side. The head came away bloody. I had no time to choose my next opponent for he chose me. A Scot had come at my right side. I had no shield there to protect me. I was only saved by his inexperience. He went for my chest but the rough ground meant that he struggled to control his lance. It hit my helmet. It made my head ring but my helmet was well made. I had no opportunity to do anything other than swing my spear at his body. We passed each other. I later discovered that Fótr had speared the knight.

I reined Dragon in for I did not want to get too far ahead of my men. Dragon was a powerful beast. He enjoyed war. His snapping jaws and his flailing hooves were deadly weapons. More knights approached but these were in an even looser formation. I saw one coming towards me. He intended to attack my spear side with his lance. At the last moment I pulled Dragon to my right so that we were shield to shield. A lance is a difficult weapon to control. He reined his horse in but I was already standing in my stirrups and with an overhand grip I stabbed down at his neck. It was not the cleanest of strikes but it tore through his ventail and into his throat. As he died his body pulled the spear from my hand.

Three more knights charged me and I did not have the time to get another spear from Fótr. I drew my sword. Glancing to my side I saw that Sir Edward had just slain a Scottish knight. His horse's muzzle was close to my horse's rump. He was close enough to aid me. The three Scottish knights thought that they had me. They had lances and I just had a sword. They saw blood on my surcoat. They did not know it was not mine!

Knowing that Sir Edward was on my right I aimed Dragon to ride between the two Scots to my left. They both thrust their lances at me. My instincts took over. I did not even look at the one to my left. I had my shield held tightly. Unless he aimed at my leg then I would be unharmed. I used my sword to smash away the lance from the knight on my right. It was relatively easy for the lance's tip wavered up and down. The lance missed me and I was able to lunge at the knight as he passed. My sword tore into his shoulder. I began to turn to attack the other Scot when I saw him fall from his saddle and Sir Ralph pulled his spear from him.

The three of us were stopped. Suddenly we heard the sound of the Scottish horns. They were withdrawing. I looked around and saw that many of their knights and mounted men at arms were between us and our own camp. The three of us turned. The knights would have to run the gamut of our swords and spears.

This time they were at a disadvantage. The ground was covered in wounded, dying and dead men. Riderless horses milled around. We did not have to move. We formed a line like beaters driving game towards hunters. One man at arms, without a spear and with his sword still in its scabbard, was so focussed on the ground that he failed to see my sword sweep towards him and take his head. I turned Dragon sideways so that I could bring my sword around into the back of a man at arms who swerved to avoid me.

Then it was over and we had won. The men of the other barons cheered. Mine did not. We had lost three men at arms. We had won but three men was too high a price. We walked our horses back to the camp. The other three leaders were there already. Their notched and bloody swords told their own tale. They were, however, joyful at the victory.

Richard de Percy said, "You were right, Sir Thomas. The plan worked."

I pointed to the Scottish camp. "And yet they have not fled the field. They will lick their wounds and try us again."

165

Barond de Vesci said, "Your archers were magnificent. They slaughtered the Scottish levy."

Baron de Clavering nodded, "We were able to attack the men at arms in the centre and we slew many. Thank you, Sir Thomas. Your advice was sage and I apologise for my comments. They were ungracious and ill-deserved."

I smiled, "Words have never hurt me. We had best see to our wounded. Have your men take the mail and weapons from their dead and recover our dead."

De Vesci said, "Why?"

"Because, if we do not then the Scots will and tomorrow we will face men in mail who would otherwise have none."

My men had already begun the task and, unlike the other conroi, had collected all the spare horses. When we returned home we would have a fine herd.

That evening as we ate the dead horses Richard de Percy said, "And what now?"

"We cannot try the same tactics tomorrow. It would not work. They will be up before dawn and they will have their own plan to defeat us. We will rise before dawn and see what they have planned. At least we are eating better than they are. We have bloodied their noses twice. If we can do so again tomorrow then they will leave."

We were up in the middle of the night and, after we had eaten, we walked our horses to the place we had begun the battle the day before. Sir Edward said, as we watched the sun rise above Rothbury. "This is unlike the Scots, lord. When we beat them then they run back across the border. Why do you think they are still here? If we fight them again then they cannot defeat us. We might not be able to beat them from the field for there are still many of them but we killed more than twenty knights this day."

"I know not. It has me puzzled too."

When the sun broke we saw the Scots arrayed before us. They had their mounted men in two blocks. One was by the river and the other, the larger one, faced us. Between them they had their warriors who fought on foot. They seemed quite belligerent still. They hurled insulst at us and some even dropped their breeks. Petr was mounted, as were the others who had standards and he suddenly said, "Lord, I can see banners approaching Rothbury."

Edward turned to me, "Now we know why they waited. They are being reinforced."

166

I shook my head. "That cannot be. Scotland is behind us. It is Morpeth and the New Castle which lie in that direction. We will wait and see."

When we saw consternation in the ranks of the Scots we knew that it was not their allies. We saw the standards. The High Sherriff had brough an army. The Scots surrendered!

The High Sherriff

Chapter 16

Robert son of Roger, the High Sherriff, Baron de Clavering, Baron de Percy and Baron de Vesci negotiated the peace. I was not upset that I was not involved. I was not a knight of Northumbria but it was obvious to me that Robert son of Roger had done this deliberately. I was not sure if it was just a snub or something more sinister. I took the opportunity of sending half of my men back to Stockton with the horses we had captured and the booty we had taken. We would catch them up. I did not want to leave without discovering more about the Sherriff. The men who left with the horses also included our wounded. Fótr led the men. He was pleased with the responsibility.

Petr was cleaning the blood from my mail when the four barons returned. Robert son of Roger, the High Sherriff was not a pleasant man. Part of it was his face. He looked like a bulldog with a down turned mouth but it was more than that. He did not speak, he hectored. The other three barons were in high spirits but the High Sherriff was not. When they spoke, I watched him.

"We made the Scots pay an indemnity. They will pay us ten thousand silver pieces!" Baron de Clavering could barely contain himself. "And we have ransom from the knights who surrendered."

Baron de Percy said, "You will be rich, Sir Thomas."

Robert son of Roger, the High Sherriff, frowned. It made him even more unpleasant to look at, "Sir Thomas is not a knight of Northumbria. He is the Bishop's man."

De Percy laughed, "Then you do not know either man, Sherriff for there is little love lost between them and, besides, we would not have won if it were not for Sir Thomas. He led us. He will get an equal share." I saw the other two barons nod vigorously.

The Sherriff was even more like a bulldog for he would not let the bone go. "His share should come to the crown."

Baron de Vesci shook his head and when he spoke there was real anger in his voice, "The Crown already gets too much. If you had arrived sooner, Sherriff, then we might not have lost the men we did. You are getting a fifth of the settlement. Do not dispute how we divide it or you may get none."

"You speak of treason, de Vesci."

"Do not push us, Sherriff. This is not treason. We divide the spoils of war amongst those who earned them! King John is many miles from here. There are barons here who feel we are over taxed for land which is not as rich as that in the south. We pay the same as those manors which yield wheat. We eat barley and oats!"

The High Sherriff looked around. We were united. He had only brought twenty knights. The bulk of the men were the one thousand men of the levy. Had the Scots known that fact they might not have surrendered. I suddenly realised how little support and power Robert son of Roger actually had. The High Sherriff of York had much more power. I saw now that this unrest among the Barons of the north was understandable.

He had to save face and so he nodded, "As Sir Thomas has helped to drive these Scottish raiders north I will agree but, Sir Thomas, in future stay close to your manor. It will be healthier for all; especially you."

His words troubled me. The last part sounded like a threat. I did not have time to get beneath his words for we all moved to Rothbury. The garrison were praised by Baron de Vesci for their hardy defence of the walls. There had been but fourteen of them. It was a remarkable feat. We ate in the Great Hall. There was not enough room for all and Sir Edward and Sir Ralph ate with the other knights at the new camp. Robert son of Roger was a taciturn man. He said little. He reminded me of Brice the Chamberlain. Perhaps these were the men the King chose to do his bidding. Maybe they were mercenaries who were more malleable than knights.

I waited until most of the barons had left the table to stand around the roaring fire for it was a chill evening. I approached the Sherriff. "What did you mean earlier when you said, *'healthier for all'*?"

"I can speak plainly now, baron, for we are alone. I meant that there are many who wish you dead. There are many who wish you gone. Your manor is where you are safe."

"You threaten me? Know that I am a knight who does not take threats well."

He gave a cruel smile, "You have a young family. The young are vulnerable. Better that you watch over them and keep your nose out of business that does not concern you."

I put my face close to his. "Do not threaten my family Sherriff. I do not fear you. If I can sink a blade into a Bishop then a mercenary like you would not make me lose a moment's sleep. Tell those who sent you with this message that if any of my family are harmed it will unleash such a wild beast that the Scots and the Vikings will seem as nothing."

He recoiled at my words. I said them quietly and coldly. Each one was like a punch to his midriff.

The Sherriff tried to save face, "The words are my own. Stay in your manor and you will be safe."

I stood upright, "And perhaps the same might be true of you Sherriff. The north is a wild and dangerous place. Who knows what dangers await?"

He nodded, "We understand each other then."

"I think so."

I had had enough of the smoky hall and I left to return to my camp. Sir Edward and Sir Ralph had left the camp fire of the knights and were with my men. When I sat I told them of the Sherriff's words, they looked at each other and then Sir Edward said, "When we ate with the other knights, the ones who came from Morpeth and the New Castle they told us that the Sherriff only brought the men when he heard that you were present at the siege. They thought that meant that he thought well of you."

Sir Ralph said, slowly, "Or perhaps he thought to do you harm. We had better keep a close watch this night on the baron."

"That begs the question, Sir Ralph, who sent the Sherriff to do Sir Thomas harm?" There was genuine concern in Edward's voice.

I thought I knew. "I think that is obvious, Edward. It is King John. He is John's man. I do not think we are in any danger here but we will ride home with caution and we will not ride back using predictable ways. I am more fearful of our home. My family was threatened." I looked into the flickering fire. "I am resolved. When we return then I put up a curtain wall and a gatehouse."

170

"Will that not give King John the opportunity to punish you?"

"No Sir Ralph, for the wall will be there to keep back the river and to join to the town wall. I will not be so foolish as to build the huge walls which Stockton once enjoyed. It will be there to prevent easy passage to the halls. We have enough men to keep a good watch. At the moment we are open and exposed. In the dark of night, it is too easy for men to move close to the hall using the shadows."

Baron de Percy came to speak with me just after dawn. "Baron, why did you not stay in the castle last night? It was more comfortable."

I decided that I could trust de Percy and I needed to confide in at least one of the other restless barons. "The High Sherriff has made threats against me and my family. I leave this morning to protect them."

De Percy did not seem surprised. "This is King John's work. He knows of the unrest here in the north. I have a small manor. De Vesci is old and de Clavering is young. You, however, have a name and reputation which would draw others to our cause. King John knows this. If he quashed you and imprisoned you that would make you a martyr and draw more to our cause. You are still the hero of Arsuf. King Richard is spoken of as the golden king. His rule meant that the country was prosperous. On the other hand, if you were killed by unknown forces then King John could say he knew nothing of it."

I shook my head, "Baron, what you say about King Richard is not true. He bled the country to pay for his war in the east."

Baron de Percy smiled, "True but compared with John his rule seems, now, to have been beneficial to England. Certainly, the barons enjoyed more freedom. Take care Sir Thomas and know that you now have powerful friends in the north. We will not abandon you."

We left early. The fastest way home would have been down the coast and across the bridge at the New Castle. That way was fraught with danger. That was the land ruled by the Sherriff. He had brought with him the lords from Morpeth, Prudhoe, Ashington and the other northern castles. Ominously none of the knights from around the Tyne were with him. My other men would be well south of the Tyne and so I decided to take us further west and use the smaller roads. We left, giving the appearance of heading for the New Castle but, once we were out of sight of the castle then we headed due south rather than south and east. We headed for Matfen. It lay south of the Roman wall and was close enough to Baron de Percy's manor that I felt safe. If we had to we could camp there but I hoped to get further south before we did.

As we rode I reflected that we had done better than we might have hoped. We had a fine horse herd now. We had enough animals for all of my men and Sir Edward's. Sir Ralph could now mount half of his men. We had chests of mail and swords. Baron de Vesci had promised that he would have our share of the reparations and ransom sent to my hall by his men. When that arrived, it would pay for the stone for my walls. We passed Matfen without incident and I decided to continue south as we had not met danger.

I made a sudden decision which surprised my men, "We will try to make Durham castle."

Sir Ralph looked shocked. "Lord, you have been threatened by the Sherriff and the Bishop is no friend of yours!"

I saw Sir Edward smile. He knew the way I thought. "Perhaps but I do not think that the Bishop is colluding with the Sherriff. The Pope has excommunicated King John. The papal interdict means that Durham is poorer as a result. I do not think that Phillip of Poitou would rebel against King John but I have a feeling that he will be more amenable than he was. Besides," I added innocently, "we need to tell him of the great victory of Rothbury!"

I know not if there were men waiting to ambush us on the road from the New Castle but we reached Durham safely. Surprisingly we were admitted although my knights and I were asked to leave our weapons with the chamberlain. Aimeric was there too and he looked unhappy at my presence. The Bishop was more cordial than he had been and, when he spoke I saw why.

"It seems, Baron, that we owe you a debt of thanks. Your heroic battle against the Scots at Rothbury has saved all of us from the predations of the Scots."

I nodded, "The news travels fast, Bishop."

"I had my knights patrolling the borders of the Palatinate. I took your words about bandits and raiders to heart. They met your men and they told us of the battle."

I smiled, "Then I could have saved myself a journey for that is one reason I came here."

"One reason?"

"In times past, before the castle of Stockton was demolished, the lord of Stockton was responsible for the manors of Hartburn, Elton and Norton. Since then they have been managed by a reeve but they have not enjoyed the protection of a lord."

The Bishop nodded, "That is true but few lords wish to farm such poor land as Norton and the other manors."

"If you would give me leave, Bishop, I would appoint men to watch the manors. I even have a lord ready to be lord of Norton."

Aimeric could not contain himself. "You must be jesting Sir Thomas! Can you be trusted?"

The Bishop said, quietly, "Peace Aimeric, Sir Thomas has not yet finished."

"No, Bishop, I have not. To improve the passage down the Tees my men have made a small cut close to Norton. It speeds the passage of ships but it has also released fertile land around Norton. If you allow me to appoint, when he is knighted, Fótr of La Flèche, then he will ensure that the yield from Norton is improved and you will have more taxes. Your coffers will be swollen." I smiled, "With the interdict I know that the Palatinate will be a little poorer than it was."

He looked me in the eyes and nodded, "And if more ships use your port then I will have increased revenue from you."

"Yes, Bishop. And, to that end I would build, by my river, a building where we could collect the taxes and, at the same time, make the town less likely to suffer inundation by building a retaining wall."

The Bishop gave me a sharp look, "This would not be a fortified wall?"

"No, Bishop. There would be a walkway along it and it would provide defence against raiding Scots but it would not constitute a threat to the crown." I chose my words very carefully.

I watched the Bishop weighing up the arguments. The attack on Rothbury by such a large army had clearly alarmed him. He nodded, "Very well but I will visit you in one year and inspect your improvements and to examine this putative knight. If I am unhappy then you will have to take down whatever has been erected."

"Of course. That is understood."

He waved over the cleric who had been listening. "Write a decree granting Sir Thomas permission to appoint a lord for Norton and to build flood defences. I will sign it and send you a copy, Sir Thomas."

"Thank you, Bishop."

He rose to escort us to our quarters. "Tell me more about this battle. The men you sent south did not know the numbers nor the reparations."

"The High Sherriff appeared and they surrendered. The reparations were punitive. I do not think that the Scots will send an army again."

"There is a but in your words."

"You are right. I fear that to get back their coin they will begin to raid again and as Northumbria is blessed with many strong castles and barons who would prosecute vigorously any incursion then I fear it would be the land to the west of here which would suffer. Your land around Auckland, Stanhope and Spennymoor."

"Then I will make plans to prevent that. I have two stout barons there. Baron Stanley and Baron Spennymoor are both strong leaders." He waved to his nephew. "Aimeric here has been desperate to prove himself as a knight. I will send him to Bishop Auckland with some of my household knights. They can keep watch for raiders. I will inform you of any danger. The new lord of Fissebourne, Sir Robert, is also keen to keep his borders safe. The next time raiders come south they may receive a rougher welcome than in times past. I will ensure that I stay closer to home in future. My people and my priests need me." There was a real change here. Perhaps I had misjudged the Bishop or, more likely, it had been his nephew, Aimeric who had been responsible. Certainly, the Bishop was being clever in sending his nephew to guard Bishop Auckland.

The meal we enjoyed with the Bishop would have been pleasant had not Aimeric been present. For some reason he seemed to resent me. I gathered that he was not as keen as his uncle implied to be taking over Bishop Auckland. He struck me as a dangerous man for he was desperate for power and his new role would make him nothing more than a glorified caretaker.

We reached home at noon the next day. Perhaps our speedy departure and erratic route south had thrown off any possible attackers but I thought that my enemies had yet to put their plan into operation. I would keep a good watch. We left Edward at Wulfestun. Sir Ralph would stay with me for the night. As we passed Norton he said, "Is Fótr ready to be a knight, lord?"

I smiled, "Were you ready, Ralph?"

He had the good grace to laugh, "No lord. It is just that, to me, Fótr will always be the young boy."

"He has grown. When we rescued the Fair Maid of Brittany that changed him. He is ready. He took the standard of the French at the battle of La Lude. I was knighted for a similar act of courage and bravery. I chose Norton for him as it is close. You had a harder task for I was a sea voyage away. I can visit him and offer advice. Besides I have little other choice. Until my knights produce sons or we find landless lords who wish a manor then my hands are tied. Baron

174

de Vesci is quite right. The northern manors are not as attractive to knights as the manors further south."

My family had been worried when we had failed to return as quickly as the others. Alfred, in particular, clung to me. I smiled, "Did Fótr not tell you that I was safe?"

"Aye father but you had to pass through Durham and we know that the Bishop is no friend to us!"

"That may be changing."

Rebekah threw herself into my arms and hugged me. She wrinkled her nose and pulled away. "You smell funny!"

I laughed. "Then I will bathe so that I do not offend you."

My wife shook her head, "The child is so precocious! She is spoiled." She glanced at Lady Ruth who just shrugged. She would not apologise for spoiling Rebekah.

We had much to do over the next weeks and months. We had stables to build and work began on the wall. Fótr would be knighted on Midsummer Day and he had much to prepare and to learn. I had no young knight to take him through what was necessary and I had to give the time to him. When the coin arrived from Baron de Vesci we used most of it immediately. I needed more men at arms and so when Captain Henry arrived we not only had goods for him to trade we had coin to buy men and horses as well as wine. I knew that there would be men who did not wish to stay in Anjou. I hoped that the lure of my name might draw them tome.

I rode with Petr and Alfred to the manors of Elton and Hartburn. I spoke with the reeves. Neither was as hardworking as Walter of Norton. I told them both of the changes which were coming and impressed upon them the need for them to become better at their jobs. Time would tell if they heeded my words. It was a moot point as I had no knights whom I could appoint.

When I spoke with Cedric the pig farmer I learned much about Hartburn. Cedric had known my grandfather. He was old but I realised he looked older than he actually was. Such was the effect of farming without a lord to protect you. "When your father was lord life was easy, Sir Thomas. The taxes were not high and you could let cattle and sheep wander for there were neither bandits nor raiders to steal them. Sir William did his best but without a lord and," he pointed to the blackened shell that had been the hall, "a castle in which we could shelter it was like taking three steps forward and two steps back. If you could do one thing for us, lord, it would be to give us a lord of the manor."

"I will try Cedric but I am much like my father and grandfather. I cannot make false promises. Know this. My men, the garrison of Stockton, will ride this manor and keep it safe until then."

"Thank you, lord. That is all we can ask."

Henry made a swift voyage to Anjou. The early summer winds were in his favour. When he returned there were just four men at arms who wished to serve and only three horses. The four men were all English and, like the ones who had come the previous year, had come from Poitou. John the War Axe was their leader. A huge man he almost rivalled Ridley the Giant in size. As soon as I spoke with them I knew they would fit in well.

John the War Axe told me a familiar tale. His lord had fought for King John and had been captured. The ransom had taken all of the money from the manor and the men at arms had been abandoned. The four who had come to me had stayed together. Some of the others had joined Poitevin lords while others had headed for the Holy Land to seek their fortune there. Some had joined the crusade against the Cathars. What concerned me more was what they told me of Anjou. It was confirmed by Henry. Some of the French counts who had been appointed by King Phillip, had old scores to settle. My three knights were not being treated well. They were over taxed. It sounded familiar. I could do nothing about it. I had trusted King Phillip and that trust was misplaced.

As Captain Henry prepared to sail to London with the wine he had bought, he would get a higher price there than in the north, I asked him about my three knights and La Flèche. "La Flèche does well enough. Sir Richard has married the daughter of the Comte de Louvain. She is older than most maids and to call her plain would be a generous overstatement,"

"Sir Richard married her for an easy life?"

"That is how I view it. Sir Henry is no fool and he is courting the niece of the Lord of Tours. He saw the wisdom of Sir Richard's marriage. It is Sir William who suffers. He now has four children and the taxes which he pays do not support the men he needs. He is using the money he accrued following you. From what I gathered he will soon be penniless."

I sent Petr back to my hall and he fetched a small chest. It was filled with coins. "I would not have my old squire suffer. When next you visit give this from me and tell him that if he needs me then send word."

"You would go to his aid?" I nodded. "Lord that would risk imprisonment or worse." There was genuine concern in his voice.

"You do not abandon those who were loyal to you. Besides I can speak with King Phillip. He promised me fair treatment for my people. Even kings are accountable for their promises."

The words of Captain Henry cast a shadow over the summer. Even Fótr's knighthood was somewhat diminished by the thought that one of his predecessors was having a difficult time. My aunt showed her truly generous nature. She bought a war horse for him and gave him one of her ladies to be his housekeeper. The hall would need much work and I gave him a small chest of coin to make it habitable and defensible. The ransoms had come in and we were now in a healthier position financially. I also gave him John the Axe and the other new men. They would be the start of his retinue. He needed a squire but, until there was a suitable candidate, then the man at arms, Peter of Tewkesbury would have to do. When Fótr left us Petr and Alfred missed him more than anyone. Despite the fact that his departure elevated Petr to first squire and Alfred to standard bearer both would have preferred him still to be in the hall.

The stables were finished and would make the conditions for our horses healthier. They were attached to the warrior hall. The wall around us took longer to build for we had to buy the stone. The gatehouse would have two towers. I hoped that they would not breach the rules laid down by the bishop. We also made part of the town wall of stone where our new wall abutted it. The walkway around the wall was, in essence, a fighting platform but as there were no crenulations I hoped that we would get away with it.

The summer that year was a good one. We did not have to endure sudden summer storms which devastated crops. The animals which had been born in spring thrived in the balmy weather. Sir Ralph became a father and that seemed to symbolise the summer. With Lady Maud pregnant too it seemed that fertility was in the air. Now that William could toddle his bigger brother and his sister seemed to enjoy playing with him. He did not just lie inertly. He could run, tumble and fall. It was good that they did so. It meant that Margaret and I had more time to talk.

We were walking by the river, one late July evening and speaking of Ralph's new son and Maud's expected baby when my wife suddenly said, "I am sorry, lord, that I have not been able to produce a fourth child."

I cuddled her, "It does not worry me. I have neither brother nor sister. The three we have, if they are all that God grants us will do. I could not ask for three finer children."

"And yet you are happy to take our son to war."

"He has seen almost eight summers."

"Which means he is just seven."

"He will not be going to war. He will carry my standard and then guard our tents."

"That sounds like war to me. Guard and carry the standard are not peaceful activities."

"There will be men at arms to watch over him. I went to battle against the Scots with my father when I was barely seven. I had had less training that Alfred. I did not come close to an enemy until we went to the Holy Land. The Battle of Arsuf was only the third time I had drawn my sword and faced an enemy. Even though we faced the Seljuk Turk I rode behind my father leading his spare horse."

"Fótr fought and was hurt!"

I could not argue with her. My former squire had been put in harm's way and that was down to me. "If I do not take him he will resent, not me, but you. Do you really want that?" She shook her head. "I swear that I will keep him safe. There is no likelihood of war at the moment. I cannot see the Scots being ready for revenge any time soon."

She squeezed my arm, "I am just a mother, I cannot help the way I am."

I kissed her and, as I did so, I saw *'Swan of Stockton'* as she tacked down the river. We walked back to the quay. When I turned she was much closer and there, waving from the side were Sir William de La Lude and Lady Marguerite. His squire and children lined the side. My knight had returned. The question was, why?

The Return of the Knight

Chapter 17

My wife had known Lady Marguerite since their time in the Baltic. Both wept as they hugged each other. I saw Johann, William's squire, with a protective arm around William's son, Henry. The other two children clung to their nurse.

I clasped William's arm. "You are here to stay or is this a visit only?"

He looked embarrassed, "I am sorry I did not seek permission lord but when…."

I waved a dismissive arm, "I told Captain Henry to tell you that you are more than welcome. There is room in the hall for we have an annex where you can have privacy and, if you and your men are not afraid of hard work then I have a manor where you can build a hall."

He looked at me in surprise. "But the Bishop of Durham…"

"Is a pragmatic man. He has seen the benefits of listening to me. Hartburn is yours if you would have it. Now come I have much to tell you and, when we eat later, you can tell me your tale. I will send for Sir Fótr and Sir Edward. They will wish to hear."

He looked surprised, "Sir Fótr? Then Johann will not be happy. He has been a squire as long."

I shrugged, "I needed a knight and he was ready. I could make Johann a knight if you wish. Elton needs a lord of the manor."

Sir William shook his head, "We come to you penniless, lord, save for the chest of coins you gave us. Johann would not take kindly to beginning life as a knight poor. We have but four horses between us all." I could tell from his voice that he was becoming upset. He must have felt that he had failed.

179

We were close to the hall and I pointed to the guest hall. "That is yours for as long as you need it. It will take time to build the hall and your wife and children can enjoy the comfort of a good roof and solid walls."

My wife had already led Lady Marguerite into the hall. Sir William, his squire and his son followed. I waved over Petr. "Ride to Norton and thence to Wulfestun. Tell my lords that I would them dine with us this night. Sir William has returned."

As he ran to the stables his father walked over. He shook his head. "His lordship has fewer men than he once had, lord."

"I know there is a tale here and I will discover it this night. Put the men in the warrior hall. I know it will be crowded …"

"Fear not, lord, we are all shield brothers. They will be welcomed."

I then went to tell the cook what we required and informed Edgar of our guests. I asked him to fetch a jug of wine and goblets. My aunt appeared. She had Rebekah's hand, "What is the commotion Thomas?" I told her." She appeared delighted. "Then there will be more children." She looked up to the ceiling. "I am sorry that you have missed this, William, you would have loved the children. I will have to enjoy them for the both of us. Come Rebekah let us go and greet the new children." For my aunt this was not an imposition. This was a joyous happenstance.

As much as I had hated to be torn away from my home in Anjou that pain had been dissipated by the happiness it had brought my aunt. It was as though she had been reborn. She still mourned her husband but, somehow, turned that grief into joy by being around children.

Sir William arrived shortly after Edgar had fetched the wine. From the way he downed the first goblet I knew that they had not enjoyed much wine on the voyage. While he slowly sipped his wine, savouring each mouthful, I told him of the battle of Rothbury, the Sherriff and the Bishop. He nodded when I had done so. He filled up his goblet, "When we called in at Dover we heard much the same. The barons there are also restless. King John just takes more and more taxes and yet gives nothing back. We heard that Robert Fitzwalter accused the King of trying to seduce his daughter and the King's response was to banish Fitzwalter from this land and confiscate his manors. How can that be just?"

"Simply put, it cannot but he gets away with it because he is King and has divine right. We have rights and one day they will be enshrined in law. However, that is a long way in the future. For now, we make you and your people comfortable. If you will have it, you can build a hall at Hartburn and be lord there."

"Of course, I will have it. It is more generous than I could have expected. I thought to return as a household knight and I would have been happy to do so."

"The days when you were a bachelor knight are long gone. You are the new lord of the manor of Hartburn. I will get Father Abelard to write the appropriate deeds."

When our wives and Lady Ruth returned we spoke of lighter matters. I commented on how much their children had grown and they expressed joy at our new additions. Lady Ruth scampered around amusing the bemused two young daughters of Sir William.

Fótr arrived quickly. Norton was just a couple of miles away. He and Johann had known each other since the Baltic. They had much to say to each other. I do not think that Johann resented Fótr; that was not in his nature. He had been with my wife when I had rescued her and I knew the youth well. He would be a worthy knight. It took Sir Edward longer to reach us for he came with his wife and his son. As his wife was pregnant he had brought a wagon.

The four ladies bubbled and chattered like magpies. The girls all fussed around the youngest child present, Edward's son, Thomas. Edward and William had much to say to each other. For the first time since I had returned to England I felt a sense of peace. My people were around me once more. True it was not all of them but there were enough to give me satisfaction.

Edgar had appreciated the nature of this reunion and the food he had ensure the cook's food was superb. The wine Captain Henry had brought on his last voyage had settled and, after being decanted, proved to be some of the best we had ever tasted. I sat with Sir William and Edward. Fótr, Johann and Petr sat with Henry and Alfred at the other end of the table. The ladies sat together. It was a most amenable arrangement. The ladies chattered. The squires and Sir Fótr spoke of knighthood and we three were able to hear what had happened in Anjou.

"It began well enough, lord. Our new overlord did not seem to notice us. Then we heard of barons in Normandy who had rebelled against King John being targeted by the French King. Many lost their manors. Some passed through La Flèche and we discovered that King Phillip and his overlords were taxing the Normans. They were driving them out and replacing them with French knights. The exception was in the land ruled by William des Roches. That did not include La Lude."

181

"King Phillip, King John, lay them in the same bed and it would be hard to tell them apart." Edward was correct.

"Sir Richard saw what was happening early on. He discovered that the daughter of the Comte de Louvain was unmarried and was over thirty years of age. She is homely and when Sir Richard heard that the Comte sought a husband for his unmarried daughter he offered to take her. To be fair she is a very pleasant lady but she is too old for children and has been unmarried for so long as to be an object of derision from the other ladies. They are well suited. Sir Richard has had the love of his life and this marriage secures him La Flèche. As soon as Sir Henry realised that was the way to become secure he courted the daughter of the Seneschal of Tours. She is a beauty and appears enamoured of Sir Henry. He will survive."

He reached for the wine and poured himself a healthy goblet.

"And you had no way to compromise?"

He shook his head. "I was advised to betroth my eldest daughter, Eleanor, to the son of the Lord of Saumur. He is but six and she is five. I would not do it. Bandits raided my land. Some of my men and farmers died. My taxes were raised. We were asked to fulfil the levy each year at harvest time. The farmers were suffering and it could not have gone on. I was contemplating returning anyway but when Captain Henry arrived then I leapt at the opportunity." He leaned back. "That is my story. I am sorry, lord, had I come back when you did, like Sir Edward, then you would not have wasted coin and my men who died fighting bandits would be alive."

Edward put his arm around my former squire. "When we look back, William, we always have perfect vision. A man makes decisions and, if they do not go right, he lives with them. You are home and Hartburn is a fine manor. It is closer to Stockton than is mine. All it lacks is a hall."

I nodded, "And tomorrow we can look at the manor and you can decide where your hall will be built."

The next morning Edward and Fótr returned to their manors and I rode out with Sir William, our squires, our two eldest sons and Sir William's men. We had more than enough horses. We rode to where Wulfstan had built his first hall and Sir Harold had enlarged it. When it had been built it had been well away from the beck which often flooded. Over the years and perhaps because of our work on the river it now flowed dangerously close to where the old hall had stood.

I said nothing for this was not my hall. I allowed Sir William and Johann to walk the site. There were, in this manor as well as mine, large patches of clay. We called it Stockton clay. It was not particularly good for making pots but worse, it did not allow the water to drain away. They found it in many places. Eventually they made their way up the valley sides. There was a large flat piece of higher ground. There were too many trees close by but they could be cut down and used for the hall and the palisade. It had a good view over the back to the south and west. Enemies could be seen from afar. To the north and the east, the ground fell gently away to the next becks. I saw in the distance the farm of Cedric the pig farmer. A hall here would please him.

He smiled, "I think here, lord. What do you say?"

"It is where I would have chosen. I would cut down that small wood for timber. The last thing you need is for cover that close to your hall and then I would dig beneath the roots and, in the autumn, set fire to them. It will make for fertile ground and stop them regrowing."

He nodded. "All we need is tools."

While you and your men mark out your walls we will return to my hall. I will send some of my men. They can help you for a few days. I will not need all of them." He cocked his head to one side. "I need to ride patrols. We were surprised by bandits once and after Rothbury some of the survivors may have fled south. And there is something else. The Sherriff made threats. He has yet to carry them out or perhaps my patrols have deterred him. Whatever the reason I will maintain them for the safety of all."

Alfred said, "Can I stay and help?" He had formed a friendship with Henry. Henry was just a year or so older.

I nodded and said to Sir William's squire, "Johann he will be a squire in training soon. Work him!"

He grinned, "Aye lord."

As we rode back across the Ox Bridge, Petr asked, "You had already chosen that site lord. Why did you not tell him to build there?"

"A man's home is a personal thing. He would never have been happy had I suggested it. He would have thought of other places he might have built. Had he suggested somewhere else then I would have explained why I did not like it but, in the end, it is his choice. When you become a knight and you have a manor then you will make the choices."

I sent more than half of my men back to help and then had Ridley and David of Wales prepare horses and arms for a patrol beyond Sadberge. There

183

were forests there. Not as extensive as the ones further north but large enough to hide bandits and brigands. We had scoured the land by the river and between Thorpe and Wulfestun but, to the west, we had not as yet ventured. Hartburn lay to the west and the arrival of Sir William meant that I had to seek bandits there now or William and his family might be in danger. The crusades, taxes and King John's vindictive nature had meant that there were fewer lords of the manor. The reeves and the burghers themselves kept the villages safe but isolated farms and dwellings were vulnerable.

As Petr and I unsaddled our horses he asked, "Lord, why are there bandits? Is it because they can find no work?"

"No, Petr, that is the excuse they give. We seek men at arms all the time. Sir Ralph is short of at least six. If these men are warriors then they could find work. If they are farmers or hunters then there are landowners who would employ them. I would. The fact that they do not have families tells me much. Do not waste your sympathy on them. They do not deserve it." I know that I sounded harsh but, in my experience the only ones who lived in the forest and deserved my attention were those with families. They were the ones who had been driven from their land and had nowhere else to go. The forest provided shelter and food.

As I went into my hall I thought about William's new manor. When Sir Harold and his son had been lords of the manor it had supported ten farms for the land was fertile. The land west of the beck which we had passed on our way to the Oxbridge had had four farms along it. Now there was one. Cedric the pig farmer and his four sons farmed the land between the two branches of the beck. They raised pigs and grew crops. The pigs thrived on the boggy Stockton clay and they rooted in the fields when the crops had been harvested. Even so, it was a hard life for them. They had no horse and his sons had to pull the plough themselves. Their animals had been taken by the bandits, brigands and Scots who had raided. Part of the land was Stockton clay but the valley sides were rich and produced good crops. Their orchard provided apples for the winter but the five of them toiled from dawn until dusk. Their children and their wives were thin. I had allowed them to trap rabbits and hares. Many lords did not. Sir William would bring hope. His men would stop raiders. When he increased his riches, he would provide sheep and cows for his people. It was what I had done when I had returned.

We left early the next morning. Alfred had begged permission to work at Hartburn. I did not mind. He would be safe there. I had six archers and four men

184

at arms. We wore no mail but we did take spears. If we found no danger then we would hunt. My archers had now grown used to the land. The Tomas brothers led the way as we passed first Hartburn and then Elton. We could have gone towards Redmarshal but there were some doughty yeoman farmers there and they prosecuted bandits vigorously. I also wanted to see Elton. If Johann was ready to be knighted then he needed a manor.

The hall still stood but the roof had collapsed in. The reeve lived in the barn. It was drier. Perhaps that explained his lack of enthusiasm for his task of managing the manor. The land itself had the potential to be rich but it was surrounded by woods and the shrubs had encroached upon the fields. It would take some serious work to clear the fields. Satisfied with what we had seen we headed down the greenway which led to the back lane. Eventually the road passed through Sadberge before forking. Sadberge was prosperous but they had a wall around their town. I had remembered it as having more people but I had been young and our memories of such times are distorted.

I spoke with the reeve as we passed. They had not seen any sign of bandits but they all farmed or worked within sight of the village. They did not venture in the woods. They eked out a living and prospered better than most. They appeared to be almost like monks. They looked in and not out. They looked after their own.

We turned north and began to make our way towards the woods which thickened out to become forests. Just before we entered I looked at the sun. It was about the third or fourth hour of the day. Once we entered the canopy of trees it would be hard to see the sun. Cedric Warbow and Dick One Arrow went to the left and right. They would ride in the trees and prevent us being surprised. We had chosen our best horses. I had Skuld. That meant they made little noise. They did not neigh unnecessarily. If they did neigh then there was danger. We walked our horses so that they did not thunder on the ground. We did not want to frighten off either bandits or game. My archers had strung bows. If there was danger then an arrow could be nocked in a heartbeat.

My archers found a small pond and we watered our horses there. My scouts examined the ground. Mordaf said. "There were men here, perhaps yesterday morning. Two were barefoot."

"Bandits?"

He shrugged, "Not all men like shoes. In our village we had one who would not wear shoes or sandals. He liked to feel the earth beneath his feet."

185

I sighed, Mordaf could find an argument in an empty room. He liked to present a different viewpoint, "But it is more likely to be a bandit than someone from your village?"

His brother grinned "Aye lord." He pointed east. "Their trail goes that way."

"Then let us follow and determine what kind of man it is."

Just then Cedric One Bow said, "Lord I have found another footprint. This one appears to be a child."

I heard Mordaf mumble, "Could be a dwarf!"

This was a puzzle. Could a child be a bandit too? "Let us proceed carefully. We will walk our horses."

Although we had a good view from the backs of our horses we could be seen easier. Being closer to the ground helped my archers to follow the trail. The trail we were following turned into a well-worn one. The tracks were harder to follow. Luckily, they occasionally stepped from the trail and we knew we were on the right track.

Suddenly Gruffyd held up his hand. When he dropped his reins and nocked an arrow we all knew that he had seen something. I wrapped Skuld's reins around the branch of a young oak. I carefully drew my sword. I waved for Petr to stay with the horses and then to Mordaf to move on. My men spread out naturally. They used whatever cover we could find. We all watched where we stepped. We spied the camp. There were children: two of them and a young mother with her arms around them. There was a man too but he was lying on the ground, held by four of the bandits. More were standing around and they were armed. The pinioned man had a bare chest and I could smell burning hair and flesh.

We had no time to waste. David of Wales looked at me and I nodded. He gave a hiss between his teeth. I could barely hear it but it must have been a signal for the archers. Six arrows flew and the four men torturing the man fell. Even as the arrows flew my four men at arms and I were racing forward. I saw that there were twelve men who were still on their feet and, as one ran at me with a sword, I realised that these were not bandits. They were well armed and clothed.

Our swords clashed. He was an experienced man at arms. Another pair of arrows flew and two more of the men fell. The man at arms tried to knee me between the legs. I was lucky. I was reaching for my dagger when he did so and his knee just jarred against my own. I stepped back with my dagger in my left hand. As he went to draw his own I swept my sword towards him. He blocked the blow with his sword but he was slightly off balance. As he reeled backwards I lunged with my dagger and caught him in the thigh. It was not a mortal wound but one which slowed him as blood seeped from his leg. I stepped forward again and feinted with my dagger towards his eyes. His head jerked back and he had to take two huge strides to keep his balance. They were to no avail for he tripped over the body of one of the men slain by my archers. Even as he fell and I raised my sword I was aware of my archers reaching ahead of me towards the woods. That glance was almost fatal. Prostrate on the ground he swept his sword towards my leg. Instinct took over. I jumped and, as I landed, rammed my sword into his throat. As I withdrew my bloody blade from his body I saw that all but three of the men were dead and my archers were pursuing the others.

Turning I saw that Ridley was unhurt but Godfrey had a bloody leg and Godwin was binding it. I shouted, "Petr, fetch the horses." There was vinegar and honey in the saddlebags of his father's horse. I turned to the man who had been tortured. His wife was holding his head. "How is he?"

"He would be dead but for you, lord." There was a sob in her voice and her two children, a small girl and boy, were clinging to their father and weeping. The man's eyes were closed but he was breathing. I had questions, many of them, but they would have to wait.

I sheathed my sword and went to the man I had slain. He wore good leather armour. There were metal studs in it. I picked up his sword. That too was a good one as was his dagger. He had a purse and in it were more than twenty silver coins. It was a leather purse and heavy. This was a mercenary. I stood. Ridley was also examining the dead as Petr brought the horses. Godwin took the honey and vinegar and Padraig the Wanderer went to his own saddle bags and took out his own honey and vinegar. He went to the man who had been tortured.

I heard the smile in his voice as he said to the children, "Let's see if we can make your father better eh? Do not fret little ones, this looks worse than it is. He will soon be as right as rain. What is your husband's name?"

"He is Aelric. I am his wife Nanna." She looked up at me, "Thank you lord."

"Speak later. Petr give them some ale. There is food in my bags."

Ridley came over, "Mercenaries, lord. They were good. If we had not had the archers with us we would have struggled." He held up the purses he had taken from the dead. None was as full as the one I had slain but they showed that these were no bandits.

"But how did they get here?" I waved my hand around. "This is a quiet area. It is why we sought bandits. They could not get work close by here." I held up the purse, "And from the coins in this purse they did not need work."

"They would have needed horses but, coming from the south, we saw no sign of them."

As if in answer we heard the neigh of horses and the creak of leather as David of Wales and his archers led a dozen horses. He shouted, "The rest are dead, lord. They had these horses tethered half a mile north of here. That is where they were running. They had come from the north east. We saw their trail clearly."

Godfrey had been seen to and the tortured man lifted his head. It was time for questions. The answers I would receive would be added to what I had seen. Here was a puzzle which needed unravelling. I went over and knelt down, "Aelric, I am Sir Thomas of Stockton. Tell me your story."

He and his wife started, "They asked about you! They thought that we had been thrown from your land. They wanted to know where they could hide close to Stockton!"

"Why would they think you were thrown from my land?"

He pointed west, "We farmed the land of Sir Thomas of Piercebridge. He was a good man. We made a living. He died without issue and the land was taken to pay taxes. We were thrown from the land. We heard from others, as we headed for the Great Road, that there were new lords of the manor in the valley of the Tees. We were heading east to see if it was true. We used the quiet ways of the woods for those who live in the settlements by the roads are not kind. They called us names and threw stones at us. They said they wanted no more poor people in their town!"

His wife said, "We are hardworking lord and it is not our fault that our lord died."

"Peace Nanna, Sir Thomas here did not do us harm. This morning four of the men you saw came into our camp. At first, they were pleasant. They smiled and laughed. They asked where we had come from. I said that we had come from the manor of Sir Thomas. That was as far as I got. One struck me. Two held me and one ran for the others. When they returned they asked me where they could hide close to Stockton. I told them that I had never been to Stockton and that my Sir Thomas lived at Piercebridge. They did not believe me and they began to burn my body. Had you not come then I would have lost an eye."

188

I stood and looked at Ridley the Giant. "We will take these folk to Stockton. Father Abelard can tend his hurts better than we. David of Wales, take your archers and back track these mercenaries. I would know whence they came."

"Aye lord."

I looked at the mercenaries' horses. Four were palfreys but the rest were sumpters and rouncys. We would be able to use them. "Do you think you can sit on a horse? It will make the journey to Stockton easier."

Aelric nodded but his wife looked fearful. Padraig smiled, "Fear not. I will lead your horse."

Petr said, "And your son can sit on my horse with me."

When they were all mounted and with Godwin and Godfrey leading the spare horses, we headed back to Stockton. Ridley said that which was on my mind, "These were killers sent for you, lord."

"The Sherriff; he implied as much but the devious snake made us think that the attack would come from the south. If, as I believe, the men came from the north east then they circumvented Wulfestun to avoid Edward. It was a clever plan. We do not keep a good watch to the west."

"Perhaps we should now, lord."

"We still do not have enough men."

Ridley nodded and then said, "Do you not think it strange that Sir William comes back to a manor which is devoid of people to farm it and we find a farmer and his family?"

"The thought had crossed my mind. Perhaps we should send men to the Great Road and see if there are others who are dispossessed. They will head for the larger towns and we both know that they are not the places for farmers and their families."

Ridley shook his head, "I thought this was a Christian land, lord. Having stones thrown at you because you are poor does not seem Christian."

"It comes from King John. He has made this a greedy and self-centred land. I do not blame the people in the villages and towns. I am disappointed but I understand. They know not how to feed themselves and four more mouths would be too much."

"Yet you will take them in, lord."

"Blame my blood."

He said quietly, "I blame nothing lord for it is to be admired."

189

I nudged Skuld so that I was riding next to Aelric. "Tonight, you will stay in my hall and your hurts will be tended to. We will feed you and see about getting you better clothes. Your journey has not been kind to you."

He nodded. "We had to sell some of our belongings to get money to buy food. It is why we headed for the woods." He hung his head, "I know how to use a bow, lord. I confess I was going to poach!"

Poaching could result in death. I smiled, "Thank you for your honesty. One of my lords is building a hall not far from my castle. He has empty farms. Would you wish to farm one?"

He nodded, "Aye lord, I would."

As I had expected the three ladies, Ruth, my wife and Lady Marguerite took the family into their care and fussed around them like hens with chicks. David of Wales and his archers returned after dark.

"Lord they came from the north. I think that two must have escaped for we found tracks heading north. We could have followed them but…"

"You did right to return. These men came from the Sherriff. I cannot prove it but I do not need to. When he sees me next then he will know that they have failed and, from now on, we keep a good watch around all of our lands. The Sherriff cannot know about our new wall and that will be a surprise for any killers."

David of Wales shook his head, "Lord, they would not try to get at you in the hall. That would be suicide. You and your squire often ride alone. When you visited Sir Edward last, you went alone. They would just watch and wait. You are a mighty warrior lord but had twelve of them caught you then you would be a dead man."

I smiled, "And you are telling me to ride with an escort."

"Until we can be sure our land is safe then aye, lord. When Sir William has built his hall then his men can keep the west safe. Sir Edward and Sir Fótr keep the north safe and the river, the sands and the sea keep us safe from the east and south."

He was right and I did as I was asked. We worked even harder on the new hall. By the time the first snows had come the roof was on. The walls were finished and there was a ditch and palisade running around it. Aelric was given the farm which lay immediately to the west of the hall. He could see its walls. It was not the best of farms for half of it was Stockton clay and could not be ploughed. Aelric showed that he knew how to farm. "Lord, if you could get goats or sheep then they would prosper there. We could use the milk to make cheese. My wife makes fine cheese."

Sir William knew the value of intelligent farmers and, now that he had horses for his men, he used some of his coin to buy from Northallerton a pair of sheep and a pair of goats. It was a small start but they were often the best ones.

We celebrated Christmas at my hall. Lady Ruth would miss Lady Marguerite and her children when they left for Hartburn at Michaelmas. It was a Christmas where we were all thankful. Aelric and Nanna's story was a warning. That could happen to any of us in a world ruled by King John.

The King comes north

Chapter 18

Spring brought hope. With the coin we had taken from the Scots we were able to replace our surcoats. In addition, we were able to provide better helmets for some of the newer men. We looked like one body now. The animals we had kept over the winter prospered. Our breeding horses foaled. People began to return to Stockton. Some had heard that there was a new lord and prosperity had returned. But it also brought a warning of our mortality. Lady Ruth fell ill. She had the coughing sickness. It was not long after Lady Marguerite and her family had left for the newly finished hall at Hartburn. Perhaps her spirits were low and that made her susceptible to illness. She was not getting any younger. She was annoyed at the fuss, "This is not the same sickness as my husband had. This is what you get in this land in the winter. I have suffered it before. I will get better. Just let an old lady do it herself."

When she recovered, at the start of March, then we were relieved. Her recovery and the new growth seemed to be reflected in the prosperity of my people. My knights all thrived. Sir Fótr had thrown himself into the running of the manor. He did, however, need a squire. There were two possibilities: Alfred and Henry, William's son. Both wished to be trained but, in the end, I decided upon Henry. We were not yet ready to knight Johann for we still had too few men. Henry's mother was tearful but she knew Fótr well. Her son would be looked after. My former squire now had a handful of men and a squire. The horses we had taken from the mercenaries meant that all of our men could now be mounted. We had no spares but that would come.

When our ship arrived from Anjou we saw that the world had changed. There were no more men coming to aid us. King Phillip had scoured the land of any English. Were it not for the merchants of La Flèche then we would have had no trade but they kept us supplied. It was sad that our former life was now just a distant memory.

It was April and we had just sent the taxes to Durham when my sentries reported knights with banners waiting for the ferry. We had visitors and they came from the south. Richard Red Leg was on the gatehouse wall and he pointed as they began to board the ferry. "I have counted at least twenty banners lord. There are more in the distance. This is a large body of lords."

I wondered what it meant. Speculation would not help. I descended and, after sending Petr to warn Edgar and my wife that we had guests I went to the quay to greet them. I knew that the first barons across would be the most important and when I saw William Marshal, the leading knight in the land, then I knew that this was, indeed, a powerful group of lords. Was I in trouble? Had I done something wrong? The fact that they had used my ferry rather than approaching stealthily gave me some hope.

I did not recognise any of the other knights save one whose livery was familiar. It was a de Ferrers! I had killed Richard de Ferrers in combat. There were members of the family in Normandy who wished me dead. I suspected the clan had returned to the safety of England now that their benefactor, King John, had lost his lands there. I would reserve judgement on this one until I had spoken with William Marshal. I had not seen the old Earl since before I had left for the Baltic crusade. He had aged. As he had served with my great grandfather I knew that he must be old. Now he looked it.

He held out his arm for me to clasp it. That was a good sign, "You have done well, Sir Thomas. I thought you were destined for a grisly end. It seems I was wrong." He lowered his voice as he waved a hand at my gatehouse, "Have you had permission for this? As I recall it was the Warlord's decision to build a castle that began all the trouble."

I smiled, "The Bishop of Durham approved."

He gave me a wry smile, "Perhaps he is just grateful that you did not stick a blade in his guts."

I smiled back, "No, my lord, thus far he has not offended me. I treat all those who do not offend me, well."

He laughed, "That is good to hear! Come, take me to your hall. We have much to say." As we walked through the gatehouse the ferry went back across the river for the rest of his lords. "I have heard good things about you. It seems that you are less reckless now and not so stiff necked."

193

"Trust me, Earl, my neck can still be stiff but I have learned to accommodate my distaste for some of those I have to follow."

He grunted. I knew not if that indicated derision or approval. My wife and Lady Ruth awaited us along with Edgar, my steward. William Marshal was an old-fashioned knight. Some said that he and my great grandfather were the only two perfect knights. He bowed, "Thank you ladies for your hospitality. I was sorry, Lady Ruth, to hear of the death of Sir William. He was a good knight."

"You are kind to say so. I believe that he is in heaven now."

He spoke to the three of us. "We will not be here long. We leave in the morning. The bulk of the army will camp in the common grazing land north of here. That meets with your approval, Baron?"

"It does. We can accommodate ten lords in my hall for we have guest quarters. My steward Edgar will show you where they are."

"Good. The days are long gone when I could sleep in a field." He turned and spoke to a knight, "De Lacy arrange it. I will go and speak with the Baron. You must still have some decent wine eh?"

"Of course. Petr fetch a jug and two goblets. We will go to my chamber. It faces west and has a pleasant aspect." I had had a window built into the west wall of my chamber. The glass was opaque but it allowed light in and I had a fire to compensate for the cold it created.

As we went up the stairs he said, "I have sympathy with you, lord. This town needs a castle. I remember when it was all that stood between us and the Scots. Your family earned the respect of all by their stoic defence."

I had two comfortable chairs in my chamber. They were stuffed with horsehair and covered in the best hides my tanners could produce. There was a fire burning. Despite the fact that it was not winter the north east of England was never warm and Anjou had spoiled me. "I pray you sit."

"This is pleasant."

Petr arrived and placed the wine on the table. He poured. "Thank you, Petr. I would have you watch the door. We would not be disturbed."

The Earl Marshal sipped the wine, "Gods but this is good."

I nodded. "The wine merchants of La Flèche keep me well supplied and I am not robbed. They were grateful for what I did."

He nodded, "Aye William des Roches spoke highly of you before he deserted the King."

"Perhaps that says more about the King than it does a valiant and true knight like William des Roches."

He shook his head, "Try thinking those thoughts without giving them air, baron!"

"I cannot help it. William was a friend and he treated me well. It was the murder of Arthur which prompted his desertion."

"That was never proved!" I cocked my head to one side. He shook his head. "The King is heading to the New Castle. He goes to war with William of Scotland."

"But I thought we were at peace."

"We were. The unwarranted attack last year, which you thwarted, might have been overlooked but Phillip seeks an alliance with King William and our spies tell us that it will happen. William still wishes to own and control Northumbria. We would have you and your knights join us. Your Sir Ralph and Sir Hugh of Northallerton are with the army already. How many others can you field?"

"There will be four of us."

"And men at arms and archers?"

"Fifty or so men at arms and forty-five archers. The days when I could field more than a hundred are long gone. It takes time to train men."

"That will be enough. We do not need your levy. The King wishes his barons to bear the brunt of the war." He lowered his voice. "He knows about the unrest here in the north east. This expedition is not only to quash the Scots but as warning to the barons of the north that any rebellion would be dealt with severely."

I emptied my goblet and refilled it. "May I speak plainly, Earl?"

He sighed and poured himself a goblet. He sat back in the chair, "As we are alone then, yes. Get it off your chest and then remain silent. That is especially true in front of the other lords. You fought many of them in Normandy and Anjou. Hugo de Ferrers is not fond of you!" He smiled as he spoke.

I began, "The High Sherriff is a vindictive man. Worse he is dangerous. I believe he sent men to do me harm." I told him of the attack and the family we had rescued.

"You have proof?"

"No, for they are dead."

"Pity!"

"In addition, the taxes are too high here in the north. We are not as rich as in the south. The Marcher Lords in Ireland and Wales are given special

195

dispensation and they have financial inducements. We are in the same position. We defend the northern march but we have nothing. The King does not listen!"

He held his hand up. "That is because he is King. He has divine right and can rule as he wishes."

"I am afraid, Earl, that it was that standpoint which cost him Anjou and Normandy. I fear Poitou will also fall."

He was silent. He drained his wine. "I will say this here, for your ears only and if this is ever repeated then I will deny it. I have sympathy with what you say. I have been punished for swearing allegiance to King Phillip. I had to do so to keep my Norman manors. I understand your viewpoint but you must be a realist. You cannot fight the King and win unless you are of royal blood."

I nodded, "And those with royal blood are either dead or incarcerated."

"Precisely. You can improve your situation greatly if you impress King John in this campaign. He may even allow you to build a castle here."

I laughed, "You do not believe that."

"No but it cannot hurt your cause to make yourself indispensable to our liege lord. De Percy and de Vesci have told me that it was you won the battle of Rothbury. You have an eye for such things. Your family blood is rich and you have inherited the Warlord's skill."

I nodded, "It is good of you to say so."

"I speak the truth. Now we leave on the morrow. The army gathers at Norham."

"We invade Scotland?"

"Aye. It will make a change to fight on Scottish soil. You join us as soon as you can. I would have you call at Durham on the way. I intend to impress upon the Bishop of his obligations. You are a Durham knight and it might just embarrass him enough to send his full force rather than a token gesture as his predecessor, Hugh de Puiset was prone to do. Do not be tardy just to make a point."

"You do me an injustice, Earl. I am not petty!"

"I apologise and one more thing; at the feast tonight, be polite to de Ferrers and the others."

"I will not suffer insults!"

"I will ensure that you are not insulted. Invite your knights too. I would meet with them before we go to war."

I sent Petr to bring Sir Edward and Sir Fótr and Ridley the Giant fetched Sir William. My patrolling archers had recently killed half a dozen deer. We would eat well!

It was my table and so I arranged the seating. My wife and aunt flanked the earl. I sat by my wife and Edward by my aunt. Fótr was next to Edward and I had Sir William next to me. It meant that Hugo de Ferrers was not within insulting distance of me. We waited for the senior knight to sit and then we sat. He leaned across my wife. "I see you have a keen eye for deploying troops, Sir Thomas." He had a wry smile upon his face.

"I have never been blessed with large numbers, lord, and so I use what I have wisely so that I incur the least damage!"

Petr, Johann, Alfred and the other squires were called upon to serve and to carve. It was a tradition. Alfred was too small to carve and he had to make do with serving meat to knights. I confess it was a task I had rarely enjoyed when I had been a squire but it had taught me valuable lessons: patience, how to cut meat and how to listen without giving away what you had heard. Johann had the last skill but Petr did not and his face showed his shock or surprise as the knights spoke in their cups. I would have to speak with him when time allowed.

My table arrangement meant that the feast went off without a problem. Hugo de Ferrers and the knights who sat close to him had their heads together and were, no doubt, slandering me. So long as I could not hear then it did not matter. The earl, his squire and Simon de Lacy were accommodated in the main hall. The rest made their way at the end of the evening to the annex. I felt safer that way.

The earl bade good night and said, "We will rise and leave early. You did well tonight and I will make enquiries about the Sherriff. I have little enough power these days but what little I have will try to discover the truth of what you say. If it was not the Sherriff then there are other enemies and that is good to know eh?"

I liked the earl. He was a throwback to the time of the Warlord. I doubted that we would see the like again and I felt sad about that.

I, of course, as the host, made certain that I was up before my guests and that I saw that they had food for their journey. The lords from the annex arrived. "Were your chambers satisfactory?"

Sir Hugo said, "Adequate, baron."

I smiled for it was grudging praise. Had he been able to find fault then he would have done so.

197

The earl arrived, "My lord, your squires have already eaten and are saddling your horses. The shortest way is through the north gate and across the Ox Bridge. You will soon find the Durham Road. It is the only remnant that we have of the Romans in the lower valley."

"Thank you for your hospitality. Sir Hugo be so good as to go and rouse the main camp. They should be up and ready to move but chivvy them anyway." He left. "Thank you, baron, I will see you at Norham." I watched them leave by the north gate and then gave orders for the muster.

My knights were keen to get to their homes. They had their goodbyes to give and then bring their men and horses back to my castle. I thought it unlikely that we would get much further north than Durham. We would need tents, baggage and servants. I asked Father Abelard to come with us for we needed a healer. There would be some with the army but I wanted one for my men. This was the first time Alfred had followed us to war. He would never be in danger but I saw the tears in his mother's eyes. Aunt Ruth was also fighting them too. He had his new helmet hanging from the saddle of his pony. I knew that he would be desperate to wear it but, in all likelihood, he would never have to.

I hugged my aunt and then Margaret, "We will be back. This is not like before. We go with the English army. I will not have the responsibility on my shoulders alone. I will just be part of the whole metal monster."

She pushed me away, "I know you, Sir Thomas. You will find some excuse to do something heroic! Don't! Come back safe with our son and your men. The Scots are not worth bleeding over."

We made a grand sight as we headed north. With banners and standards flying we were a colourful and heroic looking group. The people lined the road to cheer us and I saw Alfred with eyes wide as he took it in. The veterans like Ridley and David of Wales took it in their stride but it affected the younger warriors. Fótr and Edward joined us at the Durham road. For once we would not need scouts. William Marshal had led ten times our number just hours before us. There would be no danger and we were able to appreciate the beauty of my land.

Conversation turned to the war. For all of us this was a novel experience. We were used to fighting to hold on to our land. Now we were heading for another country and intended to take it!

"If we are to gather at Norham then it is likely we will attack Berwick." Sir William had jumped to a conclusion which was not necessarily the right one.

I said, "Norham is our northernmost castle. We could attack Berwick but it is a mighty castle. If I was asked what I thought then I would suggest Jedburgh. I

198

have seen it and there is no castle, at least not one as big as Berwick. Then I would sweep towards Edinburgh from the south. The Scottish castles line the coast. There are fewer inland."

Sir Edward asked the question which was on all of their minds. "And we fight for King John?"

I shook my head, "We fight for England. For once I agree with the King's policy. King Henry had the right idea. He cowed the Scots and with the Treaty of Falaise which made their King bow his knee to England. King Richard sold the fealty back to King William. While the treaty was in operation we were not raided. So, to answer you, Edward, yes, we fight for King John but that still does not make me like him. Nor does it make me agree with him." I laughed, "I find it amusing that he actually sent his Earl Marshal to ask me to join him."

Fótr nodded, "I had not thought of that. He needs you, lord. You can ask for whatever you want."

"Perhaps. One step at a time."

Durham was heaving. The Bishop had summoned all of his knights. There were at least a hundred banners there. I turned to the men at arms and archers. "You had better find somewhere to camp. We may be joining you."

"There is a moor north of here. We will camp there."

Amazingly we were admitted straight away. Knights parted as the four of us strode through the castle. The Bishop was seated at a table. A cleric had a roll and they were checking off names. The Bishop looked relieved when he saw me. "Sir Thomas, the Earl Marshal said that you would be here. He was adamant that I needed all of my knights."

"I think, Bishop, that when we attack the Scots there will be no one left to harm the Palatinate. Will you be riding with us?"

He looked almost afraid, "No, Sir Thomas. I have been ill recently and I will not be needed."

I wondered which of his knights would lead. Whichever of them were chosen they would have little experience of war. Few had fought the Scots and even fewer had been on crusades.

"When will we be able to leave? Norham is many miles north."

"Any knights who are not here by dawn will have to catch up for you leave tomorrow."

A knight I did not recognise pushed himself forward. He was older than I. In fact, he looked to be of an age with Lady Ruth's dead husband. "And who leads the knights of the Palatinate?"

199

The Bishop pointed a finger at me and said, "Why, Sir Thomas of Stockton of course. He is the best qualified knight here and besides the Earl Marshal suggested it. Who am I to argue?"

The older knight spluttered, "But he killed Hugh de Puiset."

Sir Edward stepped threateningly close to the knight, "And paid penance. He was forgiven when we served in the Baltic Crusade. Have you been on crusade, my lord?"

The older knight stepped back. He regretted his words immediately.

I nodded, "Then you had better have a copy for me of the knights, men at arms and archers I will lead."

"Do we need to call out the levy Sir Thomas?"

I laughed, "No Bishop; if we did then it would take six months for us to reach Norham! The knights and men at arms we have will have to do."

I was glad that I had my household knights with me. While I sat with the Bishop and checked names, they helped to organize the knights so that they would fight in conroi. Few had ever fought together and, as we collated the names, the three of them divided them into manageable groups. It was late when we finished. I would lead one hundred and twenty knights. Less than half had seen combat in the last ten years. They had just two hundred men at arms between them. The situation with archers and crossbowmen was even worse. They had but thirty archers and twenty crossbow men.

There was just the Bishop and I left in the hall. The rest had retired for we had an early morning. "It is fortunate that King John has brought his army north, Bishop. This is a poor turn out for the Palatinate."

He looked miserable, "You are right. I had thought Aimeric had ensured that my knights had maintained the men that they should. You are the only one who has fulfilled his oath. In fact, you have more than I expected."

"Then you know what you must do while I lead your men. You must visit all the lords who have not fulfilled their oath and they must be punished."

"How?"

I laughed. "That is simple, Bishop; you make them pay. They are not warriors they are merchants. They will soon realise that it is better to provide the men rather than to pay from their coffers."

We spent some time going through the documents which the Bishop had. I needed to know as much about the border as I could. The Bishop held the castle at Norham and he knew much about the places we would be likely to have to attack. I wanted that knowledge in my head before we joined the King.

200

It was a long slow journey to Norham. Had I just had my knights and men I would have been there in two days. As it was it took four. It did, however, afford me the opportunity to get to know some of the barons whom I would lead. After just a few miles and some conversation I realised that I did not like most of them. They were reluctant warriors. They whined and complained. But there were a few who appeared to have potential. Baron David of Stanley and his brother Baron Stephen of Spennymoor were two such. Their manors lay in the bleak uplands. They were prone to attacks from Scots and perhaps that was why. Neither were young men. Baron Stanley was the elder with white flecked hair. He had the squat look of a fighter. Baron Ralph of Crook, who was lord of another upland manor also had those qualities. It seemed the closer the manor was to Durham the less likely it was that they had a good lord. It must have gone back to the times of Hugh de Puiset. The manors around Durham yielded the greatest taxes and so were the ones Hugh de Puiset gave to his cronies.

Scottish War

Chapter 19

The plain before Northam was filled with tents and banners. The King was in the castle. The castle belonged to the Bishop of Durham and technically the lord would follow my banner. I did not think that would be so. When we had been five miles from the castle I had sent two of my archers to find us a dry camp site which was close to the river. There would be many horses. Good grazing would be paramount. We had brought some hay and grain but the amount we had brought was minimal.

Cedric Warbow waved us west towards a stand of trees. It was a hundred paces from the nearest horse lines. It was a mile from the castle but that did not worry me. My knights would not be expected to visit the castle. If any of them was summoned it would be me. We were so far west that we did not have to pass through the camp. We left the road and headed across the fields. It gave me the chance to look at the forces we had at our disposal. Although most were northern knights, I recognised the banners of de Percy, de Vesci and the Sherriff. There were others from further south: Hugh Bigod, the heir to Suffolk, Richard de Clare, Earl of Hertford, John de Lacey, Constable of Chester and Geoffrey de Mandeville, Earl of Essex were some of the lords whose banners I recognised. They were all powerful earls. King John was making this invasion a way of exerting his authority.

I had told my knights that David of Wales would command the archers. Sadly, only my archers were mounted. I had David of Wales make a separate camp for the archers and crossbowmen. I also had the largest single body of men at arms and so Ridley the Giant commanded them. They, too, had a separate camp. Leaving my servants to erect my tent I went with Petr and Alfred to the castle. William Marshal had stressed the need for speed. I had not been able to do so through no fault of my own. The sooner I reported the better.

My livery was known. My story was told, I had no doubt, in every hall throughout the land. My great grandfather had been famous. I was infamous. I was the hero of Arsuf who had killed a Bishop and then defied King John in Anjou. I think that even the great magnates were intrigued by me. The knights, men at arms, crossbowmen, archers and all the others stared at the three of us as we rode. Alfred was curious, "Why do they stare, father?"

"I am afraid, Alfred, that my deeds have preceded me. Men are inquisitive. It means nothing. Keep your mouth shut and your ears open. Try to avoid being the chattering magpie that you sometimes are."

Petr said, "He is getting better, lord."

"I know and I mean no criticism but King John is a dangerous man and my son has already shown a propensity for inappropriate comments."

Alfred said, quietly, "That was before I became a squire in training."

"Good. You will stay with the horses. Petr will come with me in case I need to send a message."

William Marshal must have warned the guards not to hinder my progress. We rode through the gate and I left Alfred with the horses in the Outer Ward. Petr and I walked up, through the tents towards the Inner Ward and the keep. A knight my age strode towards us. I recognised his livery, "I am William Marshal, the Earl's son. I am pleased that you have arrived." He lowered his voice. "King John was becoming anxious."

Even though it was not my fault I would not blame the men I led, "It is a long way from Durham, Sir William, and many of the men I led were on foot."

He nodded, "Come I am instructed to take you directly to the Council of War. You will not need your squire."

"Petr, return to Alfred. Water the horses and see if you can find food or grazing."

As he went off Sir William said, "I see you are an old campaigner."

I nodded, "The Holy Land, Sweden, Estonia and, latterly, Anjou and Normandy. I have learned that a knight afoot does not last long."

The keep was a sturdy one. Taken during the Civil War by the Scots when King Henry had recaptured it he had ensured that the defences were improved. The Bishop of Durham had been lax. As I entered the hall I saw a dozen knights seated around a table. King John and William Marshal were in the centre and I saw that a seat had been left for me.

I bowed, "I am sorry the journey took longer than it should, Your Majesty. No disrespect was intended. It was just a long journey."

King John said nothing but the Earl Marshal smiled and said. "We only arrived a day and a half before you. It is understandable."

King John waved an irritated hand, "Now that you are here be seated. We have much to say. There are still some men to arrive from Cumberland but as they have had an even longer journey we will not wait for them." I saw the Constable of Chester nod. "Earl Marshal."

William Marshal got to his feet. "We are planning a twin attack on the Scots. King William is at Edinburgh. He knows that we have gathered here and he is summoning his army. He will wait until he knows where we march before he commits himself. To that end Sir Thomas of Stockton will initiate our attack. He will lead the lords of the Palatinate to cross the Tweed and attack Jedburgh." All eyes were on me but I kept my face straight. I showed neither emotion nor reaction. "The castle there is a small one and its purpose is to guard the abbey. The baron will then sweep up towards Galashiels. It is hoped that the sight of the baron's banner and his reputation will make the Scots think that this is the main attack. His great grandfather and grandfather were the bane of King William when he was a young king."

There was a murmur of conversation and I took the opportunity to speak. "And how far do I go? To Edinburgh?"

King John allowed himself a rare smile, "You are a feisty cockerel, Sir Thomas. What makes you think that you will get that far?"

"The castles which the Scots have to bar our progress are along the coast. Berwick and Dunbar are mighty fortresses. As the earl says Jedburgh should not hold us up and Galashiels has no castle. From what I know the castles at Dalkeith and Lauder are the only ones which might hold us up and they lie close to Edinburgh."

I saw the earl smile. "It is good that you have prepared. You have mounted men. You will keep us informed of your progress and, more importantly, the Scottish reaction. I know that you know how to use scouts. Once we know that William is committed to an attack then we will bring the main army from Norham."

"Then you would prefer me to attack towards Lauder." He nodded. "That has a town wall and may hold us up. We have no siege train."

King John spoke for the first time, "We do not waste time on sieges. You were chosen, Sir Thomas for your skill at leading fast-moving men. Use that speed. Lauder is as close to Norham as Jedburgh. If you can be the anvil against which King William is held then we will be the hammer!"

The lords at the table banged it and cheered. I sensed that this was to garner favour rather than a genuine response.

Earl Marshal stood, "Come, I will finalise the details with you."

When we were in the Inner Ward I said, calmly and simply, "We are the bait? We are the tethered sheep upon which the wolf will feast."

To be fair to the Earl he did not attempt to deny it, "You did not think that, to win favour and have a castle once more you would just come up here and join the army chasing Scotsman over the moors, did you?" I shook my head. "I ensured that you were in command and that was for two reasons: firstly, it gave us a better chance of winning and secondly, because your destiny is in your own hands. So long as you draw the Scots to you then you have done that which was asked."

"And men will die."

He shrugged, "This is war and all men die but you, Sir Thomas, seem to lose less than most. Let us keep it that way eh?"

I nodded, "I will leave at dawn tomorrow. It is twenty miles to the Tweed. I will attack at dawn on the following day."

"Good. I will take a conroi to Berwick to make them think we attack there. The sight of an old warhorse like me may alarm them, eh?"

Petr and Alfred noticed my silence as we rode back to the camp, "Is there a problem, lord?"

"Not a problem, Petr, more of a puzzle. We have to stir up a wasps' nest and then escape without getting stung."

Petr nodded. Alfred frowned and then said, "That is impossible!"

I smiled, "And that, my son, is the puzzle."

I did not call a council of war immediately. I summoned my knights along with Ridley and David of Wales. I would have asked for Sir Ralph but he was with the Sherriff of York's men. He was not mine to command in this battle. I explained what we had to do. None seemed concerned with the enormity of the task.

"It will be easy enough to take Jedburgh. David you will take your archers and stop large numbers from escaping. Allow a couple to do so for that would bring the Scots to us. I need one of your archers to command the ones who remain."

"Will son of Robin will do. He does not suffer fools gladly."

"We use the dismounted men at arms to attack the walls and we will surround them with the horsemen. The walls are not high. No one has ever attacked Jedburgh. It is a royal residence but not a place of war. They think the presence of the monastery protects them."

Sir Edward nodded, "And that is why they have chosen you, lord." I frowned. "You killed a Bishop. They think you have no respect for the church."

I smiled, "I had not thought of that. King John is cleverer than I thought."

Sir William said, "More devious, lord."

"And when we have it?"

"Then I leave all of the men without horses and our baggage there. We will make that our fortress. When we go north we go mounted. We strike first at Galashiels and then Lauder. It is but fourteen miles to Galashiels and another five to Lauder. With luck we can drive those from Galashiels to Lauder."

"Where there is a castle or a tower at least."

I nodded, "Edward, I have no intention of attacking a castle with horsemen. We play the fearful knight. We make it look as though we are ready for a siege but David of Wales' archers will keep watch and as soon as King William appears then we withdraw. They will eagerly pursue the banner which has been the bane of Scotland. We make him attack his own walls which will be defended by our men."

"And King John?"

"A good point, Fótr; I am not sure that he will hurry. He may want our numbers thinned and me, possibly killed. If our numbers are diminished then so will the Scots and his victory will be all the greater. I am doing him a favour by drawing the Scots south. He will not have as far to travel." We spent some time working out the things I had overlooked and then I summoned the leading barons and told them of our plans. They were not thrilled!

"But we have fewer knights than the King."

I nodded, "Perhaps if all the barons had responded to the Bishop's command we might not be in this dilemma. I expect all of you to obey both my orders and my commands! Petr, my squire will use the horn to signal you and Alfred my other squire will use the standard. Make certain that you have one of your men with an eye to me. I will not be difficult to find. I will be at the van leading you."

For some reason that seemed to make them happier. I suspect some thought about being tardy. What they did not know was that I intended to have one of my men at arms at the rear watching for such actions.

"If we prosecute our attack with vigour then we will win. The battle which attacks Galashiels and Lauder will be mounted. Our speed will surprise them and we shall be able to withdraw in good order."

The Baron of Sherburn, which was close to Durham, said, somewhat sarcastically, "You seem to be confident about taking Jedburgh."

I looked at him, "Baron, I have been fighting enemies like the Scots since I was twelve years old. I may not be tactful nor does my face inspire confidence but the wounds I suffered have made me a stronger knight. If all of you were my own men then I would have total confidence in our ability to win. It is for you barons to prove that you are as good as my men at arms!"

That upset them. I saw my own knights smiling as the barons complained about impugned honour. I nodded to Ridley the Giant who banged his sword against his shield. It was like the crack of doom.

"For those who say I have impugned their honour then I make this offer; when this is over I will meet any and all of you in a place of your choosing and we will allow a trial by combat settle the matter." I smiled. "I cannot say fairer than that." They were silent. None wished to cross swords with me. "We leave at dawn. I would be camped at the Tweed before dusk. Tomorrow the knights of the Palatinate go to war."

When we were alone Sir William could not contain his laughter, "I honestly thought that some of those barons were ready to run back to Durham when you made the offer."

Sir Edward asked, "Aye, but will they fight?"

"They will fight. They may not do it as well as our men but they will fight. It is our battle which will decide the outcome of this attack. We will ride together and we will take Jedburgh."

This time, when we moved, it was faster. My words had spurred them. My archers rode ahead and ensured that the ford across the Tweed was not defended. We made a cold camp with no fires. Again, there were no complaints. I think they feared I might make good my promise earlier rather than later. Mordaf and Gruffyd scouted out the town and the abbey. They reported that although there was a greater number of sentries than we might have expected there was no sign of preparation for war. The presence of King John close to Berwick had ensured that.

My mounted archers left well before dawn. The road leading to Galashiels crossed the Jed Water north of our position. Had I so wished then I could have ensured that all of those in Jedburgh were trapped but I wanted word to reach

King William. I planned on sending the men on foot across the bridge to the south of the town while my horsemen swam the river. It was neither wide not deep. With Godwin of Battle leading the men on foot I led the horsemen to the river and I took the lead. It was Alfred who worried me. He had never crossed such a deep river. To that end I had Petr with him. He could swim but a sudden dousing in a dark river could induce panic.

When our horses scrambled up the other bank I was relieved that Alfred was there. I nodded, "Now unfurl the banner. It is imperative that the Scots see it. It is the banner which will make them panic. This is why King John chose us. They will remember the Warlord and my grandfather."

As dawn came up behind us I saw the town. The gates were closed and men stood on the walls. The walls around the abbey were unguarded and were there to deter animals rather than determined men. I halted the line. I had Baron Stanley and Baron Spennymoor leading half of the knights. I had my men and the barons I mistrusted. I would keep them close to me. My knights and men at arms would be the front rank and they the second. None of them appeared embarrassed about following men at arms. We stood in two lines and waited. Godwin would lead the men on foot, the dismounted archers and the crossbowmen against the Abbey. If the Scots sallied to destroy them then we would be able to reach them first.

As soon as the sun sparkled from the helmets and spears of Godwin's men we heard the horns and drums from inside the town and from the Abbey came the sound of a bell. A rogue cloud kept us hidden but when the light hit us I saw hands pointing at us. They did not attempt to sally forth to fight Godwin and his men.

Petr shouted, "Lord, men are leaving the abbey and heading to the town."

"Then sound the attack."

We were just four hundred paces from the town and the abbey was the same distance away. It meant we would have to charge across the men on foot who were advancing up the road. At the very least we would capture the Abbey and that was an important target. The Abbey had been founded by King David!

As we galloped towards the priests I saw that they would not make the town gate in time. The gates were still closed. I gambled. "Wheel right!" Petr sounded the horn and Alfred waved the standard. The move caught those on the walls unawares. They had crossbows but they had not yet aimed them. The gates opened as the first, younger, priests reached the town. We were just two hundred paces away. Had they had any sense they would have slammed the gates shut but they did not. They were allowing the priests and monks to enter. A few bolts flew towards us. I saw one knight, who had been slow to raise his shield, fall from his saddle. I saw why they had kept the gates open. The abbot and his senior priests were waddling along at the back. "Petr and Alfred go and take the Abbot prisoner. Johann go with them!"

I spurred Dragon hard and he leapt ahead of Edward and William's mounts. Two men in mail came from the gates with spears. Their intent was clear. They would stop us from gaining entry. I aimed Dragon at one of them and then, as I came within range of their spears I switched him to ride at the other I hurled my own spear at his chest. At three paces I could not miss and he fell backwards holding the spear. Dragon knocked two priests to the ground as Sir William speared the other guard. And then I was in the town. Panic had set in and everyone was fleeing north towards the north gate.

I reined in Dragon. I needed him calmer and I waited for my household knights and men at arms to join me. A line of Scottish knights and soldiers formed a shield wall. With their flanks anchored next to two buildings they must have thought themselves secure. They were not. The back of a horse can be an excellent place from which to throw a spear. You are throwing downwards and can often defeat a shield. This was another reason we used spears. You could not do this with a lance. Fótr's squire, Henry, handed me a spear.

My men had practised this manoeuvre although we had never actually used it. I shouted, "Cantabrian circle!"

Sir Edward joined me and my men formed two lines behind us. I knew that the other lords who were entering the gates would have no idea what we were doing. We charged towards the Scottish shield wall. Sir Edward and his column would have the advantage that their shields would protect them from the Scots. My column would not. I smiled as the Scots held their shields across their bodies and planted their spears next to their feet. They thought we intended to bowl them over. When I was five paces from them I wheeled Dragon to the left and, standing in my stirrups, hurled my spear. The Scot it struck had a surprised look as he saw the shaft of the spear sticking from his chest. He fell backwards. Sir Fótr was behind me and he hit the next man. This was the beauty of the manoeuvre, there were no wasted spears.

I rode down the length of my column and saw the Baron of Stanley. "Take your men and charge the survivors. You can ride six abreast!"

"Aye lord! An impressive attack!"

209

I reined in at the gate. Most of the other knights just milled around. The two brothers were the only ones whose men were organised and ready to attack. I saw that we had taken out the front rank of spearmen already. As the last of my men hurled their spears I heard, "Stanley and Spennymoor, for God, the Bishop and Sir Thomas of Stockton!"

A solid column of knights six men wide and ten deep charged the line. It was too much. They broke and fled. I saw that Godwin and his men had arrived, "Godwin, get your men on the walls. This is yours to defend!"

"Aye lord."

I took off my helmet and made certain that all of my men had survived. They had. We followed the knights of Stanley and Spennymoor through the town. "Padraig take a couple of men and search the dead."

"Aye lord."

When we reached the north gate, I saw people being driven back by David of Wales and his archers. They were mounted but they had nocked bows. I rode to meet him. While his men drove their prisoners into the town I reined in and spoke with my Captain of Archers. "Well?"

"We let the first two horsemen go. We slew the next ten and the rest seemed unwilling to risk a goose fletched arrow. We have twenty more horses."

"Good. When your men have eaten, give our scouts a spare horse each and send them to Galashiels. We will head there on the morrow."

Even the most taciturn of the barons was happy with the outcome. I had gambled and won. As Edward pointed out, later, as he chastised me for my recklessness, that was not always so. I had the knights who had surrendered and the monks and abbot placed, under guard in the Abbey. The abbot gave me ransom before I asked for it as did the lord of Jedburgh. The other twelve would be my prisoners until then. I used some of the other barons to escort our prisoners back to Norham. They would also tell King John that the first part of my plan had succeeded. We ate well and, confident that Godwin could hold the town for us, we retired.

Alfred and Petr shared my room. Alfred would not go to sleep. "We could go all the way to Edinburgh and take their King prisoner."

I heard Petr laugh. I spoke gently. Alfred was young. "Son, we were lucky. This was not a castle. This was a town wall and we found the gate open."

"Aye father but you destroyed a shield wall! I heard the other barons talking! They could not believe it."

"Those barons are not warriors. Do not value their opinion. So far God has smiled on us. There will be sterner tests to come. Now sleep. We leave before dawn!"

When we left the next day, I rode Skuld and Petr led Dragon. The scouts had reported that Galashiels was a hive of activity. There was no castle there and the palisade was even less impressive than Jedburgh. This time we would use my archers to gain entry. Eight of my men at arms had taken axes from the armoury at Jedburgh. We would break down the gates the old-fashioned way. My forty-five archers had plenty of arrows.

Baron Stanley and his brother asked permission to ride with me. They were interested in my retinue. "You have mounted archers. Can they fight as the Turks do, from the backs of horses?

"No, for the Turk uses a short bow made of layers of horn and wood. The war bow is too long. I mount them so that they can keep pace with my knights and men at arms."

"Your men at arms fight like knights and yet they are not knights."

I pointed at Edward, "Sir Edward was a man at arms. I knighted him. He is no different now from the days when he was as Ridley the Giant!"

Baron Spennymoor said, "And today will be like yesterday?"

I shook my head. "Do not predict what the gods of war have in store. We make plans and we hope they succeed. Make sure that you watch me when we fight. If I have to change plans then I will signal you."

The gates to Galashiels were closed. There was no obliging monastery nearby. Half of my men at arms dismounted and while the others held their shields they walked to within two hundred and fifty paces of the gatehouse. Eight of them had axes. They planted their shields in the ground and stood behind them. A few crossbow bolts flew from the walls and thudded into the shields. Arrows followed but they fell woefully short. They were not using the war bow. Confident that our movement was some sort of ruse or trick they stopped wasting arrows and bolts. The walls were lined with warriors and townsfolk.

My archers arrived. They had plenty of arrows. I nudged Skuld to walk closer so that I could observe the effect of the attack.

"Nock!" The archers had all chosen their best arrow. "Draw!" The creak from the forty-five bows was audible. David of Wales looked at me and I nodded, "Release!"

The forty-five arrows sailed towards the gatehouse. It was as though someone had built a wall of sand and the sea had swept it away as the gatehouse

211

was cleared. Even as I looked I heard the next forty-five arrows head towards the walls adjacent to the gatehouse. Some of those there were quick enough to duck or raise a shield but another twenty or so men fell. Ridley the Giant led my men at arms towards the gate only half had shields. The rest were left to protect the archers. I did not think it would be needed.

"Petr, order the barons forward."

I watched my men run the two hundred and fifty paces to the walls. Barely a handful of arrows and bolts were sent at them. My archers now had to seek targets. There was no rain of arrows but as each Scot raised his head to throw a stone or javelin at the men hacking at the gates so they were knocked form the walls. Alfred offered me a spear. "No, I shall use my sword. You wait here with David of Wales."

"Aye lord."

The sound of the axes striking the wood was like the sound of doom to Galashiels. Suddenly I saw a standard being waved. It was white. They were surrendering.

We rode through the gates. There was but one knight in the town. I realised, when I saw that the stable was empty, that the others had fled. They would be heading to Edinburgh. My plan was succeeding better than I might have hope but I did not allow myself to get too excited. King William had yet to respond and I knew that he would.

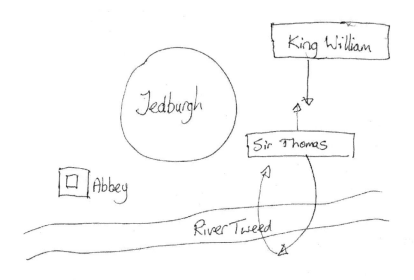

The Bane of the Scots

Chapter 20

I had the one knight we had captured sent back to Norham. He was sent via Jedburgh. The treasure of Galashiels and the weapons were also sent to Jedburgh. I took the treasure in lieu of sacking the town. I had no doubt that the good burghers would have treasure hidden away but we had enough to make my barons happy. Once again, we ate well and slept in comfortable quarters. I fear it made some of my barons complacent.

The next day we headed, not for Edinburgh and Dalkeith, but Lauder. Unlike Galashiels there was a tower. It stood on a hill. There was, however, a good wall with four well-made and defended gates. We would need a different strategy. I had sent a rider directly to Norham from Galashiels but I hoped that King John was already on the march. Our movement and our success must have reached the ears of King William. If he wanted to hold on to his throne against his many rivals he could not ignore the threat to his land.

The road along which we rode descended to a boggy stream filled piece of ground. My scouts had already reported it and so we changed to a narrower formation. We could no longer ride in three columns using the fields. We had to stick to the road. The formation meant we were strung out further along the road. It was that formation which saved us. We waited for the other conroi to form up behind as my archer scouts who had been to the north and west of us galloped in.

Cedric Warbow said, "Lord, King William and his army are just a mile away. He has many banners and horsemen. They are heading for Lauder!"

We had been anticipated. It was time for a quick decision. "Gilles, ride north and east. Find King John or the Earl Marshal. Tell them that King William advances and I will fall back to Jedburgh."

"Aye lord."

It took time to turn us around. I rode through my knights and barons so that I was at the fore. There was a fork in the road we had passed which would take us directly to Jedburgh. I spied, in the distance a wooded hill to the north of the road. I was just glad that my scouts had not spied Scots there. It was the perfect place from which to ambush.

Now the fact that we were mounted might come to our aid. Just then Walter of Coxwold galloped in from the west. "Lord, there are a large number of knights heading from the direction of Galashiels."

"How many?"

"I counted two hundred banners."

I nodded. This showed cunning. They had sent this conroi in case I was heading for Edinburgh. The King had placed himself so that he could strike at Jedburgh or Norham. If King John had played me false then we were dead.

Baron Stanhope had shown himself to be a reliable baron. I waved him over. "I will take my men and the men of Stanley and Spennymoor. We will ride to attack this conroi from Galashiels. There is a small road ahead. You take the rest of the army back to Jedburgh. Defend it!"

"Aye lord!"

"Spennymoor, Stanley, with me."

I waved Alfred forward. I dismounted Skuld and mounted Dragon. "Give the banner to Petr. Take Skuld and ride with Baron Stanhope back to Jedburgh." The old Alfred would have argued but he was growing up and he nodded. I took the spear which Petr offered me. I spurred Dragon and we headed west. The two barons and Sir Edward rose with me. "You have a plan, lord?"

"I do Edward. The last thing the Scots expect is for us to turn back to Galashiels. Our archers have saved us this day or given us the chance of salvation at least. We stand a better chance of defeating two hundred knights than more than a thousand warriors."

I had fifty knights and more than a hundred men at arms. We would be outnumbered but we had surprise on our side. We followed Stanhope until he took the fork and then we left the road. I led them across the sheep filled fields towards the wooded piece of high ground. The Scots had not used it for ambush. We would. I waved my spear and led my men there. We laboured up the slope. The woods were not thick but they hid us from view and that was what counted. We could not see the other side of the knoll but I knew that Galashiels lay in that direction.

"David of Wales dismount your men and take them to the western edge of the wood. I intend to sweep down and hit them near the road. You stop us being outflanked."

"Aye lord."

I quickly rode down the line of knights. I did not need to tell my own men what to do. They had done this before. I could trust them. It was the men of Stanley and Spennymoor I addressed. "We attack them on my command. We hit them hard and as soon as you hear Petr sound the horn three times then you withdraw and head for Jedburgh."

"And if they pursue?" The question, from Baron Stanley, was one of interest more than fear.

"My archers will engage them. They are more than skilful enough to hurt them, ride away and then join us. You must trust me, my lords. If we hit them hard enough they will flee. They will not be riding with lances or spears. Their scouts will have reported us on the Lauder Road. They know their King is coming. They are springing a trap and will be confident. The men from Jedburgh and Galashiels will have reported our numbers accurately. They will not expect an ambush."

Dick One Arrow galloped over, "Lord, they are coming. David of Wales says they are less than a mile away."

I nodded and he rode back to the archers. "Form two lines, my knights and my men at arms will be the first line. God be with us!" I took my place between Sir William and Sir Edward. Petr was behind me. "Petr, stay out of trouble. You seek no honour today. When I shout then you know what to do."

"Aye lord."

I donned my helmet and rested my spear on my cantle. The road was less than two hundred paces from us. I counted on the fact that the knights' attention would be on the road ahead. They were not far from Lauder. Knowing that King William was heading there they would be anticipating a massacre. Some would be spending the ransom already. I hoped that some would have their helmets on their cantles and their spears with their squires. If God was with us then we would win.

I waited until the leading riders had passed. Half were not wearing helmets and none had spears or lances. I saw that they were riding in a column of fours. I lowered my spear and spurred Dragon. He leapt down the slope. My knights and men at arms followed. The slope helped us to gain speed quickly. There was a danger that we might lose formation but that was a risk we would

216

have to take. We were just a hundred and twenty paces from them when they saw us. Their own noise and the fact that some of those at the front wore helmets helped us. They turned and spurred their horses. They would attack us. As I had hoped they did not have spears or lances. They would not meet us with any sort of order. I pulled back my spear as we approached.

Our speed was such that I could not be sure which knight I would strike. One almost chose himself as he rode towards me. I rammed my spear at his chest for his shield was still over his leg. In the hurry and the confusion, he had made a fatal error. My spear struck him hard just below his breastbone. Had Dragon not been such a powerful horse I might have been unhorsed myself. As it was his falling body dragged my spear from his chest and I was able to pull back and thrust again into the side of a knight who was trying to control his horse.

Then there was no-one before me and I wheeled right. I found myself riding behind a Scot who was urging his horse to get to Ridley the Giant. He never even saw me as my spear drove deep into his side. I saw then that the knights at the rear had ridden up the slope to attack the men of Stanley and Spennymoor in the flank. David of Wales timed his attack perfectly. Forty-five arrows emptied thirty saddles and the next forty-five arrows another twenty. I was about to order Petr to sound the signal to withdraw when the Scottish horn sounded twice and the eighty survivors of our attack turned and headed back to Galashiels.

"Petr, sound reform!"

My archers continued to rain arrows at the fleeing Scots. Another six fell. We had bought time and that was all. Everything now depended upon King John and William Marshal. I trusted the Earl but not the King!

As we headed south I saw that there were empty saddles. We had lost knights and men at arms. I looked at my men at arms and knights. Even though we had been the first to make contact and to begin the battle my men at arms just nursed wounds. That was a measure of the experience of the men I led.

It was dark as we approached Jedburgh. "Have the horses seen to first. They saved us today. We will camp outside the town!"

The knights under Baron Stanhope who had left first had made camp and their servants had prepared food. They were eager to know what had happened after they had left. I had no time to explain and I left my barons to do so. I went into the town with David of Wales. I found Godwin of Battle. He had not been idle. He had all of the prisoners secured in the Great Hall. That meant he only needed four men to watch them and he had chosen men who were older. The walls were well manned and there was plenty of food.

"David, I want you and your men inside the walls tomorrow. I intend to use my knights to attack the Scots and draw them onto your arrows. I may feign a withdrawal across the river. Fear not I will not abandon you."

David smiled, "The thought never entered my head."

Godwin said, "And King John?"

"William Marshal said they would come to our aid. I have to trust that."

By the time I had walked the walls and ensured that we had defences against a night attack it was almost midnight. Edward and Petr found me. "Lord you must eat and then get some rest. If you fall then we are doomed."

I nodded, absentmindedly, "The barons did well today. I was pleased."

Edward shook his head, "You did well today. I know of no other lord who could have extricated us from that trap."

"We are not out of it yet."

Baron Stanhope found me too, as I was eating some dried pork. "My lord, I beg you to rest. My men and I will watch. We were saved today because of Barons Stanley, Spennymoor and your men. If King William comes tomorrow then we will need you to lead us."

Reluctantly I slept. It was a fitful sleep and haunted by dreams. I could not remember them and they were the worst kind.

Petr shook me awake well before dawn. "Sorry, lord, Baron Stanhope said not to wake you but the scouts have returned. King William is camped just five miles away."

"You did right. How is Alfred?"

He laughed, "What do you expect lord? He is excited."

"Today I will have him in Jedburgh with Godwin."

"He will not be happy."

"But he will be alive and this day will be bloody! I would have you take care. I could not face your mother if I brought you back draped across a saddle."

"She is married to a warrior, lord. She knows."

I nodded, "Ask my captains and the leading barons to join me." I made water and drank some of the ale from the skin Petr had given me. The three leading barons and my knights arrived.

They all seemed cheerful, "What now lord?"

"Simple, we hit them when they close with the walls and then withdraw across the river. We stay close to the walls so that our archers can reap Scotsmen.

We reform on the other side and, if they try to cross, then we charge them. If they withdraw we re-cross the river and charge them again."

Baron Spennymoor said, "That is all?"

"We are too few to do more and we make the town a weight around their neck. They wish to recapture it. If they do so they have to assault its walls. We have stout men defend it. We have archers and crossbows and the men who stand behind the walls will have had three days of rest."

"And if King John does not come, what then?"

"We will have a glorious end and I will have more cause to be angry with our liege lord. Now go and prepare your men. We form three lines with our flank anchored by the town wall."

Alfred appeared., "Which horse today lord, Dragon?"

"No Alfred, I would have Dragon safe in Jedburgh with you. I will ride Skuld. She is a better swimmer and she brings me luck."

He nodded and then stopped, "I will not be with you?"

"You ride a pony. How could you survive amongst war horses?"

He thought about it and said, "One day I will not be small and I will ride a war horse too!"

As dawn broke we mounted our horses and headed for the walls. There was no sign of the enemy but they would be coming. Perhaps they would think that we had fled. King William would see less than two hundred horsemen. Our scouts had said that he had more than five hundred knights and the men on foot numbered well over two thousand. He had summoned warriors from all over his realm. Apart from the knights they had wild men from the north. Some fought bare chested. They would charge enthusiastically but, once they were broken, they would melt away like spring snow. We stood by our horses with helmets hung over our cantles. My knights and men at arms chatted easily. The other knights and mounted men at arms were more nervous and it showed in their demeanour. I could do nothing about that.

Alfred had groomed Skuld well and her coat shone in the early morning light. Petr had a spare spear for me. My sword had an edge good enough to shave with. We had done all that we could and then the Scots came. It was like a brightly coloured shadow which appeared from the north. It grew and filled the horizon. I saw some of the older knights like the Baron of Sherburn who physically moved his horse backwards when he saw them.

I mounted and turned Skuld so that I faced them. "Do not be afraid of numbers. Trust to your weapons, your horses, your mail and your skill. Most of

219

the ones we face are wild men! King John and the Earl Marshal are coming. We need to hold them for a little time is all."

A voice from the back shouted, "King John has abandoned us!"

"He has not. He asked us to do a job and we have done as we were asked. He will come. We are knights of the Palatinate. Whatever comes our way we will deal with it. Remember the orders. Hit them hard. When you hear the horn then withdraw across the river and reform."

I watched as the Scottish army formed up. I smiled. Someone was there who had fought us at Rothbury. They were ensuring tight lines. This would be no wild charge. I had heard that King William fancied himself as a knight. King Henry had dented the inflated opinion he had of himself but he would still try to use military strategy to defeat us. My worry was the discipline of the men I led. A feigned retreat could turn into a rout very easily. I had confidence in half of the knights I led. I looked to the north east. King John would be coming from that direction. I assumed he would have camped nearby. He would be far enough away from the Scots not to alarm them. We had to hold them for an hour or two. William's cautious manoeuvring suited us.

I saw that he had his knights ready to face ours while the bulk of his army were gathering to attack the walls of their town. Men on foot did not, out of choice, attack knights on horses. I looked at the sun. it was almost the third hour of the day. The Scottish knights were five hundred paces from us and four hundred from the walls of Jedburgh. Those knights on the right flank of the Scots would be in range of my archers on the walls. They would be in for a shock.

I saw the Scots close ranks. They were preparing to move. "Ready!" The Scottish horns sounded and the line moved towards us. The trick would be to hit them when we were at the gallop but allow them to have the longer ride. When they were three hundred paces from us arrows began to pick off knights and horses on their right flank.

"Forward for England and the Palatinate!"

I spurred Skuld. Unlike Dragon she did not leap forward. She had a more measured gait. The Scots were now galloping. Their line was moving inexorably away from the arrows and to their left. A gap was appearing between their right flank and their men on foot. We began to canter and there was a gap of just two hundred paces between us. We were closing rapidly. When we were a hundred paces apart Skuld's legs were opening and we were galloping. I laid my spear across my cantle. Many of the Scots had lances. They were longer but were prone to shatter upon impact. We had had the shorter ride and were still stirrup to stirrup. There were gaps in the Scottish line. Edward and Fótr were facing a single knight.

The knight I faced had a yellow shield with a blue diagonal cross. He had a full-face helmet and his shield was held, like mine, to minimise damage. He would have the first chance to hit. I watched his hand pull back. A moment later mine did too. He punched at my shield and I leaned my shoulder into it. The impact shook me and shattered the lance. I rammed my spear into his thigh. Bright blood spurted as I withdrew it. All along the line there was the sound of shattering spears and lances mixed with the crack of metal on wood and metal. Horses neighed and screamed. Men died. I had no time to see the effect of my strike for there was a second rank of knights. This line was even more ragged. The realignment as they had moved away from the archers had hurt their integrity.

I saw a knight to my right. He was heading for Sir Edward. His eyes were on Edward and his shield. My spear went into his shoulder and knocked him from his saddle. I had just recovered my spear when a third knight rode at me. He came obliquely for me. He intended to hit me on my spear side. All that I could do was to fend off the lance with my spear. As I did so Edward's spear struck him in the head and he fell from the saddle. I did not want a mêlée. I did not trust the skills of half of my knights and the Scots outnumbered us.

"Petr, sound the horn!"

I held my spear over hand and as another Scottish knight galloped at me I threw my spear at him. He was just five paces from me and did not expect it. The spear hit him in the helmet and caught in the holes of his mask. He tumbled from the saddle. As I wheeled Skuld I drew my sword and headed back for the river. I saw Petr's back before me. Glancing to my side my household knights were still there. As we passed over the site of the first impact I saw the knight I had first struck. My spear had not killed him. He had been trampled to death by horses. We had killed more of the Scots for there were many bodies lying there. I saw too many of our own Durham knights, dead. Baron Sherburn lay on the ground, skewered by a lance. He had, at least, attained some honour in his death. I glanced over my shoulder. Some knights had not heeded the call to retreat and there were knots of knights still fighting. The Scottish horns sounded reform. Skuld splashed into the river. We only had to swim for a few paces and then she found purchase and scrambled up to the other bank.

"Petr, see how many have survived."

I took off my helmet and walked Skuld back to the river so that she could drink. The last couple of knights and some riderless horses make their way towards the river. The Scots were forming up again. We had to recross the river and draw their sting. I did not want them to head for the abbey. Where was King John?

"Lord, we have lost a third of our knights and half of our men at arms."

I nodded and shouted, "Reform. We cross the river! This day is not yet done!"

This time there was no whining voices complaining. Despite our losses we had hurt them more than they had hurt us. They cheered and banged their shields. Petr handed me another spear and I walked Skuld across the river. My helmet hung from my cantle. I wanted the cool air on my face and I needed to see the enemy. As we formed up we were spotted by the Scots. They had moved closer to us and I heard their horns as they reformed. They outnumbered us by more than two to one now.

Sir William said, "If the King does not come soon all that he will find will be our corpses."

Sir Edward said, "Perhaps that was his plan all along. We decimate the Scots and all of us perish."

"That is cynical Sir Edward."

He waved a hand north, "I hear no English horns to contradict me!"

The Scottish horns sounded. I donned my helmet. "Forward!"

We began to walk towards the Scots. We would not be able to charge. Neither would the Scots. This would not be a collision at the gallop. This would be one at the canter. Our lines would be tighter and the ones at the side, Stanhope, Stanley and Spennymoor would be surrounded. The Scottish King, however, would be coming for my standard and the bane of the Scots. The slower more measured approach allowed me to see where I would be striking. The King was not in the front rank. I saw him behind his household knights. His standard, the Lion of Scotland, fluttered above his head. He was now sixty-three or so and I did not blame him for avoiding the front rank. Only the Warlord had ridden there when he had been a greybeard.

The knight who was coming for me wore King William's livery; he was a household knight. He had a lance and he rode a war horse which would tower over Skuld. I saw him pulling his arm back as we closed. This time I felt Edward's boot next to mine. Our lines would stop once we struck and spears would be useless. The lance was longer than my spear and he aimed it at my

222

head. I barely managed to raise my shield and block the blow. I thrust blindly with my spear and felt it strike flesh. I twisted and then released my grip. As I lowered my shield and drew my sword I saw that I had struck him in the side. My spear hung there. As the shaft wavered up and down so the wound would widen. Even as I looked he leaned over his saddle and then fell to the ground.

I saw King William behind him. He wore an open face helmet. We had been abandoned by King John but, perhaps, by some miracle, I could capture the King of Scotland and his standard! I shouted, "Stockton, we take the King!"

I spurred Skuld into the gap left by the knight I had struck. Other household knights tried to get at me but Edward and William had both fought alongside me for many years. Their horses formed a barrier. They used their swords to fend off the Scottish knights. King William thrust his lance at me. It was a futile gesture for he was too close to me. I hacked through it and he was left with a stump. Even as he drew his sword I heard a distant horn. I ignored it. I either captured the King or I would be butchered by the knights who were trying to get at me.

I stood in my stirrups and brought my sword down towards the King's head. I did not have the luxury of time. I could not afford to take him prisoner. I had to try to kill him. This would not be regicide for it was in battle but it was still not to be taken lightly. He blocked it with his shield. I was aware of Petr forcing his horse between Skuld and Sir Edward's. He was going for the standard. It was a brave gesture for the standard was held by a knight. As the King reeled, his sword still half way out I heard the horns again. They were closer. It was King John. I brought my sword down again and the King was forced to back his horse to avoid falling.

"Yield King William or you will die!"

He shook his head and spat his words at me, "Then I will have an honourable death but I will not yield to the spawn of the Warlord!"

He had his sword out and I smashed my own blade against it. It was a powerful blow and the sword fell from his hands. Just then Petr used my standard as a lance and punched the Scottish standard bearer in the head. He tumbled to the ground, taking the standard with him. I pressed the tip of my sword against the King's throat.

"Yield or die for King John comes! If you are dead then Scotland is his!"

Seeing the fallen standard and my sword at his throat his knights threw down their swords and shouted, "Yield, King William! We have lost!"

With hatred burning in his eyes he dropped his shield and nodded, "I surrender!"

Epilogue

We captured the great and the good of Scotland. As a result, King John made punitive demands on them. We returned to Norham with the King of Scotland as our prisoner. He was forced to pay King John ten thousand pounds of gold. It was a crippling sum. Worse his daughters were placed under the protection of King John. King William would not be able to make alliances using his daughters. It was the end of any ambitions which King William might have held. King John did not demand fealty but Scotland was no longer a power to be feared. Northumbria would never be his.

My conroi had not escaped losses. Four men at arms had fallen and Sir William and Sir Fótr had been wounded. Others had lost knights. The barons of the Palatinate had saved King John.

After the treaty had been signed and we awaited the King of Scotland's daughters I was summoned to a meeting with King John and the Earl Marshal. William Marshal was beaming. "Truly courageous and just like the Warlord! He would have been proud of you and your men. You did exactly as was asked of you and it was your capture of the standard and the King which led to our victory." I think he said what he did for the benefit of King John. Our liege lord was known for his lack of gratitude. It did not hurt to remind him.

"I thank the Earl but there were men who died at Jedburgh who might have lived had the army arrived sooner. Where were you, my lord?"

King John's eyes glared, "You question a King?"

"I was asked to draw the enemy so that they could be attacked. I did so and yet it was you who were tardy."

William Marshal stepped between us. "Thomas, you were too successful. We thought that it would take longer to take Jedburgh. Blame me for it was my error."

I nodded.

King John said, "And now, I suppose, you wish payment." He said it without any grace. It was as though he begrudged me my victory.

The Earl shook his head, "Your Majesty, he captured the King! He saved many English lives. Surely he deserves a reward."

The King looked at me as though considering and then he nodded, "What do you wish?"

What should I ask for? I knew we had had a great victory. I decided to ask for everything. He could only refuse me. "The return of my father's hereditary title and powers. I wish to be Earl of Cleveland and all that goes with it. I wish the right to put a wall around Stockton and build a keep!"

"You demand a great deal."

I nodded. He had not said no and I asked for more, "And with the title the right to lead the knights of the valley."

I saw the King chew his lip. "You may have the title and the right to lead the knights. You can build your wall but there will be no keep. I will not make Stockton a hostage to fortune."

I had got more than I had hoped. I nodded. "Thank you, Your Majesty. Know that I will defend the northern marches as my forefathers did."

William Marshal said, "I will walk out with you." Once we were in the open he said, quietly, "You did him a great service with this victory and he knows it. That is the reason you were given your title and permission to make Stockton strong. He knows that you are the strength in the area and not the Bishop."

"Thank you, Earl. I am indebted to you."

"Then take some advice from an old man. Distance yourself from those who speak of rebellion. King John is no fool and those who conspire will pay. Eh? Do not bite the hand that rewards you."

I nodded, "I would never dream of being a rebel but I may still voice my opinion, may I not?"

He shook his head, "That depends upon the company! I can see that you will never change. You remind me so much of the Warlord. God speed and the Earl Marshal of England thanks you. It was your victory and we will rightly honour you. You should know that there are many who took note of it. You will be watched very closely."

"Then I will make certain that I am a true knight."

"One more thing. I spoke with the High Sherriff. There will be no more attacks."

"Thank you, Earl Marshal. You have saved the life of the Sherriff for I do not forgive such attacks easily."

I left and joined my men. They were waiting with the treasure we had collected. We had horses, mail, weapons and coins. Sir Edward said, "Well Sir Thomas what now?"

I cocked my head to one side and smiling wagged an admonishing finger at my faithful knight, "Sir Edward, you do me wrong. I pray you address me as the Earl of Cleveland! I have the title once more!"

The clamour from my knights and my men made the sentries on the walls of Norham look for the cause of the disturbance. We turned our horses and we headed home. I still opposed the King but I was now in a position to oppose him from a more elevated station. I was no longer a baron, I was an earl. As we rode south I saw light at the end of the tunnel. That which I had lost I had almost regained. There was hope now for my family and my manor. That meant there was hope for a whole valley which had suffered at the hands of corrupt men. The Earl of Cleveland was back!

The End

Glossary

Chevauchée- a raid by mounted men
Fusil - A lozenge shape on a shield
Garth- a garth was a farm. Not to be confused with the name Garth
Groat- English coin worth four silver pennies
Luciaria-Lucerne (Switzerland)
　Mêlée- a medieval fight between knights

Nissa- Nice (Provence)
Reeve- An official who ran a manor for a lord
Rote- An English version of a lyre (also called a crowd or Crwth)
Vair- a heraldic term
Wulfestun- Wolviston (Durham)

Maps and Illustrations

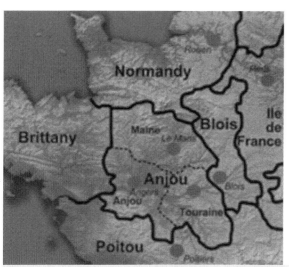

The fall of Normandy
Wikipedia Commons

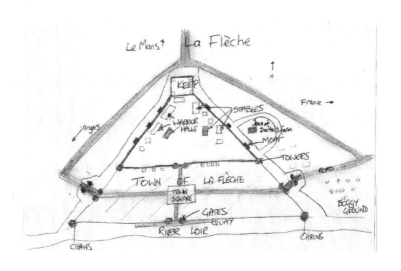

Le Mans↑ La Flèche

KEEP

STABLES

WARRIOR HALLS

Tomb of David's tomb

MOAT

TOWERS

Angers

France →

ROAD

RUINS

RUINS

BOGGY GROUND

TOWN OF LA FLÈCHE

TOWN SQUARE

GATES QUAY

RIVER LOIR

CHAINS

CHAINS

230

Historical Notes

This series of books follows the fortunes of the family of the Earl of Cleveland begun in the Anarchy. As with that series the characters in this book are, largely, fictional, but the events are all historically accurate. For those who have read the earlier books in the series the new information begins with the section: **Fall of Normandy**.

Templars

No matter where they were based the Knights Templars followed a strict routine:

- Night- Matins sleep until dawn
- 6 am Rise- Prime and then mass
- 9 am Terce
- 12 Noon Sext
- 3 pm Nones, Vespers for the dead, Vigil for the dead

There were set times to speak with their squires and see to their horses.

Prince Arthur

Arthur was born in 1187, the son of Constance of Brittany and Geoffrey II of Brittany, who died before he was born. As an infant, Arthur was second in line to the succession of his grandfather King Henry II, after his uncle Richard. King Henry died when Arthur was 2 years old, and Richard I became the new king in his place.

While Richard was away on the Third Crusade, Arthur's mother Constance made actions to make the Duchy of Brittany more independent. On 11 November 1190, Richard betrothed Arthur to a daughter of Tancred of Sicily as part of their treaty. However, Emperor Henry VI conquered the Kingdom of Sicily in 1194, so the betrothal of Arthur came to nothing.

A marriage plan, originally aiming to establish an alliance between King Richard and Philip II, King of France, to marry Arthur's elder sister Eleanor to Philip's son Louis also failed. In 1196, Constance had the young Arthur proclaimed Duke of Brittany and her co-ruler as a child of nine years. The same year, Richard again nominated Arthur as his heir and summoned him, as well as his mother Constance, to Normandy, but Ranulf de Blondeville, 6th Earl of Chester, stepfather of Arthur, abducted Constance. Richard marched to Brittany to rescue Arthur, who was then secretly carried to France to be brought up with Louis.

When Richard died on 6 April 1199, on his deathbed he proclaimed his brother John as his heir, fearing Arthur was too young to look after the throne. Arthur was only twelve years old at the time and under the influence of the French king. John immediately claimed the throne of England, but much of the French nobility were resentful at recognising him as their overlord. They preferred Arthur, who declared himself vassal of Philip. Philip recognised Arthur's right to Anjou, Maine, and Poitou. Upon Richard's death Arthur led a force to Anjou and Maine. From 18 April, he styled himself as Duke of Brittany, Count of Anjou and Earl of Richmond.

After his return to France, and with the support of Philip II, Arthur embarked on a campaign in Normandy against John in 1202. Poitou revolted in support of Arthur. The Duke of Brittany besieged his grandmother, Eleanor of Aquitaine, John's mother, in the Château de Mirebeau. John marched on Mirebeau, taking Arthur by surprise on 31 July 1202. Arthur was captured by John's barons on 1 August, and imprisoned in the Château de Falaise in Falaise, Normandy.

At the Chateau de Falaise, Arthur was guarded by Hubert de Burgh. According to contemporaneous chronicler Ralph of Coggeshall, John ordered two of his servants to mutilate the duke. Hubert de Burgh refused to let him be mutilated. The following year Arthur was transferred to Rouen, under the charge of William de Braose. Arthur vanished in April 1203.

"After King John had captured Arthur and kept him alive in prison for some time, at length, in the castle of Rouen, after dinner on the Thursday before Easter, when he was drunk and possessed by the devil ['ebrius et daemonio plenus'], he slew him with his own hand, and tying a heavy stone to the body cast it into the Seine. It was discovered by a fisherman in his net, and being dragged to the bank and recognized, was taken for secret burial, in fear of the tyrant, to the priory of Bec called Notre Dame de Pres."

Margam annals

William des Roches

In May 1199, King Philip of France met with William des Roches at Le Mans and together they attacked the border fortress of Ballon, the fortress was surrendered by Geoffrey de Brûlon, the castellan, but not before being demolished. A quarrel ensued between King Philip and William over the lordship *of the site. William was adamant that Ballon belonged rightfully to Duke Arthur, while King Philip wished to retain it as his own.*

In June 1199, King John of England launched a massive attack into Northern Maine from Argentan. On 13 September he was successful in repulsing King Philip from the fortress of Lavardin which protected the route from Le Mans to Tours. Arthur's supporters were forced to come to terms with John, and William met with the English king at Bourg-le-Roi, a fortress of the pro-John viscounts of Beaumont-en-Maine on or about 18 September. John convinced William that Arthur of Brittany was being used solely as a tool of Capetian strategy and managed to convince him to switch sides. With this, John promised him the seneschalship of Anjou. During the night, John's incumbent seneschal, Viscount Aimery, took Arthur and Constance and fled the court. They fled first to Angers, then to the court of King Philip. King John officially designated William seneschal of Anjou in December 1199 and entered Angers triumphantly on 24 June 1200.

Treaty of Le Goulet

The Treaty of Le Goulet was signed by the kings John of England and Philip II of France in May 1200 and meant to settle once and for all the claims the Norman kings of England had as Norman dukes on French lands, including, at least for a time, Brittany. Under the terms of the treaty, Philip recognised John as King of England as heir of his brother Richard I and thus formally abandoned any support for Arthur. John, meanwhile, recognised Philip as the suzerain of continental possessions of the Angevin Empire.

Philip had previously recognised John as suzerain of Anjou and the Duchy of Brittany, but with this he extorted 20,000 marks sterling in payment for recognition of John's sovereignty of Brittany. The Treaty of Le Goulet was signed by the kings John of England and Philip II of France in May 1200 and aimed to ultimately settle the claims the Angevin kings of England had on French lands. Hence, it aimed to bring an end to the war over the Duchy of Normandy and finalise the new borders of what was left of the duchy, as well as the future relationship of the king of France and the dukes of Normandy. The treaty was a victory for Philip as it asserted his legal claims to over lordship over John's French lands.

The terms of the treaty signed at le Goulet, on the Gueuleton island in the middle of the Seine river near Vernon in Normandy, included clarifications of the feudal relationships binding the monarchs. Philip recognised John as King of

England, heir of his brother Richard I, and thus formally abandoned his prior support for Arthur I, Duke of Brittany, the son of John's late brother, Geoffrey II of Brittany. John, meanwhile, formally recognised the new status of the lost Norman territories by acknowledging the Counts of Boulogne and Flanders as vassals of the kings of France, not those of England, and recognised Philip as the suzerain of the continental lands in the Angevin Empire. John also bound himself not to support any rebellions on the part of the counts of Boulogne and Flanders.

Philip had previously recognised John as suzerain of Anjou and the Duchy of Brittany, but with the treaty of le Goulet he extorted 20,000 marks sterling in payment for recognition of John's sovereignty of Brittany.

The treaty also included territorial concessions by John to Philip. The Vexin (except for Les Andelys, where Château Gaillard, vital to the defence of the region, was located) and the Évrécin in Normandy, as well as Issoudun, Graçay, and the fief of André de Chauvigny in Berry were to be removed from Angevin suzerainty and put directly into that of France.

The Duchy of Aquitaine was not included in the treaty. It was still held by John as heir to his still-living mother, Eleanor. The treaty was sealed with a marriage alliance between the Angevin and Capetian dynasties. John's niece Blanche, daughter of his sister Leonora and Alfonso VIII of Castile, married Philip's eldest son, Louis VIII of France (to be eventually known as Louis the Lion). The marriage alliance only assured a strong regent for the minority of Louis IX of France. Philip declared John deposed from his fiefs for failure to obey a summons in 1202 and war broke out again. Philip moved quickly to seize John's lands in Normandy, strengthening the French throne in the process.

John and the Lusignans

The new peace would only last for two years; war recommenced in the aftermath of John's decision in August 1200 to marry Isabella of Angoulême. In order to remarry, John first needed to abandon Isabel, Countess of Gloucester, his first wife; John accomplished this by arguing that he had failed to get the necessary papal permission to marry Isabel in the first place – as a cousin, John could not have legally wed her without this. It remains unclear why John chose to marry Isabella of Angouleme. Contemporary chroniclers argued that John had fallen deeply in love with Isabella, and John may have been motivated by desire for an apparently beautiful, if rather young, girl. On the other hand, the Angoumois lands that came with Isabella were strategically vital to John: by marrying Isabella, John was acquiring a key land route between Poitou and Gascony, which significantly strengthened his grip on Aquitaine.

Unfortunately, Isabella was already engaged to Hugh of Lusignan, an important member of a key Poitou noble family and brother of Count Raoul of Eu, who possessed lands along the sensitive eastern Normandy border. Just as John stood to benefit strategically from marrying Isabella, so the marriage threatened the interests of the Lusignans, whose own lands currently provided the key route for royal goods and troops across Aquitaine. Rather than negotiating some form of compensation, John treated Hugh "with contempt"; this resulted in a Lusignan uprising that was promptly crushed by John, who also intervened to suppress Raoul in Normandy.

Although John was the Count of Poitou and therefore the rightful feudal lord over the Lusignans, they could legitimately appeal John's actions in France to his own feudal lord, Philip. Hugh did exactly this in 1201 and Philip summoned John to attend court in Paris in 1202, citing the Le Goulet treaty to strengthen his case. John was unwilling to weaken his authority in western France in this way. He argued that he need not attend Philip's court because of his special status as the Duke of Normandy, who was exempt by feudal tradition from being called to the French court. Philip argued that he was summoning John not as the Duke of Normandy, but as the Count of Poitou, which carried no such special status. When John still refused to come, Philip declared John in breach of his feudal responsibilities, reassigned all of John's lands that fell under the French crown to Arthur – with the exception of Normandy, which he took back for himself – and began a fresh war against John.

De Ferrers

De Ferrers was a favourite of King John and also the Sherriff of Nottingham! His coat of arms was vairy or with gules. It is easier to show you rather than trying to describe it!

Eleanor Fair Maid of Brittany

I did not know the story of Eleanor until I began researching this book. Hers is a sad story. Eventually King John captured her and imprisoned her in a castle: although the exact location is uncertain. Some said Corfe and then

Bristol. When King John died his heir, Henry III continued to have her incarcerated. Her burial and her final resting place are unknown. There is a story there.

Treadmill crane

The medieval treadmill was a large wooden wheel turning around a central shaft with a treadway wide enough for two workers walking side by side. While the earlier 'compass-arm' wheel had spokes directly driven into the central shaft, the more advanced 'clasp-arm' type featured arms arranged as chords to the wheel rim, giving the possibility of using a thinner shaft and providing thus a greater mechanical advantage.

Treadmill crane- courtesy of Wikipedia.

Fall of Normandy

Prince Arthur was in Falaise and, after he was moved to Rouen he was, reputedly, killed by his uncle. That action and the ill treatment of prisoners drove William des Roches into the French camp. Between 1202 and 1204 Normandy, Brittany, Anjou and Maine were all lost. Most of Poitou also fell and only the wine rich region of Aquitaine remained in King John's hands. He never gave up on Normandy and spent the next ten years trying to retake it. He even built a fleet to defend the seaways to Bordeaux.

He might have succeeded but he had a poor relationship with the barons. They cost him Normandy and, as events turned out, almost cost him England.

King William and Scotland

King John invaded Scotland and forced William to sign the Treaty of Norham, which gave John control of William's daughters and required a payment of £10,000. This effectively crippled William's power north of the border, and by 1212 John had to intervene militarily to support the Scottish king against his internal rivals. John made no efforts to reinvigorate the Treaty of Falaise, though, and both William and Alexander in turn remained independent kings, supported by, but not owing fealty to, John.

Books used in the research:

The Crusades-David Nicholle

Crusader Castles in the Holy Land 1097-1192- David Nicolle

The Normans- David Nicolle

Norman Knight AD 950-1204- Christopher Gravett

The Norman Conquest of the North- William A Kappelle

The Knight in History- Francis Gies

The Norman Achievement- Richard F Cassady

Knights- Constance Brittain Bouchard

Knight Templar 1120-1312 -Helen Nicholson

Feudal England: Historical Studies on the Eleventh and Twelfth Centuries- J. H. Round

English Medieval Knight 1200-1300

The Scandinavian Baltic Crusades 1100-1500

For the English maps, I have used the original Ordnance survey maps. Produced by the army in the 19th century they show England before modern developments and, in most cases, are pre-industrial revolution. Produced by Cassini they are a useful tool for a historian.

I also discovered a good website http://orbis.stanford.edu/. This allows a reader to plot any two places in the Roman world and if you input the mode of transport you wish to use and the time of year it will calculate how long it would take you to travel the route. I have used it for all of my books up to the eighteenth century as the transportation system was roughly the same. The Romans would have been quicker!

Griff Hosker
December 2017

Other books

by

Griff Hosker

If you enjoyed reading this book, then why not read another one by the author?

Ancient History

The Sword of Cartimandua Series (Germania and Britannia 50A.D. – 128 A.D.)

Ulpius Felix- Roman Warrior (prequel)
Book 1 The Sword of Cartimandua
Book 2 The Horse Warriors
Book 3 Invasion Caledonia
Book 4 Roman Retreat
Book 5 Revolt of the Red Witch
Book 6 Druid's Gold
Book 7 Trajan's Hunters
Book 8 The Last Frontier
Book 9 Hero of Rome
Book 10 Roman Hawk
Book 11 Roman Treachery
Book 12 Roman Wall
Book 13 Roman Courage

The Aelfraed Series (Britain and Byzantium 1050 A.D. - 1085 A.D.
Book 1 Housecarl
Book 2 Outlaw
Book 3 Varangian

The Wolf Warrior series (Britain in the late 6th Century)
Book 1 Saxon Dawn
Book 2 Saxon Revenge
Book 3 Saxon England

Book 4 Saxon Blood
Book 5 Saxon Slayer
Book 6 Saxon Slaughter
Book 7 Saxon Bane
Book 8 Saxon Fall: Rise of the Warlord
Book 9 Saxon Throne

The Dragon Heart Series
Book 1 Viking Slave
Book 2 Viking Warrior
Book 3 Viking Jarl
Book 4 Viking Kingdom
Book 5 Viking Wolf
Book 6 Viking War
Book 7 Viking Sword
Book 8 Viking Wrath
Book 9 Viking Raid
Book 10 Viking Legend
Book 11 Viking Vengeance
Book 12 Viking Dragon
Book 13 Viking Treasure
Book 14 Viking Enemy
Book 15 Viking Witch
Bool 16 Viking Blood
Book 17 Viking Weregeld
Book 18 Viking Storm
Book 19 Viking Warband

The Norman Genesis Series
Rolf
Horseman
The Battle for a Home
Revenge of the Franks
The Land of the Northmen
Ragnvald Hrolfsson
Brothers in Blood
Lord of Rouen

The Anarchy Series England 1120-1180
English Knight
Knight of the Empress
Northern Knight
Baron of the North
Earl
King Henry's Champion
The King is Dead
Warlord of the North
Enemy at the Gate
Warlord's War
Kingmaker
Henry II
Crusader
The Welsh Marches
Irish War
Poisonous Plots

Border Knight 1182-1300
Sword for Hire
Return of the Knight
Baron's War

Modern History
The Napoleonic Horseman Series
Book 1 Chasseur a Cheval
Book 2 Napoleon's Guard
Book 3 British Light Dragoon
Book 4 Soldier Spy
Book 5 1808: The Road to Corunna
Waterloo

The Lucky Jack American Civil War series
Rebel Raiders
Confederate Rangers
The Road to Gettysburg

The British Ace Series
1914
1915 Fokker Scourge
1916 Angels over the Somme
1917 Eagles Fall
1918 We will remember them
From Arctic Snow to Desert Sand
Wings over Persia

Combined Operations series 1940-1945
Commando
Raider
Behind Enemy Lines
Dieppe
Toehold in Europe
Sword Beach
Breakout
The Battle for Antwerp
King Tiger
Beyond the Rhine

Other Books
Carnage at Cannes (a thriller)
Great Granny's Ghost (Aimed at 9-14-year-old young people)
Adventure at 63-Backpacking to Istanbul

For more information on all of the books then please visit the author's web site at http://www.griffhosker.com where there is a link to contact him.

Made in the USA
Columbia, SC
28 January 2022

54936122R00133